PRAISE FOR
don't even think
about it

"Hilarious, moving, and utterly ingenious."
—Robin Wasserman, author of *The Book of Blood
and Shadow* and *The Waking Dark*

"Finally, someone understands that if you develop
powers as a teenager, it's not the government you have to
watch out for—it's your best friends. Funny, realistic,
heartfelt, satiric, and unpredictable."
—Ned Vizzini, *New York Times* bestselling author
of *It's Kind of a Funny Story*

"It'd be great to know the deepest secrets and thoughts
of your BFFs and secret crush, right? *Wrong!* When flu
shots suddenly go awry, a group of friends gain telepathic
powers, and find out way more than they ever wanted
to know. LOL hilarious!"
—GirlsLife.com

Also by Sarah Mlynowski

The Magic in Manhattan Series

Bras & Broomsticks

Frogs & French Kisses

Spells & Sleeping Bags

Parties & Potions

Gimme a Call

don't even think about it

SARAH MLYNOWSKI

EMBER

Text copyright © 2014 by Sarah Mlynowski
Cover art copyright © 2014 by Ali Smith

All rights reserved. Published in the United States by Ember, an imprint of Random House Children's Books, a division of Penguin Random House LLC, New York. Originally published in hardcover in the United States by Delacorte Press, an imprint of Random House Children's Books, New York, in 2014.

Ember and the E colophon are registered trademarks of Penguin Random House LLC.

randomhouseteens.com

Educators and librarians, for a variety of teaching tools, visit us at RHTeachersLibrarians.com

The Library of Congress has cataloged the hardcover edition of this work as follows:
Mlynowski, Sarah.
Don't even think about it / Sarah Mlynowski. — First edition.
pages cm
Summary: "What happens when a group of Tribeca high school kids go in for flu shots . . . and end up being able to read each other's minds"
—Provided by publisher.
ISBN 978-0-385-73738-8 (hc : alk. paper) —
ISBN 978-0-385-90662-3 (glb : alk. paper) —
ISBN 978-0-449-81415-4 (ebook) [1. Extrasensory perception—Fiction.
2. High schools—Fiction. 3. Schools—Fiction. 4. TriBeCa (New York, N.Y.)—
Fiction.] I. Title. II. Title: Do not even think about it.
PZ7.M7135Do 2014
[Fic]—dc23
2012050777

ISBN 978-0-385-73739-5 (trade pbk.)

Printed in the United States of America
10 9 8 7 6 5 4 3 2 1
First Ember Edition 2015

For the ladies who lounge (and sometimes write):
Courtney, Jess, Adele, Robin, Jen, and Emily
(and when I'm very lucky, Leslie, Joanna, and Julia).
Thanks for the company and the cupcakes.

CHAPTER ONE

BEFORE

We were not always freaks.

Sure, most of us occasionally exhibited freakish behavior. But that's not the same thing.

Olivia Byrne, when she worried about something, picked the skin around her thumbnails until her fingers bled.

Cooper Miller sang badly. When he walked down the hall, when he studied, when he ate. He wasn't singing the Top 40 either—he made up tunes and lyrics about his everyday life. Walking to school. Being late to math.

Mackenzie Feldman, Cooper's girlfriend, hated needles. Not that any of us *liked* needles, but Mackenzie truly hated them. She hated them so much she'd never even gotten her ears pierced. She wore clip-ons to her own Sweet Sixteen. Or her Sweet, as we called it in Tribeca, our little downtown corner of Manhattan.

So yeah, we had certain quirks, but before October 2, which was eleven days before the Bloomberg High School carnival and eighteen days before Mackenzie's Sweet, Olivia, Cooper, Mackenzie, and the rest of us were pretty much just regular sophomores.

Even October 2, the day that changed everything, started normally enough.

We got ready for school. Most of us lived in Tribeca, within a few blocks from BHS, Bloomberg High School.

Tribeca is one of the wealthiest areas in Manhattan. Not that we were all wealthy—definitely not. Half of our parents owned our apartments; the other half rented. A bunch of us shared rooms with our siblings. If you lived in Tribeca and your parents were *really* rich or famous—like if your mom was Beyoncé or your dad ran an investment bank—you didn't go to BHS like us. You went to private school.

Anyway.

On October 2, we arrived at school, most of us on time. We locked our stuff in our lockers and headed to room 203, where 10B met for homeroom. Cooper didn't arrive on time—he was always late. He also didn't lock his locker, because he didn't bother having a lock. He could never remember the combination. And he trusted us. Back then, he trusted everyone.

We claimed our usual seats and chatted with our friends.

"Darren Lazar asked me if you were single," Renée Hinger said as she sat down beside Olivia in the middle of the room. Renée's leopard-print scarf fluttered behind her. She was also wearing a black hair band, earrings, and a silver bracelet crammed with charms. She was an accessories kind of girl. She was a busybody kind of girl. We're relieved she's not one of us. We have enough busybodies without her.

Olivia's heart skipped a beat. "What did you tell him?"

Renée laughed. "What do you think I told him? I told him you were. Unless you're involved with someone and keeping it a secret?"

Olivia had never been involved with anyone. Fifteen and never been kissed. She was afraid that when the time came she would barf all over the kisser.

Olivia did not have much confidence around boys or girls. One of the main reasons she hung around Renée was that Renée did 99.9 percent of the talking.

Of course, we didn't know the degree of her lack of confidence back then. We didn't know about her lack of kissing experience either. We didn't know any of each other's hidden thoughts or secret histories. Not like we do now.

"Do you think he's going to ask me out?" Olivia asked.

Renée twirled her scarf around her wrist. "Do you want him to ask you out?"

"I don't know." Olivia tried to picture him. He had light brown hair and red cheeks. Green eyes, maybe. Dressed well. Button-downs and the right jeans. He seemed nice. No one called him by his first name—he just went by Lazar. They had public speaking together. Her stomach clenched at the thought of the class. The next day she had to make a speech on Lyme disease, which was worth 40 percent of her grade. There was nothing that terrified her more than speaking in front of others.

"I think you guys would be perfect together," Renée continued.

"Why?" Olivia asked. "Because we're both short?"

"No, because you're both nice. And smart. And cute."

Olivia didn't say no, but she didn't say yes either. It wasn't that she didn't like Lazar. It was just that the idea of being on an actual date—where she would have to worry about what she wore, what she ate, and what she said—was incredibly stressful to her. She picked at her thumb.

Cooper came in at last, singing to himself. As usual, he looked slightly disheveled, like he'd woken up, picked up the green hoodie and jeans that were lying in a heap on his floor, and put them on.

Which is exactly what he had done. Cooper was wearing his Yankees hat. He wore it all baseball season until they were out of the running. It brought out the blue in his eyes. Not that he'd be aware of something like that. Well, not without reading our minds.

Cooper cupped his ear with his open hand. "What's up, 10B, can I get a boo-ya?"

"Boo-ya," called Nick Gaw from the side of the room. Nick was one of Cooper's good friends.

Cooper sighed with exaggerated disappointment. "That was lame, people. Lame. Lame-o. The Yankees won last night! I said give me a boo-ya!"

Mackenzie responded with a "boo-ya." She had to. That was her job as girlfriend, even if she occasionally found Cooper's antics a little embarrassing, like the time he insisted on giving her a piggyback ride down the hallway.

Cooper stood in front of Olivia's desk and wagged his finger. "Livvie, I did not hear you boo-ya. Why did I not hear you boo-ya?"

Olivia flushed. She gripped the sides of her desk. She did not like being put on the spot. Her heart sped up; her mouth felt dry. She debated. Would whatever she said sound stupid? Would she not make the right boo-ya sound? Would she sound too eager? Place too much emphasis on the *boo* and not enough on the *ya*?

But she liked Cooper. If he weren't totally out of

her league and didn't already have a girlfriend, she might have a crush on him. He was one of those people who were always smiling. Always kind. Always inclusive. Like right then, when he was trying to get her to boo-ya.

She could do it. She could! She just had to push the words out with the tip of her tongue. "Booooo-ya?"

Cooper petted her twice on the head like she was a rabbit. When he was a kid he'd had a rabbit for a whole two weeks before his dad made him return it to the pet store. He'd gotten a turtle instead. Gerald. "Well done, Livvie. Thank you for playing."

Olivia turned bright red.

Cooper made a point of talking to Olivia. She was shy, but Cooper knew that she just needed some help breaking out of her shell. Like Gerald. When he'd first gotten Gerald, the turtle had barely ventured out of his bowl. These days Gerald strutted around the loft like he was the mayor of Tribeca.

Cooper got a few more of us to boo-ya as he zigzagged his way through the desks to the empty seat in the last row by the window, right next to Mackenzie and her closest friend, Tess Demir.

"Thank you, Cooper," Ms. Velasquez said, closing the door behind her. "Now take off your hat, please."

Cooper gave our teacher a big smile. He had a small overbite from losing his retainer a month after he got it. "But, Ms. V, I didn't have a chance to wash my hair this morning."

"Then you might want to consider getting up earlier in the future," she said, taking off her blazer and slinging it over her chair.

Cooper removed his hat, revealing slept-on hair, clutched it to his chest, and finally sat down. "Let's get this party started," he said, and leaned his chair all the way back so it kissed the wall.

"Let's see who's here," Ms. Velasquez said, and called all our names. When she was done, she sat on the desk and swung her legs. "People, I have some good news and some bad news," she said. "I'll start with the bad news."

We waited.

"Those of you who are planning to get flu shots—and I think that's most of you—are scheduled to get them today at lunch," she told us.

We groaned.

Ms. Velasquez cleared her throat. "So, the good news is . . ."

Cooper made a drumroll.

Our teacher smiled. "You probably won't get the flu."

Naturally, we booed.

"What if I like the flu?" Cooper asked.

"Why would you like the flu?" Ms. Velasquez asked.

"I'd get to stay home and watch baseball," he answered.

"I wouldn't mind missing a week of school," Nick said.

We understood. His mom was a biology teacher at school. If our moms taught at our school, we'd want to stay home too.

"I'm not getting the shot," Renée declared, playing with her headband. "I never get sick. And you know, I read an article that said that they don't even work. That the pharmaceutical companies are only interested in making money off us."

We all groaned and she crossed her arms and rolled her eyes. Renée was a conspiracy theorist. She thought the government was out to get everyone.

These days we're not so sure we disagree.

"I'm skipping it too," Mackenzie said.

Mackenzie had been born a preemie, at twenty-six weeks instead of forty. She'd required a lot of surgeries. Eye surgery. Kidney surgery. Heart surgery. She didn't remember any of it, but she knew she hated any kind of needle, and she assumed the two facts were related.

"You're going to make me get it alone?" Cooper asked. "We'll do it together. I'll hold your hand. It'll be fuuuuuuun," he sang.

Mackenzie saw nothing potentially fun where needles were involved. But as usual, her boyfriend found the silver lining in everything. In coming to school. In the flu. In vaccinations.

Cooper lived in silver linings.

Ms. Velasquez tapped her fingers on her desk. "So remember, everyone. Nurse Carmichael's office.

Lunchtime. Bring your permission slips if your parents haven't already sent them back."

As Ms. Velasquez continued to talk, Olivia continued to worry. Not about the vaccination. Needles didn't scare her. She was nervous about her Lyme disease speech.

She picked her thumb. *Everything will be fine,* she told herself. *Fine, fine, fine.*

Of course, it wouldn't be fine. Not at all. But Olivia couldn't know that. It's not like she had ESP.

Ha, ha, ha.

Not yet.

Maybe you think Olivia is telling this story. Or Mackenzie, or Cooper, or someone else in our homeroom you haven't met.

It could be any of us. But it's not. It's all of us. We're telling you the story together. It's the only way we know how.

This is the story of how we became freaks.

It's how a group of *I*'s became a *we*.

CHAPTER TWO

IT HAPPENED HERE

At the beginning of lunch, we waited in line by Nurse Carmichael's office.

There were twenty-three of us. Most of homeroom 10B. 10A had gotten their shots the day before.

Adam McCall was missing—probably an ear infection. He always had ear infections.

Pi Ricci went in and came out first. Her real name was Polly, after her grandfather Paul, but her nickname was Pi because she could tell you the first thirty-nine numbers of pi. They're 3.1415926535897 93238462643383279502884l9, if you're curious.

BJ Kole went in next.

Yes, he called himself BJ.

His name was actually Brian Joseph, but he started

going by BJ in middle school. He thought it was hilarious. He was a bit of a perv.

He hurried into the nurse's office and closed the door behind him. He thought Nurse Carmichael was hot, and was always trying to come up with accidental ways to feel her up. He tried to feel everyone up.

Next in line was Jordana Brohman-Maizner. Jordana filed her nails while she waited. She kept a full manicure set in her locker. Base coat, top coat, clippers, and eleven different colors ranging from Bliss (shimmery yellow) to We Were Liars (fire-engine red).

Behind her were Olivia and Renée. Renée was still not getting the vaccination. She was only waiting in line so she wouldn't miss anything. She liked to know what everyone was up to at all times. She was the type of person who got email notifications every time her friends changed their Facebook statuses.

"Do you know that more people die from flu shots than the flu?" Renée asked.

"I'm not sure that's true," Olivia said. Actually, she was totally sure it wasn't true, because she had the Centers for Disease Control and Prevention website bookmarked on her laptop, and visited it frequently. In addition to having a lot of anxiety, Olivia was a hypochondriac.

"It's going to hurt," Renée said.

Her words didn't scare Olivia, but they terrified

Mackenzie, who was right behind them. She'd decided to do it. She couldn't believe she was really going to do it.

Mackenzie was waiting with Cooper and Tess, although Tess was busy texting Teddy on her iPhone. Teddy was Tess's best guy friend. Tess also had a massive crush on him.

"Maybe I won't get it," Mackenzie said, suddenly unsteady on her feet.

"Oh, come on," Cooper said. "It's just a pinch. You don't want to get the flu."

"Everyone else is getting the shot. I won't get the flu."

"You might. It's going around. And your Sweet is soon. You don't want to be sick and have to cancel."

Mackenzie's parents would kill her if she got the flu.

It was all booked. Her brother and sister were flying in from Stanford. Her parents had spent a small fortune in deposits. They'd gone all out. They'd booked a hotel ballroom. Hired a DJ. Hired an event planner. Mailed out gorgeous invitations. Square, black, with cursive silver print.

The few of us who'd been invited had all RSVP'd yes.

Mackenzie was excited for the party. Kind of.

Nothing was expected of her. All she had to do was dance and look pretty in her new black Herve Leger cocktail dress.

Mackenzie knew she was pretty. Ever since she was a kid, people had always told her as much. She had dirty-blond hair, dark blue eyes, a button nose, and a gymnast's body. She'd trained at the NYC Elite gymnastics studio for years. She'd tried competing back in middle school, but it wasn't for her. The night before one of her big matches, she'd stayed out late with her friends, broken curfew, been exhausted the next day, and tripped off the balance beam. Her parents had been furious. She had been relieved.

Outside the nurse's office, Cooper slung his arm around her and sang, "The needle will only hurt for a *secoooond*."

"But it's really going to hurt for that one second," Mackenzie snapped.

Cooper kissed her cheek. "I'll come in with you. And sing you a song."

He was always nice to her. Even when she wasn't nice back.

She knew she should be nicer to him. He definitely deserved it.

Mackenzie nodded to herself and to Cooper. She would do it. She would get the needle. She would do it because he wanted her to. She owed him, even if he didn't know it. The needle would be her punishment.

Back then, we didn't know she was punishing herself, or for what.

Now we know everything. Even the stuff we try to forget. Especially the stuff we try to forget.

Cooper squeezed Mackenzie's shoulder. "Then I'll get you a root beer float as a reward."

We were allowed to leave school for lunch. But we only had forty minutes, so we couldn't go far.

"Can we go to Takahachi instead?" Mackenzie asked. "I'm craving salmon rolls."

Japanese wasn't Cooper's first choice, since his mom ordered it every night. He was gluten intolerant, so there weren't too many options for him to eat—but he was a go-with-the-flow kind of guy. "Why don't we pick up Takahachi and then eat it at your place?" he asked, waggling his eyebrows. She lived a block away. No one was ever home.

"We're not going to have enough time for both after the vaccines," Mackenzie said. "Maybe tomorrow?"

Cooper was fine waiting until the next day. But he wondered if it was really going to happen then. They'd barely hooked up since he'd been back from camp. He wondered if Mackenzie was avoiding him. Although that didn't make sense—they hung out all day together at school. Why would she avoid him after hours? Did she not want to be alone with him?

The nurse's door opened. BJ came out. He had failed in his groping mission.

We all hoped Nurse Carmichael had stuck his arm with the needle really hard.

Jordana went in, barely bothering to look up from her nails.

We waited.

A few minutes later she came out looking dazed. "That was miserable," she announced. She was holding a red lollipop.

Olivia was up. She stepped eagerly toward the door. She was a big believer in vaccinations. To prevent the flu. To prevent typhoid. If only they had one to prevent social anxiety, she'd be all set.

"You really shouldn't do it," Renée said to Olivia.

"I'll be fine," Olivia said. She usually followed Renée's lead, but she couldn't in this case.

Renée sighed, looking slightly confused that Olivia wasn't listening to her. "All right. If you insist. I'm going to the cafeteria. Meet me there and we'll talk to Lazar."

Olivia's stomach clenched. She wasn't sure she was ready for that. But she said okay and then went inside the nurse's office.

Mackenzie took a deep breath. She was next.

"Hey, Mackenzie," piped up Tess. "Do you need me to help you with any Sweet stuff after school?"

Unlike her bestie, Tess was no gymnast. Or dancer. Tess was a writer. Not a professional one—not yet— but she thought that maybe one day she could be. For now she volunteered for *Bloom*, the school's twice-yearly arts journal. Tess had wavy brown hair, olive skin, and brown eyes and was well aware that she was ten pounds—eight pounds on a good day—overweight. She was well aware because her mother told her daily and not so subtly. "Why don't you go to SoulCycle, Tess?" "Are you sure you should be having that ice cream sandwich, Tess?" "You should try your bagel scooped, Tess." "I'd give you my old cute Kate Spade dress but I think it would be too tight on you, Tess." Tess tried to think of her mom's incessant nagging as white noise. White noise that would one day give her more to write about.

For now Tess was looking forward to Mackenzie's Sweet. The party was going to be epic. She was proud that the first Sweet of their class was her best friend's. Mackenzie's birthday was earlier than everyone else's because her parents had held her back a year, since she was a preemie.

It was going to be at the SoHo Tower, which was one of those celebrity hotel hot spots constantly mentioned on *TMZ*. Tess was psyched. She had already bought a dress at BCBG.

"The event planner has it covered," Mackenzie said to Tess with a flip of her hair. "But you can come over if you want."

"Sure," Tess replied.

Olivia came out a few seconds later.

"We're up," Cooper said, turning to Mackenzie. "Ready to show the needle who's boss?"

Mackenzie hesitated.

"Come on," Tess said. "It'll hurt for a second and then you'll be done."

Mackenzie turned to Olivia. "Did it hurt?"

Olivia flushed.

Mackenzie waited for a response but eventually realized she wasn't getting one. *Weirdo.* She turned to Cooper. "Let's just do this," she said, and the two of them disappeared into the nurse's office.

CHAPTER THREE

OUCH

Olivia looked at her reflection in the first-floor girls' bathroom mirror. When Mackenzie had asked her whether the vaccination hurt, she opened her mouth to say it was fine; great, even! But then she realized how insane she'd sound. Sure, she liked vaccinations—they made her feel safe and protected—but was she really going to announce that? That was not a normal thing to say. So she stood there, not responding. Which did not help in the looking-normal department.

Olivia sighed.

On the plus side, it had been nice to see Nurse Carmichael. Olivia and Nurse Carmichael were old friends.

Okay, not friends-friends. But in truth, Olivia felt

more comfortable in the nurse's office than she did in the cafeteria.

She was in the infirmary a lot.

Like, a lot, a lot.

At least twice a week.

Anytime Olivia had a cough, or a stomachache, or a hangnail, she went straight to Nurse Carmichael. Just to make sure it wasn't cancer. Or a heart attack. Or lymphangioleiomyomatosis. Which, sure, only affected one out of a million people, but it started with a cough, and if you *were* the one out of a million, then you were done-like-dinner within the year.

Olivia's father had had a heart attack when he was forty-two. Olivia had been ten. One minute they were a happy family shopping at Roosevelt Field mall; the next minute he was clutching his chest and lying on the grimy food-court floor. He was dead by the time they got to the hospital.

After that, Olivia avoided food courts. And malls. And Long Island. Her mom felt the same way—they sold their house in the suburbs and moved a few blocks from her mom's job at American Express in downtown NYC.

Olivia found Nurse Carmichael's office, with the clean white walls and posters reminding us about the dangers of meningitis, comforting.

When she'd walked in to get her shot, Olivia had said hi, Nurse Carmichael had asked how she was,

Olivia'd said she had a small headache but was otherwise fine, Olivia'd stuck out her arm, she'd gotten the shot, and Nurse Carmichael had slapped on a Band-Aid and told her she'd see her soon.

Olivia had no doubt that was true.

Then Olivia had chosen a green lollipop.

She waited until she walked away from Mackenzie and the rest of us before unwrapping it and popping it into her mouth. She hadn't wanted to look stupid sucking on it.

But now Olivia stared at her green lips and mouth in the bathroom mirror and realized she looked ridiculous. Why had she chosen green? Why, why, why? She looked like a sea monster. Or the Hulk.

She leaned over and rinsed her mouth with water. The green color stuck.

There was no way she was going to the cafeteria to talk to you-know-who. She wasn't going to talk to anyone that day. She wasn't even going to open her mouth that day if she could help it. Or the next day.

Oh no. No, no, no.

She had to open her mouth the next day. She had her speech! At eleven! What if the green didn't come out in time? What if it never came out? She held on to the edge of the sink, feeling dizzy, wishing she were anywhere but there.

* * *

Mackenzie watched as Nurse Carmichael and her giant needle crossed the room, heading straight for her.

"Cooper, you have to go first," Mackenzie said.

He pulled up his sleeve and made himself comfortable on the nurse's chair.

Nurse Carmichael aimed the needle at him. It was about to attack him. Any second. It was coming closer.

Mackenzie tried to look away. Must look away. Couldn't look away.

She definitely should have looked away.

"ARGH!!!!!"

That was Mackenzie, not Cooper. Cooper barely felt it. It was like a mosquito bite when you knew to expect a mosquito bite. And mosquito bites didn't get to Cooper. Nothing got to Cooper.

"Easy peasy," he said as the nurse pressed a Band-Aid onto his arm.

Mackenzie saw the room swim in front of her. "I don't feel well. If I'm sick, I can't get the shot, right?"

"Not if you have a temperature," the nurse said.

Mackenzie nodded. "I am pretty sure I have a fever."

Nurse Carmichael laughed. "I'll check it just in case."

The nurse pulled out the no-mouth thermometer she always used, the kind that scanned our foreheads, and took Mackenzie's temperature.

It beeped.

"No fever," Nurse Carmichael said.

"Damn it."

"You don't have to get the shot if you don't want to," the nurse said. "It's voluntary."

Mackenzie could have walked out.

We all could have walked out. Every single one of us could have turned around and walked right out the door and never looked back.

Would have, could have. Should have?

Didn't.

"No." Mackenzie took a shaky breath. "Just give me the stupid shot." She flailed her right arm out.

The nurse rolled up the arm of Mackenzie's black cashmere sweater.

"Ow!"

The nurse laughed. "That was just the alcohol."

Cooper squeezed her knee. "Close your eyes. Imagine something good. Like lunch tomorrow."

Mackenzie could do that. She closed her eyes. Imagined Cooper's lips. He did have great lips. Pink. Like he was wearing lipstick even though he wasn't. Plump. The top slightly plumper than the bottom.

But then another pair of lips crowded into her brain.

Bennett's lips.

There was a stab in her arm. Ouch.

She deserved it. She deserved the pain.

"You're done," the nurse said.

Mackenzie didn't want to open her eyes. Didn't want to face Cooper.

"Babe?" Cooper said. "We're done."

We would be, she thought, *if you knew what I did. But you never will.*

She opened her eyes.

"Don't forget your lollipop," Nurse Carmichael said.

CHAPTER FOUR

OCTOBER 3

Today was the day. Not that Olivia knew it was THE day. At the time, she just thought it was speech day.

Three hours and forty-five minutes to go.

In the fifth grade, back on Long Island, Olivia had been cast as an extra in the school play. She only had one line. One single line. She practiced that line in the shower. In her room. In her backyard. But on the night of the one-liner, she stood onstage while expectant faces stared up at her, and her mind went blank. Empty. Wiped clean. She couldn't breathe. Black spots swam in front of her eyes. The rest of the cast tried to usher her off the stage, but she couldn't move. She'd just stood there. Frozen. Like a sad, melting Popsicle.

Clearly, there were no Tony Awards in her future.

As if she would ever voluntarily step on a stage again. Thanks, but no thanks.

She rehearsed her speech in the shower. "In Ridgefield, Connecticut, Jamie Fields was innocently walking barefoot across her lawn. Little did she know that she was about to get Lyme disease."

Jamie Fields was a real person. A real dead-from-Lyme-disease person.

Olivia had chosen Lyme disease as her topic because after years of living with and being a hypochondriac, she was a champ at researching diseases, and this was one disease she was unlikely to contract, since she lived in downtown Manhattan.

She practiced while she got dressed.

She practiced on her way to the kitchen, clutching her notes.

"Morning!" her mom called. "Are you okay, honey? You look pale."

Her mother always thought she looked pale.

She *was* pale. She had straight dark brown hair and pale skin. You'd think while she was growing up, her favorite fairy-tale character would have been the similarly toned Snow White, but Olivia had never been able to relate to anyone who took food from strangers.

"I'm fine," Olivia snapped, but then she felt bad. "I'm fine," she said again in a softer tone.

"Are you sure you're feeling all right?" her mom asked. "The flu vaccine sometimes gives you symptoms."

Olivia's mom was a hypochondriac too. Her mom also had a not-so-mild case of OCD and severe anxiety. She washed her hands so often her knuckles bled. Olivia had inherited the hypochondria and anxiety but was thankfully still obsessive-compulsive free. She hoped it wouldn't come with age.

Olivia contemplated telling her mom that she was sick and staying home, but then she'd get dragged to the ER. And she knew she'd have to do the speech the next day anyway. She'd have to spend another entire day with the panic spreading down her body like an unstoppable rash. "I'm fine," Olivia said, her voice shakier than she intended.

"I poured you some juice," her mom said. "And put some banana in your granola. And put a vitamin on your napkin."

"Thanks," Olivia said, even though she was afraid that anything she ate would make her vomit.

Instead, she ran through her speech. *In Ridgefield, New York* . . .

Oh no. Not New York. Ridgefield was in Connecticut! She had forgotten where poor Jamie lived! If she couldn't remember where Jamie had contracted the disease, how was she going to remember the rest?

The clock said 8:02.

Two hours and fifty-eight minutes to go.

It was going to be a long morning.

She brushed her teeth, made sure the green tint really was gone, grabbed her bag—and notes! She had to remember her notes! Ridgefield, Connecticut!—ran to the elevator, and slid inside. There was a senior from her school already in there. Emma Dassin. Emma didn't say hi, so Olivia didn't either.

The rickety doors were about to close when Olivia heard, "Livvie! Livvie, hold on!"

Olivia pressed the *close* button, but it was too late.

Olivia's mom stuck her hands between the doors. "You forgot your hat." She held it out.

"It's October," Olivia grumbled.

"There's a breeze! And you're not feeling well. Take it."

She took it. Less embarrassing to just get it over with.

"Have a great day! Be careful crossing Broadway!"

At last the doors closed.

Olivia stared at her gray woolen hat. She didn't want a cold. But on top of everything else, she could not worry about having staticky hair.

She stuck it in her backpack just as the doors opened onto the lobby.

* * *

Homeroom. Two and a half hours before Olivia's speech.

"What's the worst that happens?" Renée asked her.

The worst? She saw it play out in her head. She would be standing in front of the class, everyone's eyes on her. Her heart rate would skyrocket. She'd be gasping for air. She'd see spots. She'd pass out and probably die.

Yes, die.

Olivia just shook her head.

"Why don't you imagine everyone in the class naked," Renée said. "Especially Lazar."

Olivia did not want to think about Lazar naked. She did not want to think about Lazar at all. Knowing there was a guy in her class who was potentially interested in her made everything worse. She picked her thumb.

BJ twisted back in his seat. "Did you say 'naked'?"

"Olivia has to present in public speaking," Renée said. "I think she should imagine everyone in the class naked."

"I *always* imagine everyone naked. I'm doing it right now." He looked from Olivia to Renée. "You both look pretty good."

"Oh, shut up," Renée said, but Olivia couldn't help noticing that she stuck out her chest.

Cooper sang his way in. "What's happening, 10B?"

"We're imagining each other naked," Renée said.

"Excellent," Cooper said, striking a He-Man pose.

Olivia smiled. Then she wished he were in her public speaking class. Not so she could picture him naked—just so he could make her laugh.

"All you have to do is focus on me," Renée said, since she was in Olivia's public speaking class. "Ignore everyone else."

Olivia was pretty sure that wouldn't help. Renée was an amazing speaker. She didn't even need notes. She just talked. And talked and talked and talked.

Ms. Velasquez strolled in. "Who's here today? Adam? You're back. Good."

"I missed my vaccination yesterday—should I get it today?" he asked.

"Yes. At lunch."

Olivia looked at her watch. It read eight-forty-five. Two hours and fifteen minutes until her speech.

* * *

It was time. *Ridgefield, Connecticut. Tick bites. Bull's-eye rash.*

"Olivia Byrne, you're up," Mr. Roth said. It didn't help that he was the scariest teacher in school both in attitude and physical appearance. He weighed about four hundred pounds, was over six feet tall, and had a permanent scowl on his face. He looked like a troll, if trolls were also giants.

Focus. Speech. Lyme disease.

She stood up. Her legs felt gummy. Her heart beat

a gazillion miles an hour. She was 99 percent sure everyone could hear it.

Olivia remembered that an irregular heartbeat was a symptom of Lyme disease. She definitely had an irregular heartbeat. Maybe she had Lyme disease after all. Maybe she'd willed it on herself. Was that possible? Was she contagious? Maybe she needed to be quarantined immediately.

The class was extra chatty. There were voices everywhere. She felt nauseated—like she was on a boat. The floor was swaying. Also, she was hot. And sweating. Her underarms were wet. Had she put on deodorant that morning? She thought she had. Yes.

She reached the front of the room. She turned around. She tried very hard not to look at Lazar, who was sitting two rows back and staring at her. He was definitely red-cheeked and cute.

Everyone in class continued to talk.

"It's so hot in here."

"Forgot my Spanish homework."

"Should have had a third cup of coffee."

"Why didn't I pee before class?"

Olivia didn't think she could do this. But she had to. Unless she refused. And failed the assignment and possibly the class.

She took a deep breath and waited for everyone to stop talking. She looked at Mr. Roth, who nodded at her to go ahead.

She looked back at the class.

"This is going to be excruciatingly boring," someone said.

Olivia cleared her throat.

"Why is she just standing there?" Olivia heard.

They were still talking. Olivia closed her mouth,
deciding to wait for everyone to shut up.

Renée looked right at her. "Come on, Olivia, you
can do it," she said.

Except Renée's mouth wasn't moving. Her mouth
was closed. Huh? Olivia was confused.

*Oh no, she's looking at me strangely. Is she going to pass
out?*

Renée was talking, but her mouth wasn't moving.
How was she doing that? She looked like a ventrilo-
quist.

Lazar was looking at her too.

She doesn't look good, he said.

Why did he ask if she was single if he didn't think
she looked good? And why wasn't his mouth moving
either?

Was she hallucinating? Did anyone else notice
what was happening?

Olivia looked around the room. Everyone was
talking, but no one was moving his or her lips.

What's wrong with her?

She looks like she's going to barf.

Oh. My. God. They were not saying these things,
Olivia realized. They were thinking them. She was
hearing what people were thinking. And they were

all thinking about her. The shock was so strong, she could barely breathe.

Voices were coming at her fast and furiously:

She's turning blue.

I really have to pee.

Why doesn't she start already?

The room began to spin. Olivia needed air.

She's going to faint!

What is happening? Olivia wondered. She saw Pi looking right at her.

I have no idea, Pi said.

Had Pi just responded to her thought? That made no sense. The room spun, like she was on the Tilt-A-Whirl. Olivia trained her eyes on Pi, a trick her dad had taught her when he took her to Disney World when she was a kid. Pick a point in the distance and stare and you won't get sick. But suddenly there were two Pis.

"Olivia!" Renée yelled.

That was the last voice Olivia heard before everything went black.

CHAPTER FIVE

I KNOW WHAT YOU'RE THINKING

We don't know why it happened to so many of us during third period. Not all of us. But a lot of us.

Eleven a.m. must have been the witching hour.

Mackenzie was sitting in calculus when it happened to her. She was thinking about Bennett. She didn't want to be thinking about Bennett. She tried to stop herself from thinking about Bennett. Did she even like Bennett? She wasn't sure.

He was a year older than she was. A junior. He went to Westside Academy. Private school. And he lived in her building.

They had spoken for the first time over a year ago, the summer before her freshman year, when she was single.

They'd met on the terrace on the eighth floor. It was August. She'd been tanning.

She tanned a lot. There were three lounge chairs on the deck, and Mackenzie always took the one on the right.

He'd taken the chair next to her. Mackenzie hadn't noticed at first. She'd been listening to music on her iPhone, but then she opened her eyes to take a sip of Diet Coke—she drank a lot of Diet Coke—and there he was, the hot guy from the elevator.

He was tall, dark-haired, and shirtless. He was wearing aviator sunglasses and using a navy T-shirt as a pillow.

"Hey," he said.

"Hey," she said back. She wished she were wearing her black Michael Kors bikini instead of her green Milly one. And just like that, she was in love. Or at least in lust.

In October, he texted her at eleven to meet him on the deck, even though you weren't allowed on the deck past ten. He had a joint with him, and she smoked for the first time. Everything went fuzzy and they hooked up on the lounge chair. The lights were off by then, so no one could see.

They hooked up on and off: on the terrace, in her room when her parents and her sister were out, in his room when his parents were. They didn't have sex, but they did everything else. They met up at least twice a week until February, Valentine's Day, when Mackenzie had to know: What was going on between them? Were they just hooking up? Were they a couple? They hung out together in the neighborhood, but he never introduced her to his friends, who mostly lived on the Upper West Side. On the weekends, he went to his parties and she went to hers. Mackenzie's friends knew about him and his friends knew about her, but they weren't official.

Mackenzie liked things that were official.

When she was a kid she'd only been part of "official" fan clubs.

She never bought purses on Canal Street. If she couldn't afford the real thing, then she'd wait until she could. She didn't like fakes. She liked labels. And she wanted the label of girlfriend.

"I'm not looking for a girlfriend," Bennett told her. They were in his room, on his bed. She was putting her shirt back on and trying to look like she didn't care. He didn't want to be her boyfriend? Whatever.

Outside she could see the eighth-floor terrace. She realized he had probably watched her suntan the entire summer before he made his way out to meet her.

She had been lying there. Easy prey. Or just easy.

She moped for a week. She wouldn't tell her parents what was wrong. Her sister, Cailin, never even asked; she was too busy with her senior year. Mackenzie wasn't sure if she didn't notice or didn't care.

Mackenzie stopped texting him. She waited for him to text her, but he didn't. Since his school was uptown, he left an hour before she did, so she hardly ever ran into him in the elevator.

She avoided the deck.

A few weeks later, Cooper and Mackenzie kissed for the first time at Jordana's birthday party. She hadn't seen it coming—they'd known each other since they were in diapers. They grew up in the 'hood together. Cooper's parents, Mackenzie's parents, and Jordana's parents used to triple-date, until Jordana's parents divorced and her dad moved to L.A.

Anyway, Jordana's party was the very first night Cooper and Mackenzie flirted. A lot.

The lights were low and they kissed in Jordana's mom's home office.

By the next morning they were a couple. Held hands. Talked every night. Hung out with each other's families. Mackenzie even invited Cooper's family to her Passover Seder. They were inseparable.

Until Cooper went to summer camp.

Mackenzie didn't mean for it to happen. Or so she convinced herself.

We aren't sure we believe her. Here are the facts: She went to the terrace. She sat in her chair. She wore her black Michael Kors bikini.

One hot August day Bennett came out and sat beside her. "Hi," he said.

"Hi," she said back.

That night he texted her to come upstairs and hang. She knew she shouldn't. She told herself, *Do not go, you know what's going to happen, you cannot cheat on Cooper.* But still she put on her cutest jeans, a lacy bra, a thong, and a tight black top Bennett had once said looked good on her. Then she went. Her heart thumped all the way up to his floor in the elevator.

They were in his bed thirty seconds after she knocked on the door.

Again, they didn't sleep together. Just everything else. In her mind, that made it less bad.

"What now?" she asked Bennett.

"What do you mean?" he asked, and she knew that nothing was different. Nothing had changed at all.

She wasn't sure what to tell Cooper. She wasn't sure why she'd done it. She loved Cooper, didn't she? True, she had felt some relief when she realized that hooking up with Bennett probably meant they were done. What she and Cooper had was too good, too easy. It was bound to end eventually.

But when Cooper showed up at her door a week later and smelled like home and hugged her so tight she thought she would burst—in a good way—she decided that she would only tell him one thing.

"I missed you" was all she said.

She felt guilty. Every day the guilt ate up a little more inside her, like a tapeworm.

That was why she'd gotten the flu shot. As punishment. She deserved it.

This was what Mackenzie was thinking about at eleven a.m. on Wednesday morning in Mr. Gilbert's calculus class. Thinking very loudly, as it turned out.

She was not paying attention to Gilbert in the

slightest. She was chewing on a pen cap and remembering. She turned to the window and realized that Tess was staring at her, eyes wide open in shock.

"What?" Mackenzie whispered.

"Did that really happen?" Tess whispered back.

Mackenzie had no idea what Tess was talking about. "Did what really happen?"

Tess leaned in closer. "You cheated on Cooper?"

Mackenzie's heart raced. "I did not." Had Bennett said something? He wouldn't. He wasn't the kind of guy to kiss and tell. Anyway, they didn't have any friends in common. And she hadn't breathed a word to *anyone*.

"You were just talking about it," Tess whispered. "Two seconds ago."

"I was not!" Mackenzie couldn't believe it. What was Tess trying to pull?

Tess shook her head. "I'm not trying to pull anything!"

"Girls," Gilbert said, turning from the whiteboard. "You're both excused."

Crap. Mackenzie was already in trouble with Gilbert for always handing in her homework late. She was in trouble with all her teachers, actually. "But—"

"Goodbye," he said. "Next time don't disrupt the class."

Mackenzie sighed. She and Tess collected their books and headed to the door.

At least, Mackenzie figured, she'd be able to find

out how Tess knew about her and Bennett. Maybe Tess was just guessing. Although Mackenzie had been thinking about it. Had she been talking out loud? Mumbling to herself? No one else had heard her. Maybe she'd been mouthing the words and Tess had read her lips. Did Tess know how to do that? Mackenzie doubted it. Tess didn't have any secret skills.

The two girls stepped outside.

Tess's eyes were bugging out of her head. She definitely knew something.

This was not good. Not good at all. Mackenzie hadn't told a single person what had happened with Bennett over the summer.

No one was supposed to know.

Even Tess. She loved Tess, but she couldn't tell her something like that. Tess looked up to her. Mackenzie liked that Tess looked up to her. And Tess would think she should tell Cooper the truth.

Mackenzie couldn't tell Cooper. He'd break up with her. And then what? She'd lose him. He'd hate her.

We can't help wondering if she wanted to lose him all along.

Still, tears burned the backs of her eyelids. Her heart raced. Her head hurt. Her mouth was really dry. She needed a Diet Coke. Or one of Bennett's joints. No, no, nothing about Bennett. That was what had gotten her into this mess in the first place.

How had Tess found out?

I can't believe she hooked up with Bennett again. He's such a user.

"Excuse me?" Mackenzie asked, hands on her hips.

Tess took a step back. "I didn't say anything."

"Yes you did. You said Bennett was a user," Mackenzie said.

Not out loud! Tess thought.

What the hell is going on? they both thought.

At that second, just down the hallway, the door to Mr. Roth's public speaking class was thrown open.

"Get Nurse Carmichael!" Lazar yelled as the entire class cleared out of the room.

Voices came from everywhere.

"Give her space!"

That must have hurt.

"She needs to breathe!"

She looks kind of dead.

Mackenzie grabbed on to Tess's hand. "I don't understand what's happening."

"Me neither," Tess said. "And it's so loud." They pressed their backs against the row of lockers to try to stay out of the way—of the people, of the voices. So many voices.

I'm hungry. Is it lunch yet?

I think I'm wearing different-colored socks.

Pi came out of the class last. Her eyes were shining as she walked by Mackenzie and Tess. She was muttering silently to herself. *I could hear her. I could hear* what she was thinking. *She could hear what I was thinking! How did that happen? Is she the only one?*

Mackenzie crossed her arms in front of her chest. *No,* Mackenzie thought. *She's not the only one.*

Pi stopped in her tracks and stared at Mackenzie. *You too?*

Me too.

And me, Tess piped up.

Pi started to laugh. *How is it that we can hear people's thoughts?*

We have no idea, Mackenzie and Tess thought at the same time.

Jinx, Mackenzie thought. *Now someone better buy me a Diet Coke.*

CHAPTER SIX

IT'S A PUZZLE
OUT THERE

Pi was the first one of us to get it. She got it before school, at seven a.m. We aren't sure why. She thinks it was because she's the smartest. We think it's because she was swimming at the time. Working out. More blood flow to her brain.

She was swimming in the downtown community pool on Warren, a few blocks from school. She swam every morning. It cleared her head. She'd read an article in *New York* magazine saying that daily exercise increased one's IQ by about ten points. She would not let ten points get away from her. She did all kinds of things that were supposed to increase IQ—ate fish with omega-3, practiced writing with her left hand, listened to classical music, taught herself chess and poker. Did sudoku. She did sudoku a lot. Sometimes she imagined boxes of numbers on white walls.

Pi had the second-highest GPA in our grade, just behind Jon Matthews. But Pi wanted to be number one. Harvard would never take two kids from one public school. And she wanted to go to Harvard. She wanted to study physics and be a physics professor. She wanted to understand the universe.

Her father was a doctor. Well, he was a researcher at Mount Sinai. He'd lost his license after a malpractice suit. It hadn't been his fault at all, but that was what happened in New York. Greed and bureaucracy got in the way of brilliance. Her mom had left him and taken a job at a hospital in Indiana when the whole thing went down. Pi had refused to move with her, deciding to stand by her dad. They didn't need her mom. She didn't need her mom. Pi would be fine—no, exceptional—without her.

On Wednesday morning, Pi was swimming laps when she kept hearing Black-Speedo Guy talking to himself about the memo he was supposed to send to his boss by noon. *Times or Arial? What says "promote me"?* She saw him there often; he always wore the same Speedo.

At first Pi stopped mid-stroke. "Excuse me!"

The guy ignored her and kept swimming.

But he also kept talking. *I need a raise. At least a hundred bucks a week. Then I could eat out more often and get cool stuff for my apartment. Like a high-def TV. Better speakers. A custom-made bobble head that looks like me and is wearing a Speedo.*

Everyone had the right to voice his ideas, Pi thought, but not when they intruded on someone else's personal space. And this was Pi's personal space. This was her morning swim.

When she reached the end of the pool, she stopped to tread water. She lifted her goggles. "Excuse me! Can you please stop?"

He didn't stop.

"Sir!" she said again, this time louder.

He stopped and turned to her. "Yes?"

"Can you please stop talking? It's making it difficult for me to concentrate."

"I'm not talking. I'm swimming."

"No, you're talking," she argued.

"No," he snapped. *"You're* talking to me." He shook his head and said, *Crazy chick. Her swimming cap is on too tight.* Then he dove under the water.

Pi held on to the edge of the pool and tried to figure out what had happened. He had said something, but his lips hadn't moved.

And on it went all morning. On the walk over to school. Getting her coffee—one cup of coffee was also rumored to increase IQ. Homeroom. She was starting to worry that she was working too hard when Olivia had her meltdown in class. It was then she realized what was happening. Olivia could hear thoughts too. Then, in the hallway, she discovered that the same thing was happening to Tess and Mackenzie.

As soon as she made that discovery, Pi moved Mackenzie and Tess down the hall so they could talk without anyone overhearing. Or without them overhearing anyone else. The farther they stood from the others, the quieter the voices in her head became.

Mackenzie hugged her arms to her chest. *What number am I thinking? Seven.*

"Seven," Pi said.

Tess's jaw dropped. "This is crazy. I heard it too. My turn." Tess closed her mouth. *Eight. No, ten. No, thirty-three and a half!*

"Eight, no, ten, no, thirty-three and a half," Mackenzie said.

"This is the coolest thing ever," Tess said, eyes dancing.

Pi glanced at the others in the hallway. "As far as I can tell, it's just happening to the four of us," she said. "You two, me, and Olivia."

"Where is Olivia?" Mackenzie asked.

"She fainted," Pi said matter-of-factly.

"From this?" Tess asked.

"Sort of," Pi said. "Not because of this, but because it freaked her out. She was doing her speech and then it kicked in and she passed out."

"Is she okay?" Tess asked.

"Probably," Pi said. She didn't want to talk about

Olivia. She wanted to talk about what was happening to them.

"But what *is* happening to us?" Mackenzie asked, throwing her hands up.

"We can hear each other's thoughts," Pi said.

"Not just each other's," Tess said, looking at the crowd in the hallway. "I can hear everyone's thoughts."

"But why is this only happening to the four of us?" Mackenzie asked, her forehead wrinkling. "It's not happening to anyone else."

Pi was deep in thought. "We're all in the same homeroom." But what else did they have in common? Nothing, as far as she could tell. The other two definitely weren't as smart as she was.

"Hey," Mackenzie said. "Just because my GPA is low doesn't make me stupid." *I just don't try.*

"Whatever," Pi said with a shrug. "It's irrelevant. What do the four of us have in common?"

Mackenzie and Tess stared at her blankly.

Suddenly all the numbers aligned. Aha! "We all got our flu shots yesterday," Pi said.

"But everyone got their flu shots," Tess said. "Most of the school got their flu shots."

"That's true," Pi said. "I need to think about this."

Mackenzie rubbed the spot on her arm where she'd gotten the vaccination. "I didn't even want the shot!"

Pi rolled her eyes. "None of us *wanted* the shot."

"No, but I really, really didn't want to get it. I just did it because . . ." *I wanted to punish myself.*

Pi didn't understand what Mackenzie meant about the punishment thing. They had telepathy. This was amazing. They were exceptional.

"I wonder how long it will last," Tess said.

Not long, Mackenzie hoped.

They watched Nurse Carmichael enter the classroom. "Maybe we should talk to the nurse about it," Tess said.

Pi considered the options. Should they seek medical advice? What if the condition was dangerous? On the other hand, once they went public they couldn't take it back. Once they went public she would surely lose control of the situation. "If it really is telepathy, maybe we don't want everyone aware that we can read their minds," she said.

"People would freak out," Tess said.

"They'd cart us off to some mental institution," Mackenzie said, turning white. "Hook us up to all kinds of tubes." *So. Many. Needles. I don't deserve that. Do I?* "Maybe we shouldn't say anything. It might go away."

Tess nodded. *If I only have one day with this ability, I want to put it to good use.*

Pi was still weighing the options. There was no real rush to tell. She could always change her mind in the morning—if it was still happening. She might as well try to explore it on her own that day. It was like poker—no reason to show the rest of the world that she had a flush. "I think for now we should keep this just between us."

"I agree," Tess said.

Mackenzie nodded.

"I'll talk to Olivia," Pi said.

I'm going to find out everyone's secret thoughts! Tess thought.

Pi caught Mackenzie scowling. *I don't want Tess knowing my secret thoughts. I don't want anyone knowing my secret thoughts.*

"Why?" Pi asked. "What are your secret thoughts?"

"Nothing," Mackenzie blurted out. *Don't think about it, don't think about it.*

Tess shook her head. *She doesn't want the whole school knowing she cheated on Cooper.*

Aha.

"Tess!" Mackenzie yelled.

Tess clamped her hand over her mouth. "I'm sorry! I didn't mean to think it!"

As if Pi cared enough to keep up with her class-mates' on-and-off-again relationships.

Mackenzie bit her lip. *Maybe I should talk to Car-michael. Maybe I want this mind reading thing to end as soon as possible. Before it ruins my life.*

"It won't ruin your life," Tess said quickly. "We won't tell anyone about the Cooper stuff. Swear."

"Swear?" Mackenzie asked.

Tess nodded.

Mackenzie turned to Pi.

"Whatever," she said. "I barely even heard any-thing. Don't worry about it." *Like I honestly care about her stupid relationship.*

"Hey!" Mackenzie said.

Pi rolled her eyes. "Sorry."

Tess linked her arm through Mackenzie's. "Let's go to the cafeteria. See what everyone's up to." *I want to find Teddy. ASAP.*

Pi had no idea who Teddy was and didn't care about that either.

"How do you not know who Teddy is?" Tess asked. "Teddy Barbosa? He's in our grade. He's my guy best friend."

Pi leaned against a locker. "I don't know. I just don't. You guys go. I'll wait for Olivia. What we should do is figure out if there are other people this is happening to. If so, round them up. Have a meet-ing."

Mackenzie nodded. "Where?"

"Club room 309. I have a key," Pi said. "I'm on the chess team."

Were we surprised by that? Not even a little.

CHAPTER SEVEN

THAT'S WHAT YOU THINK

When Olivia opened her eyes, she saw a white ceiling. She was lying on a floor. She closed her eyes again.

"Olivia?" she heard. "Can you hear me?"

"Yes," Olivia said. She opened her eyes and saw Nurse Carmichael—and then remembered what happened.

Oh. My. God.

She quickly closed her eyes again. She'd had a total breakdown. She'd hallucinated that she could hear people's thoughts! Who did that? The stress of speaking in public must have really gotten to her. She kept her eyes shut tight. "Is everyone watching me?" she asked.

"We cleared the class out. It's just you and me."

This was worse than she'd thought. "Did I faint?"

"Yes."

"How long was I out?"

"About a minute and a half. Your friend Renée caught you, so you didn't hurt anything."

"Sorry to bother you," Olivia said. "Again."

"It's no problem," Nurse Carmichael said, and Olivia finally opened her eyes.

Of all the kids who could have fainted, why does it have to be the one with the crazy mom?

Wait. What? Nurse Carmichael wasn't talking. Her lips weren't even moving.

Olivia decided she was still hallucinating. She tried to sit up, but Nurse Carmichael put a hand on her shoulder.

"Don't get up yet," Nurse Carmichael said. And then she thought, *If she passes out again, I'm going to call an ambulance.*

Olivia did not want an ambulance to come get her at school. Talk about embarrassing. "I'm fine," she said quickly. "Please don't call an ambulance."

Nurse Carmichael blinked. *Did I say that out loud?*

No, Olivia realized. But she didn't want to admit that. Because if she actually had heard it in her mind, Nurse Carmichael would definitely call an ambulance. And a shrink.

"Has this ever happened before?" Nurse Carmichael asked.

Had she ever heard voices in her head? No, she

must have meant the fainting. "When I was younger," Olivia said.

"Let's go into my office," Nurse Carmichael said. *Maybe I should call an ambulance. If I don't and she faints again, that crazy Jennifer Byrne will sue. I'll lose my job! I'll have to go back to stripping!*

Agh! That was way more info than Olivia wanted to know about Nurse Carmichael.

Olivia rubbed her throbbing temples. No way had Nurse Carmichael been a stripper. Olivia was hearing voices in her head. Hallucinations. They would go away soon. Wouldn't they? Yes. They would. Of course they would.

"Would you like me to call your mom?" Nurse Carmichael asked. *I'd rather lick a cactus needle. No, I'd rather stick a cactus needle in my eye.*

"Why don't I just rest for an hour?" Olivia asked. "There's no reason to bother my mom yet. You know how panicked she gets. It's almost lunch. I'll rest in your office until then and we'll see how I'm doing, okay?"

"Oh. Okay." Nurse Carmichael stood up. "Let's go."

Olivia sat up. The room swayed, but she placed her hands firmly on the floor to steady herself. She probably had a concussion. *Oh my god, can I die from this? I probably can.*

Nurse Carmichael reached out to help her. "Let's go." *I hope Roth isn't still out there. He terrifies me.*

Not only was she dizzy and concussed, she was still

hallucinating. It could be a stroke. Death could come at any second, if she didn't get help.

"Something weird is happening," she began as Nurse Carmichael opened the door.

"What?"

Olivia took a deep breath. She had to tell the nurse. What if she was having an aneurysm? "I hear something . . . strange."

Outside the door, the hallway was empty. Mostly. Pi was leaning over and tying her shoes.

Pi looked up. "How are you feeling?"

"Um . . . fine," Olivia said. *Besides the fact that I'm probably dying.*

"Good," Pi said. *You're not dying. Don't tell Nurse Carmichael anything. Come with me and I'll explain.*

I imagined that, Olivia tried to convince herself. *I need to go to the hospital. It is my concussion talking. I'm going to need a CAT scan.*

Pi shook her head. *You're not imagining it. I can hear you. You can hear me. Tell Nurse Carmichael you're feeling fine and come with me to the chess room.*

Olivia didn't understand what was happening. "But—"

"Everything okay, Olivia?" Nurse Carmichael asked. "Let's go."

Tell her everything's fine and that you're coming with me instead.

Olivia didn't know who to trust. Was she going crazy? Were she and Pi going crazy?

Just tell her!

Okay! But if I die of an aneurysm, it will be your fault!
"You know what, Nurse Carmichael? I'm feeling better. In fact, I think I want to get some lunch. Pi will look after me. If I have any issues, I'll go straight to your office." *If I'm not already dead.*

Nurse Carmichael looked worried. "You sure?" *I shouldn't let her go. But I really do need to run to the pharmacy to get more condoms for tonight.*

Pi and Olivia exchanged disgusted looks.

No, Olivia wasn't sure, but she nodded anyway. She needed to get away from Nurse Carmichael before she could never look the woman in the eye again.

I wonder if I have time to pick up a sexy French maid's outfit.

Olivia grimaced. Too late.

CHAPTER EIGHT

THE JUNGLE

Tess and Mackenzie had two minutes before the lunch bell. Mackenzie checked her phone and saw a text from Cooper:

Still on for my place?

No way. She could not go to Cooper's right then. She had to meet with Pi and Tess. And what if Cooper could hear her thoughts too? No, if he could, he wouldn't have sent that text. His text would have said something along the lines of *Holy shit, something weird is happening to me.*

True, he was in their homeroom. He'd gotten the same flu shot. But so far it was only happening to Pi, Tess, Olivia, and her. Maybe it was a girl thing?

Either way, they'd have to postpone their alone

time until this whole mind reading thing was cleared up.

Mackenzie texted back:

Can't today. Sorry.

"Let's do this," Tess said, eyes twinkling.

They stepped into the cafeteria. A cacophony of voices rushed at Mackenzie.

—five french fries today. Five. No more. My thighs are too—

—There's an empty seat at Jake's table! Should I take it? But Amanda said—

—Did I just get my period?—

As each thought hit Mackenzie's mind, so did a stabbing pain in her forehead.

She could hear people's thoughts. Could they hear hers?

Hello! she screamed in her head. *Can anyone hear me?*

"Yeah, me," Tess said, rubbing her forehead. "Don't shout."

"I meant besides you," Mackenzie said.

"Pi and Olivia," said Tess. "Duh."

Cooper waved to her from their regular table at the opposite end of the room. He was sitting across from Joel, one of his good friends. Joel was also one of Mackenzie's least favorite people. He'd nicknamed her Dumbie for most of second grade.

Where's Teddy? Mackenzie heard Tess wondering. *I*

need to find Teddy! This is my chance to find out how he really feels about me!

Mackenzie looked at Cooper. What if he could read her mind? He'd know she cheated on him with Bennett. He'd hate her forever. There'd be nothing she could do.

I won't say anything, Tess thought back. *I swear.*

I know you won't. But what about Pi? What about Olivia? What about anyone else this is happening to?

They both looked over at Cooper. He was dipping french fries in ketchup. He didn't seem to be stressing about anything. He looked totally normal.

"He doesn't look like he has it," Tess said.

"Do I look like I have it?" Mackenzie asked. "How do you look when you have it?"

"You look freaked out," Tess told her.

We all did have a bit of a freaked-out look to us when we first got it. Which was understandable, since it was freaky.

Cooper, on the other hand, did not look freaked out at all. He looked completely at ease as he smiled at beady-eyed Joel.

"I don't think he has it," Tess said. "But look at BJ."

BJ was sitting one table behind Cooper and did in fact look freaked out. Instead of eating the pizza in front of him, he'd placed his palms flat on the table and was frantically looking back and forth at the people around him.

Tess giggled. "Should I put him out of his misery?

Or let him wallow in it for a while? He's such a perv. I do not want to know what he's thinking at all."

"How are you going to put him out of his misery? By telling him that he probably has telepathy?"

"By telling him that he's not the only one."

"I guess," Mackenzie said. "And let him know we're meeting in the chess club room in ten minutes. But, Tess—can you check on Cooper? Make sure he's okay?" She wished she could hear what he was thinking from this end of the cafeteria. But it didn't seem to work like that. You had to be kind of close to people to hear them. Although if she could hear what he was thinking from here, then he'd be able to hear what she was thinking from *there*. If he could hear what people were thinking at all.

"You're worrying for nothing," Tess said. "Look at him, he's fine!"

Cooper waved to her again.

Mackenzie's heart sped up. "Please just check."

"Fine, give me a sec." Tess hurried over and sat down in the empty spot beside him. Mackenzie pretended to be interested in the lunch choice of tacos or grilled cheese, as she tried to digest what was happening.

A voice in her head sounded just like when the person talked out loud—but a bit muffled. Like there was a pillow over the person's mouth.

—*heard Olivia passed out*—thought Adam from homeroom as he walked by with a can of Diet Sprite.

—the tacos might look like cat barf, but they taste really good—thought a freshman who passed by her next.

She could only hear people in her immediate vicinity. As soon as Adam walked away and the freshman walked by, the freshman's thoughts kicked in.

The theme song from *Dora the Explorer* hit her next.

Unfortunately it was catchy. She couldn't help but sing along.

And then she heard someone's *If I cover my nose with my hand, will anyone notice me pick it?*

Ew, really?

Mackenzie realized Tess was waving her over. Tess was too far for Mackenzie to hear what she was thinking, so she held her breath as she walked to the table. She gave Tess a look.

He doesn't have it! Tess thought at her before jumping over to BJ.

Mackenzie exhaled.

"Hey, babe," Cooper said. "What happened to our plans?"

"I'm sorry," Mackenzie said, sitting down beside him. "I forgot I have stuff to do. I'm just going to get some food to take with me." She hated that she was lying to him again. Hadn't she told him enough lies? But she had to talk to the rest of the crew and figure out what to do. Figure out what this was.

He looked right into her eyes. *I'm so bummed she canceled on me again. I miss her.*

Crap. She leaned over and kissed him gently on the mouth. He tasted like ketchup.

"Get a room, you guys," Joel hollered. He was chewing on an oatmeal cookie. *This sucks. I'm glad I swiped it instead of coughing up the fifty cents.*

"I was hoping to," Cooper answered him, "but I'll take what I can get." He kissed Mackenzie again but then pulled back. *Maybe I can change her mind.* "We still have time. . . ."

"I can't," Mackenzie said. "I'll see you later." She stood up abruptly.

What a cold bitch. It was coming from Joel.

"At least I don't steal from the lunch lady," she barked.

He flushed. *She saw me?*

Mackenzie knew she probably shouldn't have said that. But c'mon. He'd called her a bitch.

What can we say? It wasn't the first time someone thought Mackenzie was a bitch, and it definitely wouldn't be the last.

CHAPTER NINE

US AGAINST THEM

Our first meeting took place in club room 309, the chess room.

It was small, and it had no windows since it was an interior room. It had brown carpet and smelled worse than the Chambers Street subway station in August.

Some of us sat on desks, some of us on chairs.

It was not the most organized meeting. Understandable, since on Day One we were kind of a mess. Half of us were talking out loud, the other half were thinking, and we all had headaches.

We'd rounded up eleven of us. We weren't sure if there were only eleven of us, or if we could only find eleven of us. But one thing was definite: all eleven of us were from homeroom 10B.

Who were we? We were Pi, Mackenzie, Tess, BJ, Jordana, Olivia, Nick, Isaac Philips, Levi Jenkins, Brinn Ferrero, and George Marson, who went by Mars.

The original eleven.

Pi and Olivia had walked by Nurse Carmichael's office and found Mars and Levi waiting for the nurse to get back from her condom run. Tess had found Nick, Isaac, and BJ disoriented in the cafeteria, and Olivia had found Brinn mumbling to herself in the bathroom.

I can't believe this is happening, thought Olivia now.

"It's happening," Nick said. *And my mom better not find out about it. She'll make me quit the baseball team. She'll think this is from the stress.* Nick was the only sophomore at BHS on the varsity baseball team. He glanced at the door as though his mom were about to sense something was up and run right from her biology class to the chess room.

Tess bit her lip. *Holy crap, this is ESP.*

"It's only one type of ESP," Pi said. "ESP is an umbrella term that includes all the extrasensory perceptions. We don't have clairvoyance or precognition. At least, I don't. Does anyone else?"

"I don't even know what those mean," Jordana said.

"Telepathy is when you can hear other people's thoughts. Clairvoyance is when you are aware of something happening in another location. Precognition is when you can tell the future. And then there's telekinesis, which is when you can move objects with your mind."

"No, I'm just having the first one," Tess said.

"Me too," Isaac Philips said, nodding his shock of gray hair. Yes, gray hair. He looked like his head had been colored in by a lead pencil. He was also the only publicly gay guy in our grade.

Of course, within the next few days, we'd know about anyone who was still in the closet. There were no secrets from us.

"But why are we the only ones to have any of it?" Tess asked. "What's so special about us?" *Not that I'm complaining. This is going to make a great book one day. Not that anyone would believe it. I'll have to call it fiction.*

"It must have something to do with the flu shots," Pi said, pacing the room.

"We're not the only homeroom to have gotten the shot," Isaac replied.

Vaccines come in batches, Olivia thought.

Huh? Batches? Jordana wondered while filing her nails.

Olivia turned bright red. *Everyone heard me?*

"Get used to it," Mackenzie muttered. She was sitting in the corner, giving us all death glares.

What's her problem? Levi wondered.

"Me? You're the one who's always in a bad mood," Mackenzie snapped. *Although I'd be in a bad mood too if I had those teeth.*

Some of us gasped.

Mackenzie flinched.

Mackenzie wasn't wrong. He did have terrible teeth. Probably because his parents owned a candy store on Reade Street. He'd worked there since he was a kid. He ate a lot of candy.

"Sorry," Mackenzie added. *This whole thing is pissing me off.*

We should be pissed. Our brains were just contaminated by vaccines! Brinn thought, not looking up from the notepad she was drawing in.

We all stared at Brinn. We'd never heard her talk coherently before. She was always in her own world, mumbling to herself and drawing in her notebook— usually while wearing fencing gear. She was on the fencing team but didn't seem to realize that the uniform wasn't supposed to be worn twenty-four seven. Brinn was our nerd. Sorry, Brinn, but it's true. She mumbled when she talked, her lips were so chapped they bled, and her hair looked like a bird's nest. Not that she seemed to care.

Mackenzie's not pissed because her brain's been contaminated, Jordana thought. *She's pissed because our brains have been. She doesn't want us all knowing her business.*

I don't want you all knowing my business either, Nick thought.

Pi slammed her fist against the table. "Can we try and focus, people?"

"What are we focusing on?" Levi asked. "I'm not exactly sure what we're doing."

I'm not sure why we're not in the emergency room, Olivia thought.

"I agree," Mars said. "We're hearing voices, people. That's messed up. Our brains might be melting." Mars was a piano prodigy. The day before the flu shot, he'd broken up with his girlfriend, Jill Clarke, because he didn't think they were a good fit. Jill had said she agreed. Mars was pretty hot. Dark hair, dark skin. Apparently he used to serenade her. He could sing, too, although unlike Cooper, he didn't force us all to listen to him.

"I'm not sure our best plan is to turn ourselves in immediately," Pi said. "We have to weigh the options. And I think what Olivia said about the batches was right. It was probably just our batch." *I would have realized that myself eventually.*

What a know-it-all, Mars thought.

And why is she acting like she's the boss? Levi wondered.

Pi spun around to face him. "Do you two want to run this meeting? Go ahead."

Mars cringed.

Levi rolled his eyes and sank back into his chair. Then he reached into his pocket and took out a multicolored bag of candy Runts.

"Can I have some?" Tess asked.

He passed the bag around the room.

"Let's review," Pi said. "All we know right now is that the eleven of us have developed some sort of telepathic capabilities."

We nodded.

"Let's discuss that capability for a minute, please." Pi tapped her pen against a desk. "What do we know about it?"

"The voices are like real voices," Nick said. "You hear them all, but it's hard to focus on more than one at a time."

"The closer you are to the person, the louder their voice," Mackenzie said. *I could hear Cooper really loudly.*

"You could? When? When you were getting it on?" BJ asked, arching his thick eyebrows.

Mackenzie rolled her eyes. "No. We were talking. But good theory."

"People are also louder when there's less in the way," Nick said. "Like right now, since Tess is sitting between me and Olivia, I can hear Tess's thoughts, but it's hard for me to hear Olivia's."

Good, thought Olivia.

Tess slumped in her seat. "Better?"

"Think something, Olivia!"

Olivia flushed. *My head hurts.*

Nick gave her a thumbs-up.

"We can't hear anyone outside this room," Pi said. "Maybe walls also act as interference."

BJ stretched his arms above his head. "Anyone want to test my 'thoughts are loudest when you're hooking up' theory with me?"

"No," the girls in the room said.

"Isaac?" BJ asked.

"You're not my type," Isaac responded. *He's so my type.*

Ha! BJ waggled his eyebrows. *I knew it! I'm everyone's type.*

You're not my type, Tess thought.

Olivia rubbed her temples. Her head was really killing her. She needed to go to the nurse's office to get some Tylenol. She closed her eyes. She wished she had gone home after all. The idea of everyone in the room knowing her every single thought filled her with dread.

She had dumb thoughts.

She knew she had dumb thoughts.

She didn't want everyone in the room to know all her dumb thoughts.

Wait a sec. She opened her eyes and heard—

Well, BJ, you hit on anything that moves and you're—

She closed her eyes again.

Silence.

Opened them.

—and your ears are kind of big—

Closed them.

Silence.

Opened them.

It stops when I close my eyes, Olivia thought.

Pi looked right at her. "Can you guys shut up so Olivia can talk?"

Olivia gulped. *I wasn't planning on talking.*

"Olivia," said Pi, sounding annoyed, "we're trying to learn from each other here. It doesn't help us if you hoard your discoveries. What were you thinking about your eyes?"

Olivia nodded. "I . . . I noticed that it doesn't work when you close your eyes."

"What doesn't work?" Pi asked.

"When I close my eyes, I can't hear you. The voices stop."

Why didn't I notice that? Pi wondered. "Let me try. Everyone think."

Mackenzie: *How much longer is this meeting going to last?*

Levi: *Who has the rest of my Runts?*

Pi opened her eyes. "Okay, enough. I couldn't hear any of you. Could you hear me?"

We shook our heads.

"Were you thinking things?" Nick asked.

"Of course I was thinking things," Pi huffed. "I'm always thinking things."

"So that's good news," Nick said. "If we close our eyes, we can stop listening to people and stop other people from listening to us."

He closed his eyes immediately. We all did.

"So we can still keep secrets," Jordana said. She heaved a sigh of relief. We all did.

"So what do we do now?" Nick asked.

We all opened our eyes.

That was the big question. Of course, all of us had different opinions.

Levi: *We spy on people!*

Nick: *I don't want to spy on people.*

Levi: *Then you're a moron.*

We should tell Nurse Carmichael, Olivia thought.

The next thoughts came fast and furiously, ping-ponging around the room. It was hard to tell who was saying what. It was like all of us were talking at once in a stream of consciousness.

What's Carmichael going to do? . . . She could help us. . . . How? . . . Maybe there's a reversal vaccine. . . . Maybe it's not because of the vaccine. . . . What else could it be? . . . Maybe she'll know how to get rid of it. . . . Why would you want to get rid of it? . . . Why wouldn't I? . . . We have a superpower! Why would you want to reverse it? . . . I don't want to know what other people think! . . . I do! It's awesome! . . . Where are those candy Runts? . . . We should tell Nurse Carmichael. . . . Forget Nurse Carmichael. We should go to the emergency room. . . . Or call the Men in Black. . . . There's no such thing as the Men in Black. . . . There's no such thing as ESP either. . . . If we go to the emergency room, they'll put us all in a rubber room. . . . And do experiments on us. . . . If they believe us. . . . They'd never believe us. . . . It's not so hard to prove. . . . True. We just tell them what they're thinking. . . . No one's going to like that. . . . No shit, Sherlock.

Brinn slammed her forehead on the desk and then mumbled something.

What did she say? we all wondered.

Can everyone shut up? My head is killing me.

"Me too," Mackenzie said, placing her hand on her stomach. "I feel like I'm going to puke."

"So have we agreed?" Pi asked, taking command of the room. "For now, we keep this among us?"

"I don't remember agreeing to that," Nick said.

"I think we should keep it quiet," Tess said. "Maybe not forever. But for now. Until we get a little more used to it." *Until I can use it to find out what Teddy thinks. Oops.* She looked around the room. Who had heard that?

Nick was looking right at her. He was one of Teddy's buddies. Had he heard?

Nick looked away. *Not getting involved,* he thought.

"We might as well see how we can use this," Mars said.

"Use this?" Mackenzie asked. "How do you use this?"

Tess gave her a look. "Aren't there things you want to know but no one will tell you?"

We all nodded. How could we not? Of course there were things we wanted to know.

"So let's see what we can find out," Pi said. "If we

tell other people what we can do, they'll quarantine us. No one wants his or her secrets to be public knowledge. So we have to keep this between us. That means no telling anyone. Friends. Parents. Teachers." Pi looked at Nick. "Parents who are teachers."

Don't look at me, Nick thought. *My lips are sealed.*

"What about boyfriends who are in our homeroom but don't have ESP?" Mackenzie asked.

"Do not tell Cooper," Pi insisted. "Only tell those who develop it. And we must get to them before they tell anyone else."

"Who's not here from our homeroom?" Nick asked.

Tess counted those of us who were missing on her fingers. "Sadie, Isabelle, Courtney, Rayna, the twins. There are twenty-four people in our class. And we're only eleven."

"But two didn't get the shot," Mars said. "So that makes twenty-two."

"Unless someone from one of the other classes had the batch we got," Pi reasoned. She looked at us sternly. "We all have to be on the lookout for signs."

Or on the listen-out, Olivia thought, sinking into her chair. *That was totally dumb.*

Tess laughed. *Not dumb. I thought it was funny.*

Olivia sank even farther. *They can hear me worrying about my dumbness! And now they can hear me worrying about worrying about my dumbness. It's a friggin' house of mirrors.*

"It *is* a house of mirrors," Pi said. "And we have to watch from every angle. Especially the other people in our homeroom. Got it?"

We nodded.

"We have to be a team," Pi continued. "We'll meet again tomorrow at lunch."

"I have a *Bloom* meeting," Tess said.

"Skip it," Pi ordered.

Rude, Isaac thought.

"For all we know, we might not even have telepathy anymore tomorrow," Levi said.

Olivia nodded. *Fevers after vaccines only last a day or so. Why should this last any longer?*

Pi gave her a look that was part admiration, part annoyance. *For someone who has never spoken in class, you sure have a lot to say.*

Olivia flushed.

Mackenzie turned to Olivia. "So this could all be gone by tomorrow?" Her voice sounded hopeful.

Olivia nodded. *I hope so.*

"Thank God," Mackenzie said. *Life can go back to normal.*

Brinn shook her head. Her fingers were tinged with charcoal. *Normal is boring. Who wants that?*

"Okay, everyone," Pi said. "See you tomorrow at lunch. Keep your mouths shut. If you do discover someone else, please share our discussions with them and inform them about tomorrow's meeting."

We nodded. Pi had spoken: class was dismissed.

CHAPTER TEN

THE NON-DATE
FROM HELL

Tess looked for Teddy all over school but couldn't find him.

She was psyched to finally find out if he liked her. No more wondering. She would just stand beside him and know if he felt the same or if she should move on.

But by the end of the day, Tess hadn't seen Teddy at all. Well, they'd crossed paths for a second on the stairs. Tess was going up; Teddy was going down. But there were like a hundred louder people between them, so she couldn't hear his thoughts.

She waved and tried to squirm her way toward him, but it was like rush hour on the subway, so no go.

Between sixth and seventh periods he was by his locker, so she thought maybe that was her chance, but he had some sort of French test and all he was thinking was *je pense, tu penses, il pense,* and that did not help her get a feel for if he liked her one bit, *malheureusement.*

By the time the bell rang, she knew she had to take matters into her own hands.

She texted him:

```
Hey, what are you up to later?
```

She stared at her phone. And waited. She knew in theory a watched phone never got a text, but she still stared.

Finally a text popped up—theory proven false!

```
Have practice. But want to see new
   Death Valley movie with me and
   Nick after that?
```

Tess did want to see *Death Valley.* She loved seeing horror movies, especially with Teddy. The scarier the better. When the movie was especially bloody, she had an excuse to press her face against his shoulder and breathe in his Irish Spring scent. Yum.

Usually Tess was happy to have Nick around too.

But not tonight.

Nick would hear everything she was thinking. Including thoughts about her signature sniffing-Teddy's-shoulder move.

So embarrassing.

But time could be running out. She needed to see Teddy soon. She texted back:

Sure.

She was extra pleased when she got out of the shower and saw:

Nick bailed. You still in?

Yes. She was still in.

Now, what to wear? She wanted to look pretty but casual. Not like she was trying. Normal, but really good normal. So he could see her and think she was pretty and not even notice the extra effort . . . or the extra few pounds. Or maybe even like them.

The weight was all her mom could think about. Seriously, her mom had been thinking about it as Tess ate dinner. *Maybe if she ate slower, she wouldn't be so hungry. Does she have to use that much salad dressing? Why is she taking more sweet potatoes?*

So what if she wanted a second serving of sweet potatoes? Sweet potatoes were vegetables.

She scrunched and diffused her hair and then zipped up her best jeans. Or what she thought were her best jeans.

We think her best jeans were actually the ones with the frayed bottoms.

Tess didn't know that at the time, though, so she called Mackenzie to make sure she looked good in them. "My James jeans don't make my ass look fat, do they?"

"No," Mackenzie said.

"Love you," Tess chirped. If Teddy felt the same way Tess did, soon they'd be double-dating with Mackenzie and Cooper. She couldn't wait. "What are you doing?" she asked.

"Just thinking," Mackenzie said.

"About what?" she asked. She wished their telepathy worked over the phone. Then she wouldn't have to waste time with silly questions.

"Nothing. I gotta go. Good luck."

Tess put on her best bra. It was black lace and gave her great cleavage.

None of us had seen all her bras, so we can't make an informed decision on whether it was her best.

BJ had seen one of Tess's bras. He'd felt her up during a game of seven minutes in heaven in eighth grade while they were kissing. It was a cotton white one. It had been biggish back then, but now it fit perfectly.

As Tess put on a purple shirt, she thought about what it would mean if she found out Teddy didn't like her. What if he thought she was ugly? Or fat? Did she really want to know what he thought of her? Was she opening some sort of Pandora's box? Once she knew what he thought, she wouldn't be able to erase the knowledge. It was like reading someone's diary or overhearing a private phone conversation. Once you heard, you couldn't unhear.

Tess would die if anyone read her diary. She wrote religiously. Kind of. There was an entry for every day. But she back-wrote them about once a week. She fake-dated them and used a different pen for each day of the week to make it look legit.

So did she *really* want to know what he *really* thought?

Yes. She really did.

* * *

Tess waited for him at the entrance to the theater. Teddy grabbed her in a bear hug. "Tess! Are you ready to be terrified? There will be blood. And be-headings. Many beheadings."

"Awesome," she said. "Nothing like a good behead-ing."

Tess is the best. She's just such a cutie.

Of course he had no idea that she could hear him.

Why would he? Back then people didn't ever think about their thoughts being heard. These days it's a different story.

But Tess did hear. She was thinking, *Yes! Yes! Yes! He thinks I'm the best! He thinks I'm cute!*

For the record, we don't think "cute" and "such a cutie" are interchangeable. But anyway.

As they went to buy tickets, what Tess thought was this: *If he thinks I'm cute and we're already best friends, doesn't that mean he likes me? What else does he need?*

Teddy was looking as adorable as always. His eyes reminded Tess of hot chocolate. He was in great shape too—on the bigger side, and not too thin.

Tess and Teddy had met in a creative writing class back in seventh grade. He'd had a girlfriend then who lived in the West Village. Because he had a girlfriend, they'd been able to become fast—and best—friends. But he and the girlfriend had finally broken up—after three years!—just that summer.

Tess ordered herself one ticket and then Teddy got one for himself. She wished he had offered to treat her; that would have been a sign they were on an actual date.

But they had been to the movies lots of times before. They were just friends. Best friends. At a movie. Of course, a movie date could easily change into something more in a dark theater if the mood felt right. Right?

Right.

"I'll get popcorn," Teddy said. "You get us seats."

"Will do," she said. She smiled and then entered the empty theater. There was only a handful of people already there.

She chose a seat smack in the middle.

We think that was her first mistake, by the way.

She should have sat in the last row. The last row says romance. Oh, well. Too late now.

The previews started as Teddy sat down a few minutes later. He was balancing one large popcorn and two large lemonades. They all looked precariously close to spilling.

Once he was seated, his knee was right next to hers. His arm too. They were so close. Any minute they could start kissing.

But was Teddy thinking about kissing? No. Teddy was thinking, *This preview looks awesome. I totally want to see* Iceman Revisited.

Maybe she needed more lip gloss?

Suddenly Teddy jerked in his seat. *She's here! She's here!*

Huh? She's here? Who's here? Tess looked over to see Sadie Newman and Keith Asher climbing up the stairs. Ugh. *What are* they *doing here?*

"Hey, guys," Teddy said, "come join us!"

The other people in the theater gave him dirty looks, which were accompanied by thoughts of *He better shut up!*

Tess wanted to scream, *Nooooooo! Sit somewhere else! Leave us alone!*

But she just smiled.

Sadie had curly brown hair, a big smile, a waif-like body, and huge doe eyes. You would not be surprised if you saw her on a teen book jacket, staring at the camera, looking wholesome while caught in a zombie-werewolf love triangle.

She waved and made her way toward them. She was in 10B too, but it didn't seem to Tess that any telepathy had kicked in.

Keith followed, looking vaguely annoyed.

We can't blame him. His night out with his off-and-on-again girlfriend had just become a group date with a bunch of sophomores. He was a senior. He played varsity baseball.

Keith cast a glance at Tess and gave her a brief smile. *What's her name again? Carrie?*

Tess was mortified. *He thinks my name is Carrie?* Was she that forgettable? But then Keith sat down beside Sadie, who was sitting beside Teddy, and Tess couldn't really hear anyone but Teddy. And she did not like what she was hearing.

Why is she with him? Teddy was thinking. *He's such a tool. And she's a goddess.*

Tess felt sick. Sadie was a goddess? *A goddess?!* She didn't like writing, or watching horror movies. She spent most of homeroom reading tabloids on her iPhone or picking her split ends.

"You didn't miss anything," Teddy said to Sadie. "Do you want some popcorn?"

"Sure, dude," Keith said.

I wasn't talking to you, jerkoff, Teddy thought. *I was talking to Sadie. Sadie, Sadie, Sadie.*

Tess wished he weren't talking to either of them.

She wished they weren't there. She wished *she* weren't there. She wished she were at home writing in her diary.

Mmm. She smells so good, Teddy thought. *Like straw-berries.*

Seriously? Tess thought. *Strawberries? He thinks it's good if a girl smells like fruit?*

We all know that if Teddy had thought that Tess smelled like fruit, any kind of fruit, even kiwis, she would have been over the moon. But as Tess sat in that movie theater, the only thing she wanted to do with strawberries was throw them at Sadie. Or maybe stuff them up Teddy's nose.

It continued.

When Teddy and Sadie both took popcorn at the same time, he wanted to hold her hand. He thought about her lips. He thought about what it would be like to kiss those lips. To kiss her neck. To unbutton her shirt. To lick those fingers. To—

Tess squeezed her eyes shut.

She did not want the visual, thank you very much.

Tess had no idea how she hadn't known this. They were supposed to be friends! Best friends! Why hadn't he told her he liked Sadie? And the three of them were in the same chemistry class together! How had she never noticed? The girl sat only four rows ahead of them. Was Tess that oblivious?

Tess felt crushed. Totally and completely anni-hilated. Like a truck had landed on her and then reversed and accelerated and then reversed and accelerated again until she was nothing but roadkill. She vowed never to open her eyes again.

She just couldn't believe it. Teddy didn't like her. He liked Sadie.

As if he had any chance with Sadie. She was dating a senior! She'd had sex with him, too! We all knew. Well, we were 99 percent sure. By the next day we'd have 100 percent confirmation just by sitting next to her.

Teddy tapped Tess's knee. "Don't close your eyes already! No one's even been beheaded yet!"

Tess wondered if she could volunteer to be the first. She opened her eyes.

Maybe Sadie will get scared and jump into my lap, Teddy thought.

Sadie turned to Teddy, looking startled. "Excuse me?"

Teddy beamed. *She's talking to me! Did you hear that, Keith? Huh?*

"Are you trying to talk to Keith?" Sadie whispered. "Keith, Teddy has something to tell you."

Teddy recoiled. *I do?*

Keith leaned over. "What do you want, dude?"

Teddy shook his head. *I want to punch you in the face.*

"Teddy!" Sadie shrieked. "What's wrong with you?"

"SHHHHHH!" said the woman a few rows behind them.

Great, Tess thought. *Just great.* Sadie was getting

ESP and it was Tess's job to help her. "Sadie, come with me to the bathroom?"

"Excuse me?" Sadie asked.

"Bathroom," Tess said, standing up. "Let's go."

What's she doing? Teddy wondered.

Carrie's weird, Keith thought.

Did Keith just say that out loud? Sadie wondered.

No, Tess thought. *Just come with me and I'll explain, okay?*

Sadie nervously picked at a split end. Then she nodded and followed Tess to the bathroom.

CHAPTER ELEVEN

PLEASE KEEP IT DOWN

Tess was not the only one with problems that first night.

Mars had trouble focusing on his piano lesson. It was hard to play Chopin when your teacher was making her grocery list. After his teacher left, Jill, his ex-girlfriend, dropped by his apartment to pick up a textbook she'd left behind.

"I can't stay long," she said. "I have plans." *I have no plans! I know I said it was a mutual breakup, but it wasn't! I lied! I miss you! Serenade me!* She picked up the textbook. "Later."

Levi had a shift at Candy Heaven after school, and not only did he have to listen to the kids' endless whiny chatter—"I want more gum!" "I want more chocolate!" "Ella got more jelly beans than meeeeee!"—but he had to listen to their nannies' thoughts too: *Does she never stop complaining? Why hasn't he called? Is it six o'clock yet?* He scooped a lot of gumballs with his eyes closed to block the noise. He also dropped a whole bunch on the floor by accident.

Olivia made her mom dinner. Olivia liked to cook. She made casseroles, risottos, stews. Tonight she made a chicken stir-fry. When she was done and was trying to do her math homework at her desk in the living room—there was no room for a desk in her tiny bedroom—she had to listen to her mom's OCD: *Did Olivia turn off the stove? I think she did. Maybe she didn't. I should just check. Oh, yes she did. I knew she had. But it's good to check.* Two minutes later: *What if I turned it on again by accident?*

Olivia retreated to her bedroom and spent some time Googling "flu vaccine reactions" on the family laptop. She found that most symptoms—normal symptoms, at least, like headache and sore arm—did in fact clear up on their own fairly quickly. So she had hope—*please, please, please*—that by the time she woke up the next morning, her homeroom's telepathy would be gone.

But we all agree Mackenzie had the worst evening. By far.

She knocked on her parents' door to say good night.

"Come in," they called.

Both her parents were sitting on their bed in their bathrobes.

"Night, guys," Mackenzie said, and gave them each a peck on the cheek.

"Night," her mom said. "Will you close the hallway lights?"

"Yes, I will *turn off* the lights."

Her mom was from Montreal and used weird Canadianisms like "open and close the lights." Also "washroom" and "poutine."

In case you're wondering, poutine involves french fries, gravy, and cheese curds. Those of us who have tried it claim it's delicious. Those of us who haven't are skeptical.

"Thanks, honey," her mom said. *Good thing Mackenzie is such a sound sleeper.*

Huh? Mackenzie wondered. *Why is it good I'm a sound sleeper?*

Her dad patted her mom on the leg. *I can't wait to take off Linda's robe.*

Huh? Oh no. Mackenzie slammed her eyes shut.

Her parents. Were. Going. To. Have. Sex.

Sex!

Imminently!

She backed slowly out of the room.

"Have a good sleep," her dad called.

Sleep? How was she supposed to sleep knowing what was taking place just a few feet away?

At least she wouldn't hear their thoughts once she was in her room.

She closed the door and got in her bed.

That feels soooooo good.

No. No, no, no.

They were on the other side of her wall! This wasn't supposed to happen!

She shut her eyes. Silence, thank goodness. Maybe she could just get a glass of water—

Mackenzie opened her eyes for a split second—but then heard *Her breasts look huge in that position* and immediately reclosed them.

Understandably, she refused to open them again until morning.

CHAPTER TWELVE

THE MORNING AFTER

"Olivia? Time to get up."

Her mom was standing over her. "It's after seven. Didn't your alarm go off?"

Olivia remembered that something wasn't right, but she couldn't immediately place what it was.

Then she heard her mom think, *She looks strange.*

Olivia stared. *No. No. No. No.* She could *still* hear things. Why could she still hear things? The ESP was supposed to disappear overnight! She was not supposed to hear things that morning. Would this telepathy never go away? Would she have it forever?

"Is something wrong?" her mom asked. "Are you sick?"

"Yes," Olivia said, pulling her covers over her

head. "I'm sick. Very." *I am not going to school like this. I am not going to school until this ends.*

"Poor baby," her mom said, sitting on the edge of Olivia's bed and pulling the covers off her face. Her mom frowned. *The flu shot made Olivia sick! Or what if she was infected with the actual flu before the vaccine kicked in? She is not that diligent about washing her hands. Or what if it's something else entirely? There are a lot of terrible viruses going around. Didn't the health section in the* Times *say that SARS is making a resurgence? Is it SARS? I should take her to the emergency room.*

Oh God. Olivia did not want to spend the day in the ER with her mom. But she also did not want to go to school and deal with the fact that half her homeroom could hear her thoughts.

"Can I just stay in bed for now? Maybe take a day of rest and see how I feel? And if I'm not better by this afternoon, then we can go to the emergency room?" Oops. Her mom hadn't said the emergency room part out loud.

Her mother considered, not noticing the mistake. "Okay. I can stay home from work." *What if she collapses when I'm not here?*

"I won't—" She stopped herself. "I'll be fine here. I'll rest. I'll call you if I need anything."

Her mother hesitated. *I do have a meeting today. But what if she needs me?*

"I'll be fine. Promise." If her mom was staying

home, then she was going to school. Her mom's crazy made Olivia feel even crazier.

"Okay, honey," her mom said finally. "Call me if you need anything." *I'll call her every hour to check in. Maybe we can Skype so I can monitor her color.*

Olivia's phone buzzed next to her bed, and she twisted around to see what it said. She didn't usually get texts this early.

It was from Pi. She had started a group chat. It was to all of us. It said:

```
I'll assume nothing has changed?
  Meeting still on for lunch.
  Everyone be there.
```

Olivia thought the text sounded vaguely threatening.

We all thought the text sounded vaguely threatening.

"What's wrong?" her mother asked. "Who's it from?" She tried to sneak a peek at the message, but Olivia turned her phone over quickly.

She debated what to do. She really wanted to hide under her covers. But she needed to find out what was happening to her. "You know what? I'm feeling much better."

Her mother eyed her phone suspiciously. "Already?"

"Yeah. I must have had a nightmare or something. I'm fine. Really."

"Hmm." *I think she should stay home just in case. It could still be SARS.*

"Mom! I'm not sick. Feel my head."

Her mother pressed her palm against Olivia's forehead. Indeed, she had no fever. "You don't feel warm. . . ."

"Because I'm not. I have a lot of work I shouldn't miss today," Olivia rushed to explain. "If I need to, I'll stop by Nurse Carmichael's, 'kay?"

Her mom paused, considering. Then she nodded. Sucker.

* * *

So we went to school.

By this time there were more of us. Twenty-one, to be exact. The telepathy had kicked in for almost everyone in our homeroom over the course of twenty-four hours.

Courtney Hunter got it while she was watching TV with her parents. She didn't have her own TV in her room, which was annoying. Her parents wanted her to bond with them over shows and have family time together. They liked to watch all the trendy shows about murdered teenagers and boys with paranormal powers on the CW and ABC Family. She sat in the middle.

I wish Una would wear her hair like that, her dad thought.

Una was her mom.

"What did you say?" Courtney asked.

Her dad kept his eyes on the TV. "Nothing."

I wish Gerry had abs like that, her mom thought.

"What did you say?" Courtney asked her mom.

"Nothing," her mom said.

Courtney started feeling sick. "Stop being weird!" she cried. But the thoughts kept coming.

Eventually she started screaming that she could hear what they were thinking, and they gave each other a look.

Is she on drugs? they both thought at the same time.

"I am not on drugs!" she yelled.

Her parents looked at each other in alarm.

"I think we need to check your room," her dad said.

"I am not on drugs!" she yelled again. Not at that moment. Even though she'd never had ADD she occasionally popped an Adderall. Just to help her concentrate when she had an exam. She took maybe one a week. Two, max. Luckily she was out, so her parents wouldn't find any.

They went to check her room while she watched the end of the show.

* * *

Isabelle Griffin got it during dinner. She was alone and had ordered pizza from Dean's, and when the food showed up, she could hear the delivery guy's thoughts. When her parents and brother came home, she could hear their thoughts too, and she freaked out. She started hyperventilating. Her mom didn't understand what was wrong—"What do you mean you can hear my thoughts?" And she called their doctor's office, which paged Dr. Coven, who called back seven minutes later.

"She's hearing voices," Isabelle's mom told her, her voice trembling.

Dr. Coven thought Isabelle was either on drugs or having a psychotic episode, and instructed her mother to take her to the ER immediately. The two of them took a taxi to St. Luke's emergency room. While her mom was filling out paperwork, Isabelle texted her friend Jordana:

At hospital. Losing my mind.

Isabelle's phone rang two seconds later.

"You're not crazy," Jordana said, and explained.

Isabelle wasn't sure she believed Jordana, but then Jordana conferenced in Pi, and Pi explained how it all worked and about the eye closing and everything and ordered Isabelle to hightail it out of the ER.

Isabelle told her mom that she was feeling better, that the voices were gone, that all she needed was a good night's sleep, but the ER nurse was already calling her name, and so she had no choice but to get checked out.

Isabelle peed in a cup and got her blood drawn so they could run a toxicology report and do drug tests. Meanwhile, Jordana and Pi kept texting her.

Don't tell them anything.

Did they figure it out?

What's happening over there?

The tests all came back clean. The nurse couldn't find anything wrong with her.

* * *

Anojah Kolar got it over breakfast. She told her dad that she could hear his thoughts, but he didn't believe her. He asked her if she needed a new glasses prescription. LensCrafters was having a sale.

Dave and Daniel Zacow, the twins, both got it in the elevator. They were the only ones in the elevator at the time, so at first they thought they were finally developing twin powers, which people were always asking them about. Anyway, when they stepped out of the elevator, they realized they could hear their doorman's thoughts too.

"Morning, Dave. Morning, Daniel," he said. *Good thing they're always together, because I never remember who's who.*

Edward Williams wasn't that surprised when he

started hearing thoughts. He had always expected something paranormal to happen to him, but he'd always thought it would come in the form of him turning into a vampire. He watched and read a lot of vampire stuff. *True Blood*. Anything by Anne Rice. *Fright Night*—the original and the remake. He once put together a list of the top hundred vampire movies for his blog. He even read the Twilight books. He had to after he found out the lead guy was named Edward. He wanted to live forever and bite girls' necks and, well, sparkle.

Sergei Relov and Michelle Barak both got it on their way to school.

Sergei stopped in the park to call his girlfriend in Toronto. There were only a few people there that early and they weren't too chatty, so at first Sergei thought the extra voices were from cell phone interference. He hung up and called her again. It didn't help.

Michelle got it on the subway. Unlike most of us, she did not live in Tribeca. She lived in a small four-floor walkup in Midtown. But BHS was a better school than the one in her area and she had gotten in, so she took the subway there and back every day. When the telepathy kicked in, the subway got loud. Very loud. But hey—it was rush hour. Very loud was to be expected.

Rayna Romero got it right before homeroom while standing in the middle of the hallway. One second she was minding her own business, walking to class, and the next second voices were attacking her at full volume.

"Late night last night?"

He looks like shit.

"Wait for me one sec?"

I have a wedgie.

"Did you do your calc homework?"

She better let me copy.

"Will is such a loser."

Is everyone staring at my zit?

Rayna didn't understand what was going on. *Why is it so loud in here? Where are all the voices coming from?*

Rayna wanted to go to homeroom, but she couldn't move. She was *never* late for homeroom. She was never late for anything. She didn't like being late and she didn't like surprises. But that morning she just stood there. Suddenly she had a splitting headache.

The bell rang, making it worse.

Rayna, it's going to be okay, she heard from somewhere. She wasn't sure where the voice was coming from. She looked around. No one was talking to her. Tess was standing in front of her, but her lips weren't moving.

Rayna, we need to go to homeroom, the voice said—the voice that was talking to her.

I don't want to go to homeroom! I want this to stop! Rayna's eyes were wild. Terrified. *But I can't concentrate. There are so many thoughts!*

"Excuse me!" a senior yelled as he stood behind her. "You're in the way!" *Honk! Honk! I wish I had a horn on my nose.* He eventually walked around her.

Rayna, close your eyes, the nice voice said. *Trust me, just close them.*

Rayna did what she was told, thinking maybe she was dreaming. She had a lot of weird dreams. Sometimes she flew through the hallway stark naked except for her days-of-the-week underwear.

As soon as she closed her eyes, the voices halved. *Better,* she thought. At least the real voices weren't so rude.

"It's going to be okay," the nice voice said, but this time it wasn't muffled and was accompanied by a hand on her arm.

She opened her eyes to see that Tess was talking to her. "What's happening? I really don't like surprises."

"Follow me to homeroom," Tess said. "We'll explain."

Unfortunately for Rayna, this wasn't the only shocker she would get that day. That night, while she downed a plate of cheese ravioli and breadsticks with her parents and younger sister, she would telepathically discover that she had been born with a sixth finger on her left hand, which had been promptly removed and never spoken of again.

Um, surprise?

CHAPTER THIRTEEN

SOMETHING FUNNY'S GOING ON AROUND HERE

Cooper sang to himself as he hurried up the stairs to school. As usual, he was late. This time he was late because Ashley, his three-year-old sister, would not let go of the leg of his jeans. She hadn't wanted him to leave. "Let's play Spider-Man!" she'd hollered. When she finally let go, she insisted on going with him to the elevator to press the button. He adored his sister, but she made it infinitely more difficult to leave the apartment.

He slept in by accident. He'd been up late the night before. The baseball game had gone into extra innings. Finally, the Yankees had beaten Baltimore in the eleventh, 4–3. They needed to win two more games to go to the American League Championship

Series. After the game was over, he'd had trouble falling asleep. He'd been thinking about Mackenzie and trying to figure out what was going on with her. Something was up; he just wasn't sure what. When they'd spoken the night before, she had sounded distant.

"You okay?" he'd asked.

"Yeah. Fine," she'd said, her voice clipped.

It was with this in mind that he dumped his books into his locker and hurried to homeroom. He was looking forward to seeing her.

"What's up, 10B!" Cooper sang. "Can I get a boo-ya?"

Usually we responded to his chant. On this day, though, we just stared at him. No one said a word. Not even Nick or Mackenzie.

He tried again. "10B! I cannot hear your boo-ya!"

Again we didn't respond.

He looked confused. He *was* confused. Understandably. Every day for all of September at least some of us had responded to his boo-ya. That day we were all too busy mentally talking to each other.

And what we were saying was this: Everyone in our homeroom could read minds. Everyone except Renée, Adam McCall, and Cooper.

I get why Renée and Adam can't—they didn't get the vaccine. But why can't Cooper do it?

He got the shot, didn't he?

He did!

Did anyone see him get the shot?

Mackenzie did. She went in with him.

Mackenzie was in the back row. Tess was sitting to her right. Cooper would take the spot on her left.

Levi, BJ, and Courtney were all in the row in front of her.

Yes, Mackenzie thought. *I just hope it didn't work on him. Damn, I didn't mean to think that!*

Mackenzie's glad he doesn't have it! Courtney thought.

Why? thought BJ.

I don't know! replied Courtney.

Stop thinking about me! Mackenzie ordered.

Mackenzie always thinks everything is about her, Courtney thought.

Excuse me? I do not.

Why wouldn't you want Cooper to have it? BJ asked, twisting around to look at her. *Unless there's something you're not telling him. Did you lie to him? Did you cheat on him?*

The name *Bennett* popped into Mackenzie's head before she could stop it. She clenched her eyes closed immediately, but it was too late.

Way too late.

"Bennett who goes to Westside?" Courtney blurted out.

Oh no, oh no, oh no. Mackenzie didn't want to give anything else away, but she wanted—she *needed*—to know what the others were thinking. She opened her eyes.

"What about Bennett who goes to Westside? I know a Bennett who goes to Westside," said Jordana, who was sitting next to Courtney.

He's the guy Mackenzie cheated on Cooper with. He lives in her building. He's hot.

BJ shook his head in dismay. *Mackenzie cheated on Cooper with a private-school guy? Rough. Cooper doesn't deserve that.*

Mackenzie cheated on Cooper!

Why would she cheat on Cooper?

Slut!

Bitch!

Mackenzie gripped Tess's hand.

It wasn't me, I swear, Tess thought.

BJ was staring at both of them. *So it's true?*

Can you just stop thinking about this, please? Mackenzie begged. She spotted Nick in the front of the classroom. Nick was friends with Cooper. Not best friends, but good friends. Was he listening to this?

Don't worry, Tess thought. *Nick won't say anything. He's staying out of people's business. He didn't say anything to Teddy about me.*

Mackenzie put her head down on the desk and closed her eyes. She wanted this to stop.

"Hey, babe, what's wrong?" Cooper asked, finally taking the seat beside her. "Headache?"

She opened her eyes and stared at his trusting face.

"You have no idea," she said.

CHAPTER FOURTEEN

AND WE MEET AGAIN

Like the rest of us, Olivia walked out of homeroom with a pounding headache.

Unfortunately, she had public speaking next. She hadn't seen Mr. Roth since the previous day's telepathy-induced panic attack. She had her speech with her, but she didn't think she could do it that day. She prayed her teacher would give her a break.

"Let's just stroll by Lazar's locker," Renée said. *They are going to be the cutest couple.*

Olivia was too tired to argue. And anyway, at this point she was happy to surround herself with people who could not read her mind. Homeroom had been one of the most stressful classes of her life.

She was even too stressed to worry about Lazar. To worry what he thought of her. To worry if he thought she was cute. Or if he thought she was a total moron.

She'd felt awful for Mackenzie. Everyone in homeroom had been thinking about her and Cooper. She felt bad for Cooper too, of course. The whole situation was miserable. If she'd been in either of their places, she would have just about died.

She hated that the people in her homeroom could hear her thoughts. She did not want them to know that the only kissing experience she had was with her pillow. She didn't want everyone knowing when she had to pee. Or when she had a stomachache. She had lots of stomachaches. At her next doctor's appointment she was going to ask them to check for Crohn's disease.

She didn't want everyone knowing anything.

She was planning on avoiding the other people with ESP at all costs. Since there were about two hundred people in her grade, only a few students in each of her classes would have ESP.

But she'd still have to listen to everyone else's thoughts, including Renée's. And all of Renée's Olivia-related opinions.

Olivia really should go out with Lazar. A boyfriend would make her so happy. She should also not tie her hair back in a half ponytail. It's so sixth grade.

"You should really wear your hair down," Renée said. "Have you thought about bangs?"

At least Olivia could trust Renée to say what she thought.

"There he is," Renée said. *I should get him to walk with us to public speaking!*

Olivia stopped in her tracks. *No! Wait!*

"Hey, Lazar!" Renée said. "Come walk with us!"

Argh.

Lazar looked up, first noticing Renée. *She is such a pest.*

Olivia tried not to laugh. She *was* a pest. But at least she was honest.

Then he looked at Olivia. *Oh! It's Olivia!*

Olivia stood up straighter. *Yes, it is. Thank you for noticing.*

I hope she's feeling better. What happened in class yesterday was insane. I've never seen anyone faint before.

Olivia felt her cheeks burn. Great. Just great. Now all he saw when he looked at her was a freak of nature.

"Hi," he said, looking into Olivia's eyes. He had splotches of red on his cheeks. "How are you feeling?"

"Oh, um—" Her throat closed up. She hated talking to guys. What if she said the wrong thing?

She looks better, he thought. *She looks good.*

Olivia blushed. *I look good? He thinks I look good!*

Wait, what was the question? Oh right—"I'm feeling better. Thanks. Thank you."

"Good to hear. That was one scary fall," he said, still looking into her eyes. *She has great eyes. They're so expressive.*

He's complimenting my eyes! "Thanks," she said. Then she realized that he hadn't actually said that aloud. What had he said aloud? Oh! Her fall. That was one scary fall. "Yes," she said finally. "It was one scary fall. But I'll live."

He was still staring at her intently. *She's pretty.*

Hmm, Olivia thought. *Maybe hearing what people think won't be as bad as I thought.*

* * *

Tess also had a headache. And now she had chemistry class with Teddy and Sadie.

She would have to talk to Teddy. She would have to look at Teddy. She would have to listen to Teddy.

She would have to be lab partners with Teddy.

"Sorry you missed so much of the movie last night," Teddy said to Tess as she slid into the seat beside him. "Is everything okay?"

"Yup," she muttered.

Sadie walked in and waved.

"Hi," Sadie said, about to approach them. Sadie had texted Tess twenty times since the night before.

And left five phone messages. It was super annoying. Tess would prefer not to chat with the girl who had stolen the heart of the guy she liked. She did not want to be best friends with her either. She wanted nothing to do with her. But since she wasn't a bitch, she'd had no choice but to help Sadie through her breakdown at the movies.

First she'd whisked Sadie away to the bathroom. "What is wrong with me?" Sadie had asked Tess, tears overflowing from her doe-like eyes.

So Tess explained. About how it was happening to everyone in their homeroom. That they were not the only ones. That they were meeting the next day to talk about it at lunch and to decide what to do.

Meanwhile Tess was thinking, *You better not like Teddy!*

And Sadie said, "What? Huh? Teddy?"

Then two other girls stormed into the bathroom and it got noisy. Tess had stepped back so that the other girls were between them and she could compose her thoughts while Sadie was distracted by the noise.

Tess did not want Sadie to know that Teddy thought she smelled like strawberries. She did not want Sadie to know anything about Teddy at all. He was *her* Teddy. Even if Sadie was dating Keith, it was still possible that she could fall madly in love with Teddy, right? Even if he was a sophomore and Keith was a senior? Unlikely, yes, but still possible.

Teddy was smart and funny and cute. No. Tess would not let herself think nice things about Teddy. Sadie would hear, and it would just encourage her to like him.

Other than physically putting other people between her and Sadie, or maybe hiding in the bathroom stall, Tess wasn't sure how she could stop Sadie from hearing her. She couldn't exactly close her eyes in the middle of a discussion.

The strangers went into stalls.

Tess decided to try something. "Everything is going to be fine," she said. "Don't worry. It's a little overwhelming at first, but you get used to it." Tess realized that if she kept talking, then Sadie would focus on what she was saying. Not on her thoughts. Also, if she forced herself to keep talking, then she wouldn't be able to think at the same time.

"And it stops when you close your eyes," Tess added.

Sadie slammed her eyes shut.

Tess took a deep breath. Ahhh. Free play. *You better not like Teddy! He's mine, mine, mine!*

Sadie opened her eyes. "I think I want to go to sleep."

"No worries," Tess said, backing away. "I'll tell Keith you're not feeling well. You can call me if you have any questions. Or text me."

Afterward, Tess had snuck back into the dark theater and told the boys that Sadie wasn't feeling well.

I can't believe she's making me miss the movie, Tess heard Keith think. Then, *I guess this means no sex tonight.*

Ass.

Oh no! Teddy thought. *This was our time together!*

Tess told Teddy that she had to deal with a family issue and spent the rest of the movie eating popcorn and sitting on the wooden bench outside the theater, reading and answering texts from Sadie.

```
Sadie: I can hear my parents too?
Tess: Yup.
Sadie: And my doorman?
Tess: Everyone.
Sadie: Do you think it'll be gone
   by tomorrow?
Tess: I hope so.
```

Obviously it was not gone by the next day, because there they were in chemistry and it was still happening.

As soon as Sadie stepped inside the classroom, Teddy's brain went into overdrive. *She's here! Awesome. I hope she's feeling better. Her hair is so shiny.*

Barf, barf, barf, Tess thought, but then got nervous. What if Sadie had heard her mentally barfing? Also, Renée was sitting in the front row. But Tess couldn't remember if Renée had gotten the shot. She didn't think so. She'd gone on and on about it all being some government conspiracy.

As Sadie stepped up to her, Tess started to panic. She did not want Sadie to know that Teddy was obsessed with her. No, no, no! She had purposefully kept as far away from Sadie as she could all morning so that she wouldn't accidentally give away Teddy's feelings. It hadn't been easy. After the previous night, Sadie thought Tess was her new best friend.

But as soon as Sadie walked down the aisle, she'd be standing next to Teddy and would know everything, because surely Teddy would blab on and on and on about the stupid strawberries.

Without thinking, Tess squeezed her way in front of Teddy so that she was between him and Sadie. Hopefully Sadie wouldn't be able to hear Teddy's thoughts over Tess's. And yeah, Sadie would still be able to hear Tess's thoughts, but maybe she could camouflage them better than Teddy could. "Excuse me," she said to him.

What's Tess doing? Teddy wondered.

Just go with it, she told him, even though she knew he couldn't hear. And now that she was between Sadie and Teddy, she gave Sadie a tight smile. "How are you?"

Sadie shrugged. "You know. Homeroom was crazy."

"No kidding."

Do you think it'll go away soon? Sadie asked. *I don't like it.*

Me neither, Tess thought.

Teddy's thoughts jumped into her head. *Why are they just standing there staring at each other?*

Oh, right, Tess thought. *This must look super odd.* "Let's chat at lunch," she told Sadie.

"But—" Sadie stopped. *I'm feeling so alone. I really want to talk.*

"We'll talk at lunch," Tess said.

"You guys are going for lunch together?" Teddy asked eagerly. "Want some company?"

Seriously? "We have a meeting at lunch," Tess said.

"What meeting?" Teddy asked.

Good question, Tess thought. She looked at Sadie. *Any ideas?*

Telepathy club?

Gee, thanks, Sadie. "Communications club," Tess said.

"Oh. Cool. Never heard of it," Teddy said. "Does it need new members? I'm looking for a club to join."

How about Pathetic R Us? Tess thought.

Why is he pathetic? Sadie wondered. *Aren't you guys best friends?*

Don't think it, don't think it, don't think it, Tess thought.

Don't think what? Sadie asked while Teddy thought, *It would be great to be in a club with Sadie. Get some quality time with her.*

Tess wished they'd both shut up.

Sadie blinked. *What's your problem?*

Tess couldn't take it anymore. *He likes you, okay? He likes you. Teddy likes you. Are you happy now?*

Sadie's jaw dropped. "I didn't know."

Teddy leaned against the table. "You don't know if they take new members?"

Sadie blushed. "No, I didn't know that—" Her voice trailed off. *But why are you so mad? Do you like him or something?*

Yes! I've liked him forever! And he's obsessed with you.

Her lips made an O. *I'm sorry!*

Me too. Tess turned to Teddy. "The club is by invitation only." *And you are not invited.*

* * *

Third period, Pi had a surprise quiz in precalc.

She was not prepared.

It was unusual for Pi not to be prepared. She was an over-preparer. She didn't have the second-highest GPA in her class for no reason. She had it because she had goals.

She wanted to get a perfect GPA.

She wanted to go to Harvard.

She wanted to be exceptional.

She wanted her mother to realize Pi was exceptional and to know she'd had nothing to do with it.

Second in your class was not exceptional.

First in your class was exceptional.

But Jon Matthews was number one, not her. It seemed to come easy to him too. He definitely wasn't as studious as Pi was. Plus he was in Glee Club. And he played in a band called Demon. And he had a girlfriend. How did he have time for all those things? And to still be number one? It was impossible to understand. Pi barely had time for anything except being number two. She studied all the time. Even having to play on the chess team stressed her out, but she needed *at least one* extracurricular to get into Harvard.

Jon barely seemed to break a sweat. Yet he was still number one.

Pi needed to study. Hard. That's why she wasn't prepared. She hadn't had time. Normally she reviewed her precalc notes at night. She practiced. But last night she'd been too busy exploring her new talent.

Anyway, who cared about a little math test when she could hear what people were thinking? Jon couldn't do that.

She could hear the person on her left: *X plus . . . no, that's not right.*

The person to her right: *Eight to the power of . . .*

The person behind her: *I'm never going to finish on time, must focus!*

She could even hear her teacher, Mr. Irving: *What should I make for dinner tonight? Maybe a peanut butter and pickle sandwich? Or cream cheese and canned tuna?*

For the record, we all agree that both are absolutely disgusting dinner choices.

Anyway.

As far as Pi could tell, no one else could do what we could do. She had Googled and Googled and Googled some more. She had read studies from medical journals. She had gone to the library.

She really *was* extraordinary.

Well, *we* really were extraordinary.

She'd debated telling other people. Like her dad. The world. Her mom. But if people knew what she could do, they would probably try to stop her from doing it. And they'd assume that her success was because of her telepathy and not because of her hard work. Perhaps it was better to use the ESP to give her a leg up, to help her be exceptional without anyone knowing how she was doing it.

She stared back at her test. She knew most of the answers. Even though she hadn't prepared, she was still smart. But she needed to get all the answers right.

Too bad she had surrounded herself with idiots. If she had sat closer to Jon, she'd have gotten every answer correct. Talk about giving herself a leg up. She looked around to see where her nemesis was sitting. He was a few rows behind her and diagonal. Maybe if she maneuvered a bit, she could get a straight line to him and there would be less interference?

She fidgeted and wiggled. She heard the girl in

red. The guy in black. She never cared enough to remember anyone's name. She knew Jon's and her teachers' and that was enough.

She felt like she was playing with the antennae on a radio, trying to get the signals right.

If she angled her body to the left and tilted her head to the right, she could hear him more clearly. . . .

Next, Jon thought. *Number fourteen.*

It worked! She could hear him!

Hold on—he was already on number fourteen? She was only on number ten! She shouldn't have wasted so much time.

He was staring at the equation. *Hmm. What's the value of y?*

And then he worked through the problem.

And Pi could hear him working through the problem.

She scribbled as he thought.

She knew he'd done it right. It was so effortless for him.

Fifteen.

All she had to do was listen.

CHAPTER FIFTEEN

MEETING NUMBER TWO

Our second meeting took place at lunchtime again, back in the chess room. We pushed desks and pulled out chairs so that we formed a circle. We could all hear each other. No interference.

Everyone in our homeroom who had gotten the vaccine was there. Everyone except Cooper.

"Are you sure he doesn't have it?" Pi asked Mackenzie.

"I'm sure," Mackenzie said. *I'd have heard it if he had it. Wouldn't I have?*

Yes, Pi thought.

"But why is he the only one not to have it?" Tess asked. "It makes no sense."

"What's different about Cooper?" Pi asked Mackenzie.

What's different about Cooper? Mackenzie wondered. *He likes to sing. He's nice to everybody.*

"He has a gluten allergy," Nick said. "Maybe that has something to do with it."

"Oh," Mackenzie said. "Right!"

Way to know your own boyfriend, Courtney thought.

Whoa! Tess thought. *Way to be bitchy.*

That could be it, Pi thought. "Does anyone else here have a gluten allergy?"

No one did.

"Different allergies could affect the processing time," Pi reasoned. "Maybe his system is slower to digest the vaccine."

"Or maybe he's not getting it at all," Mackenzie said hopefully.

"You're going to have to tell him," Jordana said while filing her nails.

"No one is telling anyone anything," Pi said forcefully.

"Not about us," Jordana said. "About you and Bennett. We all know."

The entire circle stared at Mackenzie. *Is this really happening? Am I really sitting on a desk discussing with practically my entire homeroom whether I should tell my boyfriend that I cheated on him?*

Yes, Brinn thought while drawing in her notebook. She was wearing her white fencing jacket over jeans. *It's really happening.*

"He's going to find out eventually," said BJ. "Wouldn't you rather he hear it from you?"

Tess put her arm around Mackenzie. "This is really between the two of them. It's none of anyone else's business."

"But now we're lying too," Courtney said. "We're involved. I feel bad even looking at him."

"Gimme a break," Mackenzie snapped. "Are you saying I'm the only one here with a secret? You've never lied about something? Stolen something? Taken an Addie before a test?"

Courtney turned pink. *How did she know?*

Now we were all looking at Courtney.

"Taking an Addie is cheating," Tess said.

"Exactly," Mackenzie said. "I'm sure other people have cheated on tests too."

Pi turned red. *Like last period.*

Now we were all looking at her.

"You?" Tess shrieked. "Cheated? Aren't you like the smartest person in our grade?"

"The second smartest," Pi said in a small voice. "I didn't really cheat. I just . . ." Her voice trailed off.

Levi snickered. *Pi? Speechless? There's a first.*

"That just proves my point," Mackenzie said, looking meaningfully around the room. "We all have secrets. And they're all going to come out. So it's in all of our best interests to *keep* secrets."

"Are you threatening us?" Courtney asked. "One

of us tells Cooper about Bennett, and you tell the principal I've taken an occasional Adderall to help me through an exam?"

"She didn't threaten anything," Pi said. "She was just informing us that that's the way it is. So it's agreed? Our secrets stay secret."

We all nodded. Some of us less convincingly than others.

Olivia was the least convincing of us all. *This is all getting a little crazy. Maybe it's time to call the CDC after all.*

"What's the CDC?" Courtney asked her.

Olivia flushed. "Centers for Disease Control and Prevention."

"Why would we call them?" Jordana asked.

Olivia cleared her throat. "They have a Vaccine Adverse Event Reporting System. Where people and doctors can call in to report possible side effects to vaccines."

Rayna nodded. "Then maybe they could make it stop." She was still shaken from her hallway experience that morning.

She would be even more shaken that night after her discovery at dinner. She would spend the next twenty-four hours wiggling her left hand.

"Why would you want to stop it?" Courtney asked.

"They'd want to stop it if they knew we had it," Levi said. He took out a paper bag with CANDY

HEAVEN stamped across it and started munching on jelly beans. "No one would want us to use it."

Jordana smoothed the sides of her hair. "No one wants us using it on them."

"That's why I want to tell someone," Rayna said. "So they can make it stop."

Pi was clearly getting agitated. "Right now it's in our control. As soon as we tell someone, it's out of our control." She glared at Isabelle. "We almost lost control last night."

"Not my fault," Isabelle said. "No one told me what was happening until I got to the hospital."

"I think we should take a vote," Rayna said. "Who wants to tell and who doesn't?"

"Tell who?" Nick asked.

"The CDS or whoever," Rayna said.

"CDC," Olivia corrected her.

Pi gave them both dirty looks.

"Let's do it," Mars said. "Who wants to tell?"

On *tell,* twelve of us raised our hands. The twelve included Olivia, Mackenzie, Rayna, and Tess. On *don't tell,* nine of us shot up our arms.

"*Tell* it is," Levi said.

Pi glared at Tess, Mackenzie, and Olivia. "What happened to you guys? I thought you agreed with me."

Mackenzie shook her head. "I want this to end. And we're not going to be able to end it without help."

She thinks she can end it before Cooper finds out.

Good luck with that!

He's so finding out.

"Well, I'm finding out all kinds of stuff I don't want to know," Tess said, looking sadly at Sadie.

"It's not my fault," Sadie whimpered.

What happened with them?

Tess is in love with Teddy, but Teddy's in love with Sadie.

Isn't Sadie still dating Keith?

Sadie nodded. "Exactly my point."

Pi looked at Olivia. "And what about you?"

"It's too overwhelming," Olivia said softly. She kept her eyes on the floor. "I can't handle all my thoughts being so public."

She's shy.

She'll have to get over that.

"I understand you're shy," Pi said. "But what do you think is going to happen if we go public? We're all going to be on display. No one will care if you're shy."

Jordana shrugged. "Can someone explain why we have to be in agreement? If some of us want to tell, we can tell. It doesn't hurt the others."

"Not true," Pi said. "If Rayna tells the CDC what's happening—"

"No one would believe her anyway," Jordana said.

Pi paced around the inside of the circle. "They may not believe her at first. But eventually they would.

She could prove it. And they'd figure out how it happened and they'd suspect all of us have it."

"But Rayna could say it's just her," Jordana added.

Pi shook her head. *And then Rayna gets all the glory?*

I don't want the glory, Rayna thought. *I want it to stop.*

Jordana looked at Pi. "I don't get it. If fame is the goal, we're better off telling people. We'd be on the news."

We'd be on 60 Minutes*!*

We'd be on the cover of Time *magazine!*

We'd definitely be on TMZ*!*

Pi looked around the room. "Is that the kind of fame we want? For everyone to think we're weirdos? For everyone to be afraid of us? No one will want to stand next to us. No one will want to talk to us."

Oh God, Olivia thought. *I don't want that at all.*

"Exactly," Pi said to her. "You're not evaluating this situation properly. You have to think about all the advantages we have."

Like cheating off of Jon Matthews and not getting caught? Brinn thought, still drawing.

Pi flushed. "Well, yeah. But I'm not talking about cheating on tests. Think beyond that. We can excel in our fields. We can be the best."

"I don't want to cheat to get ahead," Nick said. "My mom would beat me."

Really?

Is she a strict teacher?

Never had her.

Should we call social services?

Nick slapped his palm against his forehead. "She doesn't really beat me. It was a figure of speech."

Pi kept going: "It's not just about school. Think of the edge you'll have in everything. In relationships. You'll always have the upper hand. You'll always know if someone is about to break up with you. You'll always know what your parents are really planning. What they're thinking."

I had enough of that last night, Mackenzie thought. *Your breasts look good in that position? Seriously?*

BJ leaned in. "You and Cooper?"

"No," Mackenzie muttered. "Forget it." *My parents. Ewwwwwwww!*

Your dad lucked out, BJ thought. *I've seen your mom and she's a MILF.*

Mackenzie closed her eyes. "Yes. I heard my parents. Having sex. In their room. Can we move on now?"

"You could hear through a wall?" Pi asked. "I thought we couldn't do that."

Mackenzie shrugged. "I did it."

Pi pursed her lips. *I can't do that. Why can't I do that?*

Jordana laughed. *Maybe Mackenzie has super ESP or something.*

Mackenzie opened her eyes. *Great. Just great. I want this thing gone.*

There is no way Mackenzie has more advanced ESP

than I do. Maybe she had a hole in her wall or something.
Pi shook her head. "You're not seeing the big picture.
Let's think of our careers. We'll be the best at what-
ever we want to be. Anyone want to be a lawyer?"

Jordana raised her hand. Her nails were bright
yellow.

"You will always know if your client did it. You will
always know what the jury is thinking. Say you're a
judge. You will always know the truth. Think about
any job. This capability will give you an advantage."

What if I want to be a doctor? Olivia wondered.

Pi nodded. "You'll know your patient's symptoms
without him having to say a word."

"Except if he's in a coma," Levi said.

"You can open his eyes," Pi said. "Check his vitals,
read his thoughts."

"I could be an amazing psychologist," Courtney
said.

Levi snickered again. *You want to be a shrink? Are
you going to prescribe all your patients Adderall?*

F you.

"Does anyone have a pet? Has it worked on them?"
Tess wondered.

I got a lot of barking from my dog.

"I do not want to know what my fish are thinking,"
Levi said. "I've killed five of them."

Sicko!

He probably fed them gummy bears.

I always knew he had it in him.

Levi looked offended. "Not on purpose! We have floor-to-ceiling windows! Our apartment is too cold!"

"Think about teaching," Pi continued. "You'd be amazing. You'd always know if your students were getting the lesson. And paying attention. Or cheating."

We were all quiet for a few minutes as we thought over the options. Even Tess and Olivia were nodding.

Slowly all of us were agreeing with Pi.

"We're assuming the telepathy isn't going to disappear," Jordana said.

"That's true," Pi said. "It might. I say we use it while we can."

Nick sat up straighter. "We could still use it to be awesome even if other people know we have it."

"Not if they're afraid of us," Pi said.

"Not if we're in a rubber room," Levi added.

"Should we take a revote?" Pi asked. "All in favor of keeping this a secret?"

Almost all of us raised our hands. Even Tess. Even Olivia. Everyone except Mackenzie.

"C'mon, Mackenzie," Nick said. "We have to all be in this together."

She doesn't have much bargaining power at the moment, does she?

You'd think she'd be afraid of pissing us off.

Pi stared Mackenzie down. "Mackenzie, are we a team or aren't we?"

I don't have much choice here, do I? Mackenzie wondered. *Anyway, even if we get rid of the telepathy, my secret is already out of the bag.*

Excellent point, Pi thought back. "One last vote. Are we all in it together?"

And we all raised our hands, Mackenzie included. We would not tell.

CHAPTER SIXTEEN

JUST IGNORE ME

We didn't wait long to use our ESP to take over the world. Domination began during gym class.

At BHS, the gym classes were made up of two homerooms. We were combined with 10A.

The girls were playing volleyball inside the gym. The boys were playing a New York version of touch football in the park.

Even though we were matches in physical strength and coordination, they weren't exactly fair games. Not once we figured out how to position ourselves properly to minimize interference. Here's how volleyball went:

Leora from 10A prepared to serve. She looked across the court and tried to psych us out. *I guess I'll serve short to Olivia. She's the weakest.*

Olivia: *Ah! She's shooting it to me!*

Jordana: *I'll get it!* Jordana was our best player.

Leora served.

Jordana swooped in and popped it to Courtney, who slammed it back over the net.

One of them: *I'm hitting it to the open area between Brinn and Courtney!*

Brinn: *I got it!*

Jordana: *Hit it back to the area between Shoshana and Jill!*

Point!

Us: *Tip it!*

Point!

Us: *Cut shot!*

Point!

We kicked ass.

Our boys did just as well. We knew all of 10A's plays and kept intercepting the ball.

And sure, football was just football. Volleyball was just volleyball. Gym volleyball, and gym football, so even more irrelevant. But still. Our dominance over our opponents continued after school.

The BHS chess team had a match against Stuyvesant.

Pi's opponent was a senior named Rick. He was their best player.

Let's try a pirc defense, he thought, moving his pawn to the middle.

I don't think so, Pi thought. She laughed inside her

head. Since she was the only one from 10B on the chess team, no one could hear.

Her opponent didn't stand a chance. Pi was able to block all his moves. She knew what was coming.

She won three games in a row.

Nick kicked ass at baseball practice.

Brinn kicked ass at fencing.

Dave and Daniel kicked ass at their wrestling practice. It was easy to block moves when you knew what they were. But when they had to wrestle each other, they ended up standing still, eyes locked, in a stupor.

Daniel: *I'm going for your legs.*

Dave: *Then I'm going for a whizzer!*

Daniel: *You suck at whizzers.*

Dave: *You suck at takedowns!*

Daniel: *You're ugly.*

Dave: *No, you're ugly!*

Daniel: *I'm kind of hungry, actually.*

Dave: *What do you think Mom is making for dinner?*

Mackenzie and Tess didn't have extracurriculars on Thursdays. Instead, they'd crossed the West Side Highway and were sitting on a bench in Battery Park sipping chocolate milk shakes from Shake Shack and gazing at the Hudson River. They could kind of see the Statue of Liberty from where they were, but it required some twisting. And they were too tired to do much twisting.

Tess took a big gulp of her shake and sighed. "This is not going to help me look good in my dress at your

Sweet. It's already a little tight. You are a very bad influence."

Mackenzie took a long sip. "I've practically forgotten about my Sweet with all the insanity going on. So I think we earned these today."

"That was a rough lunch," Tess said, shivering. "This whole thing is crazy."

"I know."

"I'm glad you're going through it with me, though," Tess said. "We're lucky to have each other." She tried to imagine what it would be like if she had no one to talk to about what was happening. No, it would be too horrible.

"It really would be," Mackenzie said. Her phone buzzed with a text.

"Who is it?" Tess asked.

"Cooper," Mackenzie said. "He wants to know what I'm up to."

"Tell him to meet us."

Mackenzie shook her head. "I can't deal with him right now. Not in person. It's too stressful."

"I know what you mean," Tess said. "That's how I feel about Teddy."

Mackenzie sighed. *Not exactly the same thing.*

Tess felt like she'd been slapped. *I didn't say it was the same thing.*

Instead of answering, Mackenzie typed a text back into her phone. "I'm telling him I'm busy with you."

Poor Cooper, Tess thought.

"That doesn't help."

"Sorry," Tess said. "Are you going to tell him about Bennett?" Tess's feelings were still hurt that Mackenzie hadn't confided in her. Tess always told Mackenzie everything. About how weight-obsessed her mom had gotten since her dad dumped her. About how Tess had been bulimic for about ten minutes back in eighth grade. About how she stalked her dad's new girlfriend on Facebook.

I'm sorry. You like to share. I don't. "I guess I'll have to tell him," Mackenzie said eventually. "He's going to find out anyway."

"Not if he doesn't get it," Tess said. Maybe his gluten allergy had blocked it from appearing at all.

"Maybe. But with so many people knowing . . ." She stared into the water. "He's bound to find out."

"What do you think he'll do?" Tess wondered.

"I think he'll break up with me."

Yeah, Tess thought. *I guess so.*

Mackenzie flinched. Her phone buzzed again.

Tess heard Mackenzie read herself the message: *Are you guys in Battery Park? I think I see you.*

He saw them?

Mackenzie stiffened. *Damn, he's here.*

They both turned and spotted him waving from the other side of the grass, near the apartments.

Mackenzie waved back. *So much for avoiding him.*

He jogged toward them, a huge smile on his face. "What's up, laaaaadies?" he sang.

Tess felt suddenly out of place. *Do you want me to go?*

Please don't, Mackenzie thought. "Hi."

He kissed her on the lips. "Mmm. You taste like milk shake."

Mackenzie offered him her paper cup. "Want?"

"Yes, please." He took a big slurp. "Hey, Tess, what's shaking?"

"Besides the milk? Not much," Tess said. "Just enjoying the weather." It was a beautiful evening. But still, she felt awkward. *Mackenzie, are you sure you don't want me to go? Now would be a good time to tell him.*

Mackenzie's eyes widened. *No! Don't go! I can't tell him now!*

Okay, okay, I won't. Tess leaned back on the bench just as her phone rang. She looked at the caller ID. "It's Teddy."

"Tell him to come meet us," Cooper said. *Of course she will, she loves him.*

Tess's heart stopped. *How does he know that? Mackenzie, did you tell him?*

Oops. Will she know if I lie?

Mackenzie! Tess flushed. The phone rang again.

Tess ignored it. She wished Teddy didn't exist. She would not call him back. She was done with him. She looked at Mackenzie. *What should I do?*

Mackenzie leaned her head back against the bench. *Maybe he'd feel differently if he knew how you felt.*

I doubt it.

"You ladies are quiet today," Cooper said. He lay down on the bench and put his head on Mackenzie's lap. "Speaking of which, what was up with everyone in homeroom this morning?"

"What do you mean?" Mackenzie asked. She turned to Tess. *Why don't you just tell him that you want to jump him?*

I'm not going to do that! Tess cried. Well, she cried it inside her head. She picked up her legs off the ground and hugged them to her chest.

"Seriously?" Cooper asked. "You didn't notice everyone was acting weird? There was a lot of staring going on." *It was like a zombie invasion.*

"I didn't notice anything," Mackenzie said.

Mackenzie, Tess thought, *if I jump him, then he'll know I like him. What's the point of that if I know he doesn't like me?*

"Then you'd know for sure," Mackenzie said.

Cooper blinked in confusion. "Then you'd know what for sure?"

Mackenzie!!!! Tess wailed.

Sorry, sorry. "Just talking to myself," she said. *This is too confusing. I can't keep up two conversations at the same time. Can we discuss this later?*

Tess sighed. *Whatever. I should probably go.*

"No!" Mackenzie yelled.

Cooper blinked again. "No, what?" *What is up with her today?*

Mackenzie shook her head. "No, I didn't realize what time it was. I have to get home."

"Already?" Cooper asked. "It's only five." *She's definitely acting weird. Maybe she has her period?*

Tess rolled her eyes. *I hate when guys blame weird moods on periods.*

Mackenzie sighed. *They're usually right, though. I'm a bitch when I get my period.*

You can be bitchy even when you don't have your period, Tess thought.

Mackenzie blinked. *True. I didn't know you thought so, though.*

Tess bit her lip. *I didn't mean that. You're not bitchy. Only a little bitchy. To everyone. Including me. Crap. I didn't mean that either. Yes I did. No I didn't. All right, I did. I just didn't want you to know I did.* "I'm starving," Tess said, desperately wanting to think of something besides Mackenzie's bitchiness. "I think I'm going to go back to Shake Shack and pick up a cheeseburger."

That's not going to help with the dress, Mackenzie thought.

Tess froze. *See? Bitchy.*

I really did not mean to think that out loud.

Tess shook her head. *You just meant to think it to yourself? Best friends aren't supposed to think you need to diet.*

You said you were having trouble fitting into the dress! Eating a cheeseburger isn't going to help! That's not a secret! And a best friend isn't supposed to call you a bitch either!

I called you bitchy, not a bitch!

We agree. Like cute and cutie, bitch and bitchy are not the same thing.

"I'm going to finish this unless you stop me," Cooper said. He took the top off the milk shake and downed what was left, giving himself a milk shake mustache.

"I'm off," Tess said. *This whole conversation is upsetting.* "I have a ton of homework," she lied.

"Me too," Mackenzie said quickly. *I'm a horrible person.*

No you're not, Tess thought.

Cooper sat up. "I'll walk you both back. Unless you want to watch the baseball game with me?"

"So much homework," they both said. *Boring,* they both thought. They looked at each other and smiled.

"Where's your team spirit?" Cooper asked.

"I have to finish an English essay," Mackenzie said.

"When's it due?" Cooper asked.

Mackenzie shrugged. "Yesterday."

Cooper laughed.

Tess knew Mackenzie wasn't kidding. Mackenzie handed in everything late. Even when Tess offered to help.

All three stood up. Mackenzie put her hand on her friend's arm. *Tess, I'm sorry. Let's both get cheeseburgers. My treat.*

I'm sorry I called you bitchy.

I am occasionally bitchy. But you're not fat.

Swear?

Yes! You're not skinny, but you're not fat.

The thought felt like a kick to Tess's stomach. But could she blame Mackenzie? She wasn't wrong.

I'm sorry! I didn't mean to think that! You're very pretty! If you went to the gym twice a week, you'd be gorgeous! Shit, shit, shit. I'm sorry! I can't help it!

Tess knew that Mackenzie was gorgeous. Everyone knew that Mackenzie was gorgeous. But Tess had always hoped that Mackenzie had thought Tess was gorgeous too. As is.

Mackenzie looked straight at Tess. *I'm sorry. Really. You're a much better friend than I am. I don't deserve you.*

"I said, where's your team spirit?" bellowed Cooper.

When did I ever have team spirit? Tess thought. *Go home, Cooper!*

Mackenzie giggled, which made Tess start giggling too.

Cooper took Mackenzie's hand and smiled. *Now she's in a good mood. Maybe she doesn't have her period after all.*

Which made Mackenzie and Tess laugh harder.

CHAPTER SEVENTEEN

SWEET WHISPERS
IN YOUR EAR

Mackenzie's phone rang at eleven-thirty. She was fast asleep. She'd made sure to go to bed and shut her eyes long before her parents even started looking sleepy.

"Hello?" she whispered.

"You're not going to believe what just happened," Cooper said.

"New York lost?" Mackenzie asked.

"No. They won. Three to two. Go Yankees. It was something weird. Really weird."

Mackenzie jackknifed in her bed. "What?" She prayed it was something innocuous. Like his TV wasn't working.

"Ashley woke up and came into my room and I

walked her back to bed. She kept talking about which princess she should be for Halloween—Cinderella, Belle, or Aurora—but her mouth wasn't moving. It was like I was reading her thoughts. I'm losing it, huh?"

She didn't know what to say. She had to tell him. She had to tell him about the telepathy. She had to tell him about Bennett. She had to tell him everything and pray that he loved her enough to forgive her.

She couldn't tell him part one without part two, could she? No. Because if she told him part one, about the telepathy, he would want to know why she hadn't told him to begin with. He had called her as soon as he noticed something strange. He'd wonder why she hadn't called him.

He would hate that their whole homeroom knew about Bennett. Everyone but him.

He wouldn't be mad. He would be hurt.

She had to tell him. She opened her mouth to tell him.

Then she closed it.

She didn't want to be the one to hurt him. She didn't want to be the one to burst his the-world-is-wonderful bubble. She was thankful that thoughts could not be heard over the phone. She said, "Yup. You're losing it. But I'm impressed you know the names Belle and Aurora."

"Of course I do. I have a three-year-old sister. She's

obsessed with them. Also with trick-or-treating." Mackenzie heard him take a short breath. "So what do you think about the fact that I hallucinated hearing my sister's thoughts? Do you think my neighbor was smoking pot in his bathroom again and the fumes were leaking into my room?"

She forced a laugh. "That guy is such a stoner."

"It's like I was in a science fiction novel or something."

"I can tell my mom," she said, trying to keep her voice light. "It sounds like a perfect TV show." Mackenzie's mom was an exec at NBC.

"Prime time?"

"Definitely."

"Will I get a producer credit?"

"Greedy, aren't you?"

"Did I wake you up?" he asked. "I know I said goodnight an hour ago."

"Yeah," she said. "But I don't mind. Are you in bed?"

"Not yet."

Since Cooper wasn't dwelling on his newfound power, Mackenzie assumed he didn't believe it had really happened. He didn't know the truth yet. He'd find out—but not tonight. "Wanna fall asleep on the phone?" she asked. They hadn't done that in a while. Since before the summer. This might be their last time. She felt a tightening in her chest.

"'Kay," he said. "I just need to brush my teeth. Should I call you back in five?"

"No," she said, afraid of losing the connection. "Don't hang up. I don't mind hearing you get ready for bed."

"Then here we go," he said.

She heard the water run and then the sound of his electric toothbrush.

"ARGH ARGH ARGH," he said.

She laughed. "Am I supposed to understand that?"

"I ran out of toothpaste the other day and found an extra tube under Ash's sink. It has Cinderella on it and is bubble gum flavored."

She laughed again. "Is it delicious?"

"Very. Frankly, I don't know why anyone uses anything else."

"I like my Crest Extra Whitening."

"And you do have a beautiful smile."

"Why, thank you." Would he still think she had a beautiful smile the next day?

She heard the sound of tinkling. "Are you peeing?" she asked.

"Why, yes I am. You said you didn't mind if I got ready on the phone."

"I didn't realize that included peeing."

"It's part of the bedtime routine."

She could still hear the tinkling sound. "That is the longest pee in the history of mankind," she said.

Maybe it would go on forever. Then they'd never have to go to sleep, and they'd never have to wake up and face the rest of the world.

"Ashley and I had to have our glass of warm milk before bed. It's also part of the routine."

"What's the rest of your routine?" Mackenzie asked.

"Milk, potty, teeth brush, change into pajamas, book, bed. Well, that's Ashley's. Mine is just teeth, pee, take off pants and shirt, bed, mind read."

There was another opening. She took a deep breath. "Maybe you really can read minds."

He snorted. "Yeah, right. Hallucinating seems more likely now that I've said it out loud. What's your bedtime routine? Wait. Let me guess. Change into sexy lingerie, teeth, pee, bed?"

Opening closed. She felt a whoosh of relief. "You forgot face wash. Don't you and your sister face wash?"

"No, we do not. I wash my face in the shower. She washes hers in the bath. We have good skin. We're lucky."

I'm lucky, Mackenzie thought sadly. *Lucky to have you.*

"Are you ready yet?" she asked.

"One sec. Turning off lights. Getting into bed. Finding comfy spot. Okay. Ready. Hi."

"Hi," she said. She felt a weight on her chest. This could be their last phone call. Unless he didn't really have telepathy. Maybe it was a fluke. Maybe he really was hallucinating. Maybe he hadn't really heard his sister.

Poor Mackenzie. Now she was the one hallucinating.

She knew she should tell him. She had to tell him. She didn't tell him.

"Love you," she said instead.

"I love you too," he replied.

Mackenzie fell asleep with the phone in her hand.

* * *

When she woke up the next morning, the phone was dead.

It was late already—after eight.

She got out of bed, her heart thumping. This was the day. She knew this was the day. She charged her phone while she showered.

She had to talk to Cooper. Why hadn't she told him the night before? She should have told him everything the night before.

We can't help but agree. She should have told him everything when she had the chance. Could have, should have, didn't.

Mackenzie's cell only had a few bars, but she called him anyway. It went straight to voice mail.

His phone had died too.

Shit, shit, shit.

She had to get to him before he got to homeroom. Where should she find him? Should she sprint to his apartment or find him at his locker?

She ran the five blocks to school. She'd meet him at his locker. Then she'd tell him. She'd tell him everything.

CHAPTER EIGHTEEN

START SPREADING THE NEWS

Cooper was late. So late he didn't even have time to go to his locker. He went straight to homeroom.

It was warm for October anyway, so he didn't even have a jacket.

It was a beautiful day.

The Yankees had won.

He and Mackenzie had had one of those perfect nighttime conversations that they hadn't had since before the summer. The kind when you talked late into the night with someone and the whole world but the two of you disappeared. The night before, everyone but them had disappeared.

Sure, the thing with his sister had been a bit weird. He could have sworn she was talking to him but her lips weren't moving. It was like there was a recording of her playing from somewhere in the room.

Maybe it had been one of her dolls talking? A lot of them did weird things like clap and dance. Maybe they talked too.

His alarm had gone off that morning and he had hit the sleep button a million times. He'd looked briefly for his cell but hadn't been able to find it. It was probably dead somewhere under his duvet. No biggie. He'd thrown on a pair of cleanish-looking jeans, a gray shirt, and his Yankees hat, then brushed his teeth and grabbed an apple.

His mother and sister were already up by then. His dad was in Chicago for work. Or maybe it was Denver. He was always somewhere.

"Coop, Coop, Coop," his sister cheered. "Come sit next to me."

Cooper's sister had dimples and corkscrew curls, and a cute personality to match. She was always smiling and singing to herself. Just like her big brother.

"He's already late," his mom said. She worked, but only half days now. She dropped Ashley off at school just before nine, went to work, and picked her up at one.

"What's up, my favorite ladies?" Cooper sang. He kissed his mom on the cheek and then his sister on the forehead.

I'm fucking exhausted, he heard his mom say.

He looked back at her in surprise and laughed. "Mom, Ashley heard that."

"Sorry?" His mom poured herself a cup of coffee.

"She repeats everything," Cooper said.

"What are you talking about?" His mom took a long sip, no milk, no sugar.

"I repeat everything," Ashley said.

"Never mind," Cooper said. "I gotta go. I'm late!"

"Have a good day!" his sister cheered. "Good day, good day, day, good day!"

"You guys, too," he said.

I'll try to stay awake, his mom said.

Huh? He turned back to her. "Mom, you okay?"

"Yes, honey, I'm fine." She gave him a smile. "See you later."

He knew he should probably run to school, but he was enjoying the sky. And the red and orange leaves on the trees in Washington Market Park. There was nothing better than fall in New York. It was so crisp and colorful and full of life.

Maybe he could take Ashley apple picking that weekend. Maybe Mackenzie would even want to come.

Everyone was chatting as they walked down the streets. Other students, parents, toddlers, nannies, babies in strollers. People were even singing to themselves. It was a merry, lively, louder-than-usual morning. He had a bit of a headache, but he was in too good a mood to let that bother him.

He stepped through the school doors just as the bell rang. He said hello to people as he walked through the hallways, and they said hello back. It was louder than it normally was, but he didn't really notice.

"What's up, 10B!" he cheered as he stepped into homeroom. He looked around for Mackenzie, but she wasn't there yet.

Everyone stared at him.

Does he have it yet?

I wonder why he doesn't have it.

"Have what?" Cooper asked.

He heard that!

He has it!

Cooper looked around the room, but no one was talking. It sounded like they were talking. But their mouths weren't moving. He was thoroughly confused.

He must have just gotten it.

He doesn't know what's going on.

Someone should tell him.

Where's Mackenzie?

He's not going to want to talk to Mackenzie in about five seconds.

Does she know he has it?

Cooper grabbed hold of a nearby desk. He felt woozy. Something strange was happening, but he wasn't sure what. Why was he hearing voices? He looked at Isaac and Nick and Pi, and they stared back at him.

It seemed to him like everyone was watching him.

He was right. We *were* all watching him.

"It's so quiet in here. Has anyone read any good books lately? I need a rec," Renée piped up from her desk.

Poor Renée.

Maybe she'll get it too. Cooper did.

Yeah, but Cooper got the vaccine, she didn't.

Right.

So now she's the only one?

Adam McCall didn't get it either.

He's not here again.

He's sick.

He's always sick.

Well, then, maybe he should have gotten the vaccine.

Voices were coming from everywhere. Who was talking? Where were they coming from? Where was Mackenzie? He didn't understand what was happening.

Olivia, who was sitting next to Renée, stood up. "Cooper, why don't you sit down?" *My turn to be kind. And brave.*

She held on to his arm and brought him to the back of the room, where he always sat. "Don't panic," she said.

"I don't understand," he said. "What's going on?"

Olivia looked right into his eyes. *We can't talk about it here in front of Renée. She doesn't know. But you can hear me, right? Nod if you can hear me.*

He nodded. He didn't know how he was hearing her when she wasn't talking, but he heard her.

We're not sure what happened or why, but we think there was something in the flu vaccine that is giving us telepathy. Nod if you got that. And don't talk. Just think.

He nodded. *But what does that mean?*

Nick's desk was the seat right in front of him. *We can hear each other's thoughts,* Nick thought.

Just each other's? Cooper asked.

No, Olivia told him. *Everyone's. We can hear everyone's thoughts.*

Voices, voices, everywhere.

It's so cool, another voice added. *You're going to love it.*

You can make it stop, too! If you close your eyes, you can't hear. If someone else closes their eyes, you can't hear them either.

It's like if you're listening to the radio in your car and you close the window. No one can hear it.

Cooper wasn't sure what he could hear. He was insanely overwhelmed. Thoughts were swirling around him, everywhere.

Who has this again? he wondered.

Us!

Who's "us"?

Just our homeroom.

Mackenzie too?

Yes, Mackenzie too.

Mackenzie can hear through walls.

That's bullshit.

It's true! I can a little bit too. If I'm pressed up against them.

Cooper's hands were fists. *But why didn't she tell me? Why didn't anyone tell me?*

The room was silent. "BJ, shut up," Nick barked.

Everyone who was sitting next to BJ gave him a look.

"I didn't hear him," Cooper said.

He's blocked by other people, Nick said. *You can hear the people around you best.*

"But what did he say?" Cooper asked. He looked at BJ, who had the desk in front of Nick.

He's going to find out anyway, BJ thought, leaning to one side.

Cooper heard him that time. "I'm going to find out what?"

Renée stood up and glared. "Have you guys all been taken over by aliens or something? Cooper, what are you talking about?"

Cooper shook his head. "I have no idea."

Ms. Velasquez walked in and closed the door. "Morning, everyone."

We were all still watching Cooper. And BJ.

Cooper looked at Olivia for help. *What are they talking about?*

Don't think about it, don't think about it, don't think about it, Olivia repeated to herself. Then she closed her eyes.

He stood up and surveyed the room. *You mean there's more? Mind reading isn't all that's going on?* He looked at Nick. *Someone better tell me what's going on. C'mon. Tell me!*

Nick sighed. *Mackenzie hooked up with some tool this summer.*

Cooper gripped the sides of his desk. *No she didn't.*

Nick shrugged. *That's what everyone's saying. Sorry, man.*

We're all on your side.

She's a bitch.

Slut.

Give her a break. She's sorry.

Cooper's head hurt. *Mackenzie wouldn't do that.*

She did it.

"Can everyone sit down, please?" Ms. Velasquez asked. "Cooper, please take off your hat. No song for us today?"

Cooper didn't want to sit down. He didn't want to sing. He didn't want to take off his hat. He wanted to go home. He wanted it to be the day before. He wanted to be back in bed with Mackenzie's voice on the phone. Quiet. Just them.

The door opened and Mackenzie was there. We all looked up at her. She looked back at Cooper.

She didn't need to hear it to know that he knew.

CHAPTER NINETEEN

FLIRT

We felt terrible about what had happened to Cooper.

We loved Cooper.

But we couldn't spend too much energy thinking about him, because we all had our own stuff to deal with.

In Olivia's case: public speaking class.

"Olivia," Mr. Roth barked, waving her over to his desk. "I'm expecting you to redo your speech next week. Thursday."

Argh. She had to try again? Hadn't once been enough? "If you want me to," she squeaked.

Poor girl. She's clearly terrified. But she has to keep trying. It's like falling off a bicycle. Or in my case, learning to tango. At first I was terrible. But now I'm the Monday night king of Calesita's. "Yes," he said sternly. "You must."

Aw. We hadn't realized Mr. Roth was secretly a softy. Or a dancer. Olé!

Renée had already taken a seat in front of Lazar but then gone to chat with a friend at the back of the room. Olivia took the empty seat next to her.

She could feel Lazar watching her as she sat down. She told herself to be bold. She looked back and gave him a smile.

"Hey," he said. *She looks great today.*

She did? She was wearing her regular jeans but had spent a few minutes putting on some blush, eyeliner, and pastel pink eye shadow that morning. "Hi," she said back, but then realized that her voice was really low, so she said it again but louder. "Hi."

Lazar straightened his shoulders. *Do it. Do it. Do it.*

Olivia wondered what he was going to do. Was it possible he wanted to ask her out?

He looked down at the floor. *What if she's busy?*

He was going to ask her out! He was!

She probably has plans. It's already Friday.

She wanted to shout at him that she had no plans. Ever. *Ask me out! Ask me out!* For a second she wished he could read minds. Or that she could implant her thoughts into someone else's head.

Unfortunately for Olivia, we didn't figure out how to do that until much, much later.

"Hey, all," Renée said. "Olivia, what was going on

in homeroom today? Why did you tell Cooper not to panic?"

Olivia swiveled back to Renée. "I didn't say that," she lied.

"Yes you did. Didn't you? Class was seriously weird. Did something happen between Cooper and Mackenzie? They both looked like they wanted to cry." *I wonder what happened,* thought Renée. *Maybe it's about her Sweet? I don't understand why I wasn't invited. It doesn't make any sense. Maybe my invitation got lost in the mail. It happens all the time. I should tell her I never got it.*

Olivia was embarrassed on her friend's behalf. But all she said was "I don't know what happened." She hadn't been invited either. She didn't really care—it wasn't like she and Mackenzie were friends. And anyway, parties gave her major anxiety. On the other hand, it would be fun to slow dance with Lazar.

Mr. Roth banged his fist on his desk, signaling that they'd all better shut up.

I'll talk to her after class, Lazar thought.

Yes! Olivia thought. *You should!*

So at the end of class she waited.

I should ask her now, he thought. *Before she leaves.*

"Come on," Renée said, standing up.

"You go ahead," Olivia hurried to say.

"Are you talking to Mr. Roth again?" Renée asked. "Do you need me to talk to him for you?" *I'm so his favorite.*

"Oh, um, I'm okay, thanks."

"I can wait with you."

"I'm good."

Renée looked from her to Lazar. *Maybe she wants to talk to Lazar. Should I stay and facilitate? She might need my help.*

I'm not going to ask in front of Renée, Lazar thought.

Renée put her hands on her hips. *Is it possible she wants to talk to him alone? That's so unlike her.*

It was unlike her. Or unlike the old her. The old her would have avoided him altogether because the anxiety of a date would have made her pick her fingers apart. ESP was making her brave. "Goodbye, Renée!" Olivia said more forcefully. "I'll meet up with you later." Olivia wasn't sure how else to get her friend to take the hint.

Renée smiled. *She does want to talk to him alone!* "Okay! See you later!" She sashayed out.

Finally.

Olivia waited.

Lazar cleared his throat. "Olivia?"

"Yes?" Olivia said. She turned around to face him. She tried to look surprised.

Oh no, she looks like she doesn't want to talk to me.

No! No! I do want to talk to you! She tried to make her face look unsurprised. Expecting.

She looks like she's in a hurry.

Ahhhh! What was wrong with her face?

Maybe I shouldn't ask her out. He stood up. "Have a good weekend."

No, no, no. That was not how this was supposed to go. "Um, you too," she said. But then she added, "Wait!"

He stopped.

She took a deep breath. "What are you doing this weekend?"

"Oh, I have tickets to see *Men of Paris* on Saturday. They're great seats. Fifth row." *She's probably busy.*

I'm not busy! I'm wide open! I have no idea what Men of Paris *is, but I like Lazar, I like men, and I like Paris—in theory, anyway, since I've never been—so what's not to enjoy?* "Is that a . . . play?"

"Uh, yeah. It's a play. It's Off Broadway. Jacob Irvinston directed?" *How could she not know that?* Time Out New York *gave it five stars!*

"Oh," she said. "I know it. *Time Out New York* gave it a five-star review, right? I really want to see it."

"You do?" He eyed her skeptically.

"Yes. I wish you had an extra ticket. I would love to go. This weekend. With you." She couldn't believe she'd just said that. But she had. The words had flown from her mouth.

He blinked. "You would?"

She nodded.

It's like she's reading my mind. "Well, I have an extra ticket. Would you like to come with me?"

"Yes!"

In truth, she was dying to know if it was a musical, because she really did love musicals and was kind of bored at non-musicals, but she decided not to ask. Either way, she was going to a play. With a guy. *Oh my goodness, I just asked a guy out.*

As they collected their books and walked out of class, Olivia felt a wee bit guilty that Lazar didn't know she was reading his mind. But not too guilty. It wasn't like she *asked* to be able to read his mind.

And she wasn't trying to trick him. She was trying to date him.

CHAPTER TWENTY

THE TRUTH HURTS

Cooper avoided Mackenzie all morning.

At lunch she cornered him by his locker. "Please talk to me."

He shrugged. "What's there to say?"

"I'm sorry. It was a totally horrible thing to do."

No kidding, thought Jordana. She was filing her nails one locker over.

"Can we go somewhere private to talk?" Mackenzie asked. *Please don't shut me out.*

We had decided not to have a meeting at lunch that day. Pi and a few other 10Bers had an American history test and they wanted to prep then.

Instead, we were all meeting after school at Sadie's apartment on Duane Street.

He shook his head. "Sure, now you want to go somewhere private."

"Let's go to my place," she offered.

I can't be in your room. It would hurt too much.

His thought pierced her heart.

"Let's go to the gazebo."

The gazebo was in Washington Market Park, only a few blocks from school. They walked out together, him a few steps ahead, not looking back.

They were both quiet. All she kept thinking was *I'm sorry, I'm sorry, I'm sorry.* All he kept thinking was *I can't believe this is happening,* over and over again.

When they got to the gazebo, they sat beside each other, not speaking.

Finally he turned to her. "Did you sleep with him?"

"No," she said quickly. *No! I didn't!*

"What did you do, then?"

"I . . ." She wanted to lie, but she couldn't. He would know.

"So your first instinct is to lie to me? Great." *Does she always lie?*

"No! I don't! I just . . . I don't want to hurt you."

"But you did hook up with him," he said. *How could she do that?*

"Yes." *I'm sorry.*

"While we were together." *Why would she do that?*

"Yes." *I'm sorry.*

"And you didn't tell me." *Liar.*

"No." She felt tears well up in her eyes. Was their relationship really going to end? Just like that?

"Why?"

She shook her head. Was he asking why she had hooked up with Bennett or why she hadn't told him? She wasn't sure she knew the answer to number one, but she definitely knew the answer to number two. "I knew you'd break up with me, and I didn't want that to happen."

He sighed. "Too late now." *It's so over. I can't even look at you.*

Pain exploded in her chest. "Please, Cooper. We don't have to break up. It was months ago." She put her hand on his arm. "Please. Don't. We are so good together. I screwed up."

We agree. She really did screw up. Big-time. Huge-time.

"I would change it if I could," she babbled. "I would go back and change it." She would change everything. She didn't want to be the kind of girl who cheated on her boyfriend. She didn't want to be a bitch. She wanted to be sweet. She wanted to be worthy. She couldn't lose him. She just couldn't. She loved him. She really did. "I love you."

He shook his head. *I still love you.*

"See! You do! I know you do!"

"Stop it," he said, and closed his eyes. "I don't. I *loved* you."

The past tense crushed her.

He opened his eyes and said, "Mackenzie, we're done."

"No, don't say that! You can't say that." She wanted to push the words back into his mouth. His beautiful mouth, with the top lip slightly plumper than the bottom. They couldn't break up. She couldn't not see him. Her Sweet was in two weeks. Would he not even come?

He knocked the back of his head against the gazebo pole. *So this is about your Sweet?*

"No! I don't care about my Sweet. I just care about you being there with me."

The idea of having a huge party without him by her side—maybe without him even there—was beyond depressing. She'd cancel it if he wanted her to. She really didn't care about it. She didn't think she ever had.

I can't stay with her. I can't.

She put her hand on his knee. "Yes you can," she whispered. "You can."

He shook his head and closed his eyes again. "I don't want you reading my mind."

She hated being shut out. "Cooper, please. We can get over this. Together."

He kept his eyes closed. "Can you go? I want to be alone."

"I don't want you to be alone. I want us to be together."

"It's not up to you."

Okay, I'll go. She stood up. *But I love you.*

His eyes were still closed. He didn't hear.

CHAPTER TWENTY-ONE

PEEKABOO

That afternoon was the American history test. Pi sat down in the front row, like she always did.

Courtney came in and sat down next to her—for the first time ever.

Two seconds later, Daniel came in and sat on the other side of her. When Dave came in next and sat directly behind her, Pi blew up.

"Seriously?" she asked. "None of you have ever sat next to me before."

Dave laughed. *Might as well use what we got.*

I studied for this! Pi felt indignant.

I studied too, Courtney thought. *But you're smarter than me.*

Pi glared at her. *Taking an Adderall doesn't count as studying.*

Courtney shook her head. *I'm out. And anyway, I'm too afraid to mix them with the telepathy. I don't want any more side effects. I could start speaking in tongues or something.*

Pi crossed her arms over her chest. *I'm not letting you cheat off me. It's not right.*

Um, excuse me, thought Dave, *didn't you cheat off Jon Matthews just yesterday?*

Pi wasn't sure what to say to that. It was true.

Dave continued: *If you're allowed to cheat, why aren't we?*

Rationally, Pi knew he had a point. But still. It didn't seem fair.

Mr. Johnson burst into the room. "Morning, everyone!" he chirped. "I hope you're all ready. It's a tough one."

Good thing we have a secret weapon, Daniel thought.

Pi narrowed her eyes. *You do not have a secret weapon!*

As Mr. Johnson passed out the papers, Pi tried to block hers with her arms. As if that would help.

She looked at number one: *Which state was one of the original American colonies? A. Ohio. B. Vermont. C. Rhode Island. D. Maine.* She marked C.

Way to go, cheered Dave.

Thanks, Pi, thought Courtney.

Pi was annoyed. Very annoyed. She read number two and then tried to close her eyes before the answer came to her. *D. Battle of Fort Charlotte!* But it was too late.

Thanks again, thought Courtney.

Pi couldn't work like this. Not with the chorus commenting on her every move.

Daniel coughed. *Actually, I think the answer might be C. Wasn't it the Battle of Cape Spartel?*

She looked back down at her paper. *No. You're wrong.*

Pi wondered if maybe she should think about the wrong answers on purpose.

Daniel coughed again. *That's a real asshole thing to do.*

It totally is, thought Courtney. *What happened to us against them? Being a united front?*

Don't you want to help us? asked Dave. *We're all Espies here.*

Espies? Pi asked.

People with ESP? It has a nice ring to it.

It did have a nice ring to it. But still. *No,* Pi thought. *I want to get the highest grade in the class. If we all hand in the same thing, that isn't going to happen. Don't you think Mr. Johnson will be suspicious?*

So I'll get some wrong, Dave thought. *There are twenty multiple-choice questions and two short essays. You normally get perfect, right?*

Pi straightened her shoulders. *Almost.*

Out of the corner of her eye she could see Daniel

twirling his pencil between his fingers. *We'll dumb down our essays. Make some spelling mistakes. Use our own words. You'll still get the highest grade in the class. It'll be fine.*

Pi gave a small shake of her head. *It'll mess up the curve. Don't you normally fail?*

No!

Cs, then.

Daniel was now thumping his pencil against the desk. *I'll get two of the multiple choice wrong, then, 'kay? Happy?*

Pi sighed. Did she have a choice? What was she going to do, complain? *Fine. Copy if you want. But stop annoying me. I need to focus.*

With an audible sigh, she tried to block out our voices and looked back down at the test.

We cheered. *Thank you, Pi! We love you, Pi!*

As a token of our appreciation, she received *The Big Book of Sudoku* the next day.

CHAPTER TWENTY-TWO

WE KNOW EVERYTHING

It took us a while to file into Sadie's apartment.

She lived on the ninth floor, and there was only one elevator.

There were twenty-two of us.

It was one of those elevators that opened directly into the apartment. And it was a really nice apartment. Like *really* nice. It was the whole ninth floor, plus a wraparound outdoor terrace. Terraces in New York are rare but coveted. Sadie even had a barbecue on hers.

While we waited for everyone to come upstairs, we gossiped.

Because after three days of being Espies—yup, Dave's nickname stuck—we had accumulated a lot of secrets.

Emma Dassin, the senior who lived in Olivia's building, had missed her period and was going to get a pregnancy test after school. She hadn't told her boyfriend. She had told her best friend. Her best friend thought it was Emma's own fault for not using a condom. Meanwhile all the best friend had eaten all day was half an apple. She was seriously anorexic.

There was the freshman who dropped his retainer in a toilet in the second-floor school bathroom and then—wait for it—put said retainer straight back into his mouth.

The other freshman who still wet his bed. He had an appointment with a urologist on Wednesday.

The junior who had walked in on his stepmother taking a shower.

The sophomore who had stolen a glitter pen from the Duane Reade pharmacy on Greenwich. She stole something every day. Sometimes from Duane Reade, sometimes from Whole Foods. Her dad ran a hedge fund, so it definitely wasn't because she couldn't afford the stuff.

Hey, Rayna, do you ever shoplift? Six-finger discount!

So not funny.

A little funny.

We passed around secrets like trading cards until everyone arrived.

All twenty-two of us. Even a sad-looking Cooper. Even Mackenzie.

We sat in as much of a circle as we could. We were on couches, the carpet, chairs; some of us even sat on the glass coffee table, which was probably not a great idea. A buzz of comments—out loud and in our heads—flew around like we were in a real-life Twitter.

"We have an hour," Sadie said.

What happens then?

Keith coming over for some lovin'?

"My parents come home," Sadie said.

Was Sadie the first one of us to lose her virginity?

I think she was!

"Do you mind?" Sadie asked, turning red.

The first girl, maybe. Wasn't it BJ?

"Of course it was," BJ said. *I wish.*

I bet they have a lot of sex.

Who?

Keith and Sadie.

"I have a lot of sex. A lot," BJ says. *At least a little.*

Anojah fiddled with her glasses and thought, *But Sadie hates kissing Keith because he has bad breath.*

"Omigod!" Sadie yelled. "Can you guys shut up?"

Anojah blushed. "I'm sorry! I heard you thinking about it this morning!"

"Thinking about what?" Jordana asked, moving in closer. "Did I miss something?"

Sadie fidgeted in her chair. "Can we talk about something else, please? Anyone want a drink?"

"I'll take a beer," one of the twins said.

"Um, no," Sadie said. "My parents would shoot me. We have Vitaminwater."

"Do you have any chips?" Nick asked.

"Salt and vinegar."

"Perfect."

"I could use something sweet," Courtney said.

Levi pulled a paper bag out of his backpack. "I have gummy bears."

"No, I want chocolate." *Maybe we should send someone on a brownie run to Tribeca Treats.*

"So go, Courtney," Mars said. "You're the one who wants something sweet."

I don't want to miss anything.

"It's just down the street," Sadie said.

"I have a Twix," Tess said. "You can have that." She glanced at Mackenzie. *Since apparently I should be on a diet.*

Mackenzie gave her a look. *I never said that!*

Tess shrugged.

"I thought we made up," Mackenzie whispered.

"We did," Tess whispered back. "Don't worry about it." *I'm still pissed. I can't help it.*

Pi stood up. "Now that the all-important snack issue is settled, let's get down to business. How is everyone feeling?"

"I'm still getting headaches," Courtney said, chomping on the Twix.

Levi nodded. "Me too."

"Mine are getting better," said Courtney.

Anojah reached behind her glasses and rubbed her eyes. "My voices are really loud. And my head is still killing me."

Pi tilted her head to the side. "I wonder if it has something to do with your glasses."

"What do you mean?"

"Well, we can't hear other people's thoughts if our eyes are closed. And no one can hear us if our eyes are closed either. So it seems transmission is coming through the eyes. Have you noticed a difference when you take your glasses off?"

Anojah pushed them on top of her head like sunglasses. "Someone think something."

Hey, babe!

How vile was the lasagna in the cafeteria today?

Not as vile as the chicken potpie.

Anojah blinked repeatedly. "That was so much better. Quieter. Much."

Pi smiled smugly. "There you go."

Anojah rubbed her eyes again. "But what am I supposed to do? Walk around blind?"

"Speaking of blind," Mars said, "have any of you tried hearing Keren Korb's thoughts? I couldn't. She was a dead zone."

Interesting, thought Pi.

Keren was the only vision-impaired kid at our

school. She was a senior and had short bright pink hair and wore pitch-black sunglasses everywhere she went.

"I noticed that," Jordana said. "I guess her blindness is shutting us out."

Anojah waved her hand. "Can we get back to me and *my* blindness? Pi, what should I do?"

"I can't fix everything," Pi barked.

She's grumpy because of what happened in American history.

Heard about that.

Lucky.

I wish Pi were in my classes.

Pi put her hands on her hips. "Speaking about what happened in American history, we have to be extra careful. We don't want to get caught."

"We won't," Dave and Daniel said simultaneously.

Maybe they did have twin powers.

"I'd like to talk about something," Cooper announced.

We all swiveled to face him.

Is he mad at us for not telling him about Mackenzie?

He must be so embarrassed.

I'm surprised he even showed up.

From his seat on the couch, Cooper looked around the room. "I don't understand why we're keeping this a secret."

"Because we're not ready for other people to know about it yet," Pi said, sounding impatient.

"But it's wrong," Cooper continued. "We're lying."

Haven't we already had this discussion?

He's just pissed because of Mackenzie.

Mackenzie blushed.

"This isn't about Mackenzie," Cooper said forcibly. "Although it does suck that every one of you knew and no one told me. I don't like living a lie."

"Well, you're too late," Pi said. "We voted and that's what we decided to do."

Cooper got up. "I think I'm going home."

Way to be a baby.

"I'm just tired, okay? It's been a long day." *I want to watch the game. I don't want to be here.*

We nodded. We understood.

Pi crossed her arms. "You're not going to say anything, right?"

"I won't say anything. I just need to think." *In private,* he added. He pressed the button to the elevator and it opened immediately.

Mackenzie got in with him. The door closed.

He's never going to forgive her.

Would you?

No way.

I don't know. If it was really a mistake, maybe.

People do make mistakes.

And she's pretty hot.

"Is there anything else we need to discuss?" Sadie asked, glancing at the clock on the DVR. "It's getting late." *Keith is going to be here in fifteen minutes.*

"Do we really need to have so many of these top-secret meetings?" Jordana asked. "My friends think I'm ditching them."

I'm surprised more people haven't been suspicious.

What are they going to suspect?

That we're up to something.

We are up to something.

"We don't have to meet this weekend," Pi said.

Daniel stretched his arms above his head until they popped. "Good. What's everyone up to?"

"Olivia has a date," BJ said.

Olivia blushed. *How does he know?*

Seriously? You've been thinking about it all day.

"I can't believe he's taking you to *Boys of Paris*," Courtney said. "Snore."

"It's *Men of Paris*, and it got a rave in the *Times*," Sadie said.

Tess stood up and glanced at Olivia. *I'm not a play person.*

Me neither, Olivia admitted. *But I'm excited for the night.*

Good luck, Tess thought. *Can't wait to hear how it goes.*

Thanks. Good luck with Teddy. I hope he realizes how awesome you are.

The intercom near the elevator door buzzed.

Sadie pressed a button. "Hello?" she said.

"Keith is here," said the doorman. "Should I send him up?"

Shoot! He's early! "Oh! Tell him I'll come down in a minute?"

"He says he needs to use your bathroom."

Classy.

Sadie pressed the intercom button. "I guess . . . send him up?"

We felt the vibration of the elevator moving back up the floors.

"Won't he wonder why we're all here?" Jordana asked.

Sadie pulled on a split end. "I told him I was taking a nap. He's gonna wonder why I lied."

"Is there another way out?" Tess asked.

Her eyes darted around the room. "There's a fire exit out the back of the apartment. Do you guys mind taking the stairs?"

"Of course not!" Olivia said.

I mind! We're nine floors up!

Come on, let's move.

Sadie opened the door to the stairwell for us and we silently followed Pi and filed out.

The staircase was grungy. Since there was only one tenant per floor, every landing seemed to be used for recyclables and storing oversized suitcases. We snaked down and around the staircase.

"I'm getting dizzy," Courtney complained.

"It's too dark in here," Jordana said.

"*Shhh!*" Pi ordered.

This is so creepy.

Do you think we're the first people to ever use this staircase?

Hopefully. It's in case of fire.

Or sneaking your homeroom out to hide your secret ESP meeting.

Tess tripped over a tricycle and into Olivia, who fell against Mars.

"Sorry!" Tess whispered.

This could turn into a really unfortunate game of dominoes.

Don't even joke.

Couldn't Sadie have just told him we have a homeroom project?

That would have been easier.

They're so hooking up right now.

Then I hope he brought breath mints.

A few of us giggled. Pi pushed the stairwell door open and led us into the light.

CHAPTER TWENTY-THREE

THE BIG NIGHT OUT

Lazar picked Olivia up at six. They were going to get pizza first and then take the subway to the theater district.

Olivia was a nervous mess. She had never been on a real date before. She had never even been on a pretend date.

She'd spent the day trying to distract herself with television. She'd started with repeats of *House, Grey's Anatomy,* and *Mystery Diagnosis,* but then somehow ended up watching hours of the OWN network. She admired Oprah but found the woman a mystery. How did anyone have so much confidence that they could tell other people how to live their *best* life? How did she not doubt herself? How could she stand the entire world watching and gossiping about her every move? How did she know what to wear on TV?

Wait a sec. Did Oprah have ESP?

Olivia turned off the TV and went through her closet, eventually settling on a light green dress and black heels. She definitely looked like she was going on a date. She hoped she wouldn't trip walking down the subway stairs.

She doubted Oprah worried about tripping down subway stairs.

We doubt Oprah ever takes the subway.

"He goes to school with you, right?" Olivia's mom asked.

"Yes, Mom."

I don't understand who this Lazar character is. She's never mentioned him before. What if he tries something? Should I call his parents?

A half hour later there was a buzz from downstairs. "I'm coming down!" she called into the intercom.

Her mom popped up beside her. "No way. Tell him to come up."

Olivia pressed the intercom again. "Actually, can you come up?"

"Sure."

"You're not wearing those heels, are you?" her mom asked.

Olivia twirled her foot. "I am. What's wrong with them?"

"Aren't you taking the subway? That's a lot of walking. And a lot of stairs. I don't want you to trip."

"I won't trip, Mom. I know how to walk." It was one thing when Olivia worried about it, another thing when her mom did.

As she waited, her heart beat hard, too hard, in her chest. Was she having a heart attack? Could teenagers have heart attacks? She wasn't sure. She wished she had time to Google it. Maybe she should make an appointment with a cardiologist.

She quickly opened the door when Lazar knocked.

"Hi," he said. *Oh, so pretty.*

She blushed. "Hi."

"This is my mom," Olivia said, motioning behind her.

He nodded. "Hello, Mrs. Byrne. Nice to meet you."

"You too," Olivia's mother said. *At least he's polite. Short, though.*

"Mom!" Olivia yelled.

Startled, Olivia's mom asked, "What?"

Oops. "Nothing. Um, we're going."

"Okay, have fun. Be careful on the subway. Especially in those heels."

They all looked down at her shoes.

I wish she was wearing flats, Lazar thought. *I don't want her to be taller than me.*

Oh. Olivia hadn't thought of that. "You know what?" she said. "Mom, you're probably right. Be right back." She ran to her room, changed into her boots, and ran back, praying that her mom hadn't said anything too embarrassing.

Better, Lazar thought, and opened her front door.

Hey! The date was going to be easier than she'd thought. All she had to do was listen.

He better not try anything too advanced for her, thought her mom. *He looks like a nice boy. But it's always the ones who look clean-cut who end up being the sociopaths. Hmm. She's not wearing a sweater? Does she want to get pneumonia?* "Olivia, don't forget to take a—"

"Goodbye, Mom," Olivia sang. She blew her mom a kiss and closed the door behind her.

CHAPTER TWENTY-FOUR

IT ALL SUCKS

Cooper was depressed.

It was Saturday night and he was lying on his bed, watching the baseball game on the TV above his desk.

The Yankees were losing 3–0. It was the bottom of the ninth. Jeter was at bat with two outs. He needed a home run.

If they lost this game, the Yankees were out of the series.

Strike one!

Damn.

"Come on!" he yelled. "Do it!"

Cooper's iPhone rang. It was Mackenzie. Again.

He didn't answer. He didn't want to talk to her. He didn't know what he wanted.

No, that wasn't true. He wanted his world to go back to normal.

He wished Mackenzie had never cheated on him. He wished she had never lied to him. He wished he had never gotten a stupid flu shot. He wished the Yankees were winning.

But it wasn't just Mackenzie who was a liar.

Everyone was full of shit.

The day before, he had arrived home after the meeting feeling numb. When he'd unlocked the door, he'd felt a flood of relief at the sight of his mom and sister.

"It's good to see you," he said.

But Ashley didn't even look up from the TV. She was watching *Cinderella II*. She was thinking, *Funny mousies funny mousies.*

"I'm home," he said. "Do I get a hug?"

Ashley motioned to him to be quiet. "Shhh!"

His mother looked up briefly from her laptop. "Hi, honey," she said, and then returned to the screen. *I can't believe how high this bill is. How am I going to pay for it?*

When he strolled over to the kitchen to get a snack, his mom slammed her laptop shut. *Not for his eyes.*

Huh? What bill couldn't he see? Was his mother keeping secrets from him, too?

She looked up and smiled. "How was your day?" *What should I make for dinner? Can we order in Japanese again or does that make me a bad mom?*

"Fine," Cooper said. "Do you want to order Japanese?" Might as well make life easy for her. He grabbed a cheese stick from the fridge. "Is Dad back tonight?"

"He has to stay over the weekend," his mom said.

"Again? How come?"

His mom traced her fingers along the table. "His project," she said, but then she thought, *His floozy.*

Cooper almost choked on his cheese stick. "His what?"

"Project," his mom repeated. "Some big deal he's working on in Chicago."

Cooper hadn't known what to do with himself. He kept standing up and sitting down, standing up and sitting down. His mother had definitely thought *floozy.* Was his father having an affair? No. It couldn't be. There was no way he was finding out that both his girlfriend and his father were having affairs. That was too insane.

He couldn't think about it. If he didn't think about it, it wasn't happening.

Except he couldn't *stop* thinking about it.

He told his mother he wasn't feeling well, and had spent most of the past twenty-four hours in bed.

His life was falling apart. His girlfriend had cheated on him. His father seemed to be cheating on his mother. And his mother . . . well, she was hiding something.

Everyone was a liar. Except Ashley. And Gerald. But turtles couldn't talk. All Cooper could hear from him was a low squeaking sound.

At least Ashley had told it like it was. She didn't want to be interrupted during her movie, so she'd told him to be quiet.

But she was only three.

Strike two!

One day he'd woken up happy and the next day everything was fake. Everything was a lie. He was surrounded by liars.

And he was no better. He was pretending he couldn't hear his mom. He was a fake, just like them.

Cooper watched Jeter get ready for the next pitch. His phone buzzed.

`Please forgive me. I love you.`

Strike three!

The Yankees' season was over.

Most of us were bummed by the news, but Cooper was the only one to throw his phone at the TV.

CHAPTER TWENTY-FIVE

BRAVO

The date went perfectly. How could it not? Olivia didn't have to worry about screwing up. Every concern Lazar had, Olivia heard.

If she doesn't walk faster, we're going to be late.

Olivia walked faster.

She has a pretty smile.

Olivia smiled more.

What did she just say? She speaks so softly.

Olivia spoke up.

I wonder what her favorite band is. I hope she likes Delivery.

"I just love Delivery! They're the best."

"Did you like the new Thomas Allen movie?" *It was so amateur. I hope she didn't like it.*

"No way," Olivia said. "It was so amateur."

We know—we can't believe she used the word *amateur* either.

But Lazar nodded, his eyes wide. *It's like she's taking the words right out of my mouth!*

Which she was.

He thought she was amazing—which she knew because, well, she could hear what he was thinking.

His thoughts weren't the only ones she could hear.

The man sitting in the row in front of her at the show: *Did I gain weight or are these seats getting smaller?*

The tourist beside her: *Sleeping with my psychiatrist may have been a bad idea.*

One of the actors onstage: *Maybe I should try out for* American Idol.

The twelve-year-old sitting diagonally from her: *This is so boring. Is it almost intermission?*

Olivia agreed. Five stars or not, *Men of Paris* was excruciatingly boring. She couldn't help wondering if the five had been out of ten.

Listening to the people around her was much more entertaining.

Lazar especially. *That guy is too tall to play Pierre. He's a giant. Couldn't they have found someone shorter? He can barely stand up straight. He's like the Leaning Tower of Pisa.*

And then even more interesting: *I want to kiss her.* Oh! Yay!

But did he mean now? Or did he mean he wanted to kiss her later? Like when he was walking her home?

He wasn't going to kiss her right now, was he? When they were still at the show? That seemed like a strange thing to do.

Olivia peered at the other members of the audience. No one else was kissing. It was an Off Broadway theater, after all. That seemed disrespectful. Worse than chewing gum, and she knew she wasn't supposed to do that. She had thrown hers in the garbage bin outside.

By the way, we agree: making out at an Off Broadway show is unacceptable. Even if you're in the back row.

But Olivia wanted Lazar to kiss her. She was pretty sure. He was nice. Or nice-ish. At the very least, he was the first guy to show interest in her.

Maybe I'll take her hand first, Lazar thought.

That sounded like a decent idea. She realized her hands were in her lap, so she tried to subtly lift the one next to him and rest it on the arm of her seat.

He took the bait and grabbed her hand. His fingers were colder than she had expected. And long. They were nice fingers. She liked the way they held hers.

His hand intertwined with hers—the way he moved his thumb in circles on her palm every now and then—made the boring second half of the play go by much faster.

* * *

They were walking back from the subway stop. They were holding hands again. Hers aligned perfectly with his, since she was wearing flats.

I'm going to do it, he thought.

Olivia cheered silently.

I should wait until we're outside her building.

Good idea, she thought.

Or maybe I should do it now.

She swallowed. Hard. *Now?*

Right now. Olivia's heart raced in a way that could not have been healthy.

They were on the corner of Church and Murray waiting for the light. *Now! I'm going to do it now!*

Seriously? she wondered. There was no one else waiting at the light with them, but there were definitely people on the streets. She wasn't really a make-out-in-the-streets kind of girl. She wondered if she should stop him. Did she want him to kiss her? Did that mean they were a couple? Did she even like him? Did she want her first kiss to take place while waiting for the light?

He put his arm around her shoulder and pulled her toward him. *Here I go!* He closed his eyes and his lips pressed against hers.

She closed her eyes too.

Suddenly they were kissing. His lips were soft and sweet.

They stayed there for a few minutes until he pulled away and she opened her eyes.

She did it! She had her first kiss! And it was nice!

He was smiling. *That was good,* he thought. *Although I wish she'd use more tongue. Two stars.*

Olivia felt herself turn red. Two stars? She was a bad kisser! She finally had her first kiss at the age of fifteen and she wasn't even good at it! She'd failed! Was she going to get another chance? Or was that it? She tried to hear his thoughts, but all he was thinking about was the best way to get to her house. *Around the block or cut through the park?*

Oblivious to her panic, Lazar took her hand and led her across the street. They didn't say anything until they got to her door.

"I had a really great time," he said.

"Me too," Olivia responded.

I guess I should kiss her again, he thought.

Yes! Olivia thought. *You should!* But she wondered, what did that mean to use more tongue? She knew what it meant, technically, but how was she going to do it? Just stick it in there?

He leaned in toward her and then closed his eyes as his lips pressed against hers. She opened her mouth and gently let her tongue trail into his mouth and meet his. His tongue was sandpapery, but she swirled it back and forth. Was that right? She opened her eyes in case his eyes were open and then she'd be able to hear, get a progress report maybe, but no, his eyes were closed.

But then they opened.

Why are her eyes open?

Oops. She closed them.

A few minutes later, when her tongue started to get tired, she pulled away and opened her eyes.

That was awesome, he thought. *Five stars.*

Now, that's a rave review.

CHAPTER TWENTY-SIX

NEW PLAN

Pi called an Espies meeting for Monday before school. She texted us all the night before, instructing us to meet her in the chess room at seven-thirty. It was early. Very early.

But we all showed up—all except Cooper.

We weren't surprised. He was never on time, and anyway, he kind of hated us right then.

"He doesn't hate you," Mackenzie said, sipping a Starbucks pumpkin spice latte. "He hates me."

We nodded.

"He just needs some alone time," Nick explained.

Pi paced the room. "Okay, people, I want to chat about our booth at the carnival on Saturday. We have a bit of a problem."

Once a year, BHS students put on a carnival in the gym to raise money for the library. Every homeroom had a booth. The entire neighborhood came by to support the school.

"What?" we asked.

We're supposed to do the fortune-telling booth.

We laughed. We couldn't help it.

"So what?" Courtney asked.

"We can't tell people their fortunes," Pi said. "We'd give ourselves away."

Nick shook his head. "Am I missing something? Did we develop clairvoyance when I wasn't paying attention?"

"No, we didn't," Pi said. "At least, I didn't. No one else did, did they?"

We shook our heads.

Pi looked at Mackenzie suspiciously. *I bet she can't really hear through walls.*

I can.

Whatever, thought Pi. "The fortune-telling booth is still too risky. Reading minds. Telling fortunes. Too close. We should do something else."

She gives us a few test answers and she thinks she's in charge?

"I *am* in charge," Pi said huffily. "I don't see anyone else taking the leadership role. And we need a leader. If someone else thinks he or she could do a better job, please feel free to step up."

We looked at each other and shrugged.

"We should have a nail-polish booth," Jordana chirped.

"11C is doing nail polish," Sadie said. "Keith's homeroom. They're also doing back massages."

Good thing they're not doing a kissing booth. Keith would scare everyone away.

Shut up!

BJ groaned. "A kissing booth! Why didn't we think of that?"

"What about bobbing for apples?" asked Anojah, squinting at the rest of us. She was always squinting without her glasses.

Brinn mumbled something.

"What?" Pi barked. "Can you just think, please? I can't understand you when you talk."

Brinn rolled her eyes. *Whatever you say, Polly. Do you know that your real name means "bitter"?*

I'd prefer you call me Pi, thank you very much.

"Who gave you that nickname, anyway?" Levi asked.

"My fourth-grade teacher," Pi said, but first she thought, *I gave it to myself.*

We all smirked.

"What I was trying to say," Brinn said super-slowly, "is that we already got approval for the fortune-telling booth. It's too late to change."

"Argh," Pi groaned. "Well, then, our fortune-teller needs to be someone who can't read minds. So we don't give ourselves away."

We all thought it at the same time—Renée. There wasn't much choice.

"So we're settled?" Pi asked. "Someone tell Renée."

I guess that's me, Olivia thought.

Pi banged her fists on the table. "Good."

Were her eyes always purple?

Pi turned around. "What was that?"

Dave stared more closely at Pi. "Your eyes are looking purplish."

She motioned to her blue shirt. "They're blue. Maybe it's the shirt."

Daniel looked at her a little more closely. "No, I don't think that's it."

"You know," Levi said, "I've noticed that my eyes are getting a little purple too."

Maybe you've been eating too many purple jelly beans, Courtney thought.

"Does anyone have a mirror?" Pi asked. "Jordana?"

What, I'm so vain that I must have a mirror?

Yes, thought Pi, *exactly.*

My money's on Jordana having a mirror.

What's the big deal? Anojah wondered. *I have a mirror.*

But does Jordana?

I really want to say I don't, Jordana thought. *But I do.* She pulled out a silver Kate Spade compact mirror and handed it to Pi. *Just in case I ever have spinach in my teeth.*

If she'd had spinach in her teeth, we would have

noticed. And she would have heard us noticing it. But anyway.

Pi studied her reflection. *My eyes are vaguely purple. How did I not notice that?*

You clearly don't spend enough time in front of a mirror, Jordana thought, and a bunch of us giggled.

"Some of us have more important things to worry about than how we look," Pi snapped. "Is this happening to anyone else?"

We checked out each other's eyes. Tess's were still brown. So were Olivia's. She stopped at Mackenzie's. "Yours have a purplish glint."

"They do?"

"The purple eyes must have something to do with the ESP," Tess said.

Pi snorted. *Thank you, Captain Obvious.*

I knew we were turning into vampires, thought Edward.

"We are not turning into vampires!" Jordana screamed.

"We'll see," said Edward.

"I don't want my eyes to turn purple," Rayna whined. "I like my eyes the way they are."

Purple eyes are seriously weird.

Creepy.

I think it's cool.

Better than the boring brown color I have now.

I was thinking of getting colored contacts, but this is free.

Pi needed time to think about it. "I guess there's nothing we can do but—"

Keep an eye on it? Olivia thought.

BJ and Tess laughed.

Pi gave a tight smile. Having purple eyes was highly unusual. It would certainly set them apart from everyone else.

Mackenzie's next thought said it all: *It means we won't be able to keep this a secret.*

CHAPTER TWENTY-SEVEN

SLAMMING DOORS

Mackenzie was not having a good week. No one was talking to her, at least not out loud.

It had started on the way to homeroom on Monday. Tess was wearing her favorite jeans and a new pair of boots.

No tall boots with those jeans, thought Mackenzie. *Why can't she see it makes her thighs look huge?*

It was involuntary. Mackenzie would never have said such a mean thing in a million years. But Tess snapped, "You really do think I'm fat, don't you? You think it all the time."

"I do not!"

"You think I should lose ten pounds! You know I'm a perfectly healthy weight, but you think this kind of crap all the time. It's like you're siding with my mom."

"Your mom is crazy. I'm not siding with her," Mackenzie said, but she couldn't help thinking, *Eight pounds, maybe.*

"You are such a liar," Tess said, shaking her head. *At least my mom tells me what she thinks, ugly as it is.*

Instead of sitting with Mackenzie in homeroom, Tess went to the front of the class and sat next to Olivia, of all people. When had she ever spoken to Olivia?

At least Olivia doesn't think I'm a pig, Tess barked.

"I don't think you're a pig!" Mackenzie yelled. Of course we all heard.

And then weighed in.

No pun intended.

She's definitely not a pig. I think she's pretty.

She's okay.

She could lose five pounds.

But what if it was five pounds of boobs? That would be a travesty. She has good boobs.

You could lose five pounds.

Me? I'm a growing boy.

Leave her alone.

Can't you judge a girl on her brains? Or her sense of humor?

Do you want her to become anorexic?

Then she'd definitely have no boobs. Or ass. And her ass looks hot in those jeans. She's bootylicious.

You are an animal, BJ.

I'm a healthy, normal, growing boy.

Was that a double entendre?

Double what? Think English.

Gross.

Tess was horrified.

Mackenzie sat through homeroom by herself.

Now everyone thought she was a horrible slut *and* a bad friend.

And Mackenzie couldn't help agreeing. She was a terrible friend. She was a terrible girlfriend. She missed Cooper so much she ached. She never thought she'd miss him this much. How could she have cheated on him? How could she have been so careless about their relationship? Why hadn't she told him—fought for him—when she'd had the chance?

When she got back her English essay during sixth period, she was reminded that not only was she a bad friend and girlfriend, she was dumb too.

C-.

With the note: *More effort, please! And hand it in on time!*

The only thing Mackenzie was good at was being pretty.

By the end of Tuesday, Mackenzie was exhausted and miserable. Plus it was raining.

She staggered back to her apartment and into her elevator. She pressed the *close* button so she wouldn't get stuck listening to the French thoughts of one of the many Parisians who lived in her building. Nothing was more annoying than listening to someone rant in a language she couldn't understand.

The door started to close when a knapsack swung inside.

A gray knapsack.

She knew that knapsack.

It was Bennett's. Which meant—

"Hey," he said, his voice husky.

"Hey," she replied, heart instantly in her throat.

He raised an eyebrow. "Haven't seen you in a while."

She tried to sound cool. "I've been around."

"We must keep missing each other."

She felt him checking her out. *She's looking hot. Maybe she'll come over?*

"So what are you up to today?" he asked.

Was he serious? Did he really think she was going to run into his arms after what had happened the past summer? "Not hanging out with you," she snapped.

He laughed. "Am I that obvious?" He reached over and tugged at her sleeve. The touch made her jump.

"Yes?" she said.

She seems mad at me.

Was she? It wasn't his fault that she'd hooked up

with him. It wasn't his fault she was weak. He never made her any promises. He was single. He'd never done anything wrong, really.

The elevator stopped on her floor. "Wait—it missed you. Aren't you on fifteen?"

He glanced at the panel. "Oops. Forgot to press it. I was distracted by your beauty."

"What a charmer," she said, stepping out.

I'm not giving up yet. This time I won't blow her off for Victoria. I'm done being played by that crazy chick. He held the elevator open with his hand. "What are you up to tonight?"

Victoria? Who was Victoria? Had he blown her off because he'd been pining after some girl? "Test tomorrow," she said eventually. It wasn't a lie. She did have a physics test. Too bad Pi wasn't in her class. But Jon Matthews was. She refused to sit next to him, though.

She was done with cheating.

We must admit, we were impressed with her ethical resolve. Even if it was too little, too late.

Bennett held the elevator door open. "And this weekend?"

"Carnival," she said.

The elevator banged against his hand and then reopened. "Right. And next weekend is your Sweet. I got your invite."

Oh God. She'd forgotten that she'd sent him an

invite. She'd done it weeks earlier, before everything had happened.

Why had she sent him one? It wasn't long after they'd hooked up. She'd already started to feel guilty, so why had she invited him? Had she wanted him to show up? What had she thought would happen?

Mackenzie felt like crying. And now her Sweet was next week. The event planner was coming over later to go over details. Her sister and brother were coming in. Her mom had booked them a million spa appointments that weekend.

They'd bought her a Louis Vuitton clutch too. The one she'd wanted forever, with the classic design. They hadn't given it to her yet—it was a surprise—but it wasn't like they could keep secrets from her. Not anymore.

She didn't deserve it. She didn't deserve any of it. She was a horrible person.

The Sweet was supposed to be the best night of her life, or at least one of the best nights of her life, and it was all a hot mess. Cooper wasn't talking to her. Her best friend wasn't talking to her. What if no one showed up? She looked back at Bennett. Would he show up? "Are you coming?"

"Maybe," he said. *Depends what I have going on.*

He was such a jerk.

"I'll see you when I see you," she said, and walked away.

I think I—

The elevator door closed and she had to wonder how he'd finished that sentence.

She wondered if it was *I think I made the biggest mistake of my life.*

Then they'd be thinking the same thing. In his case, letting her go. In her case, letting him in.

CHAPTER TWENTY-EIGHT

PARTY ON

Olivia was having a great week. Really great. Possibly the best week ever.

Before she'd gotten ESP, she'd spent a lot of time and energy worrying about what people thought of her, but to her relief, she was discovering that most people—well, the non-telepathic kind, anyway—didn't think about her at all. Plus she had a boyfriend. A cute boyfriend! They weren't soul mates just yet, but Olivia knew that a true connection took time to build. Time and telepathy.

For the first time in a long time, Olivia also had a ton of friends. Tess had sat next to her in homeroom. Even Jordana and Courtney said hi to her between classes.

It might have been rough for some of us, but for Olivia, having the Espies was the besties.

Ha, ha.

Of course, Olivia didn't ditch Renée. She would never do something like that. At least there were no surprises with Renée—her internal thoughts weren't that different from what she said aloud. Both were overconfident and self-deluded.

"I'm going to be an amazing fortune-teller," she'd bragged to Olivia on Wednesday morning in home-room. She stood up and tossed her striped red-and-orange scarf over her shoulder. *I think I'll have a real gift for it.*

Renée really thought she knew what was best. At all times.

Renée knew what Olivia should order for lunch in the cafeteria. "Do not get the chicken burger. The cook never cooks the chicken properly." *One day the whole school is going to get food poisoning.*

Renée knew what colors looked best on Olivia. "You should buy more green. It's very flattering on you." *I'm lucky I can pull off almost every color.*

And of course, Renée had known that Olivia would make a good couple with Lazar. In that case, Olivia was grateful for her friend's overbearing know-it-all-ness.

Life was good.

Not for everyone, though.

Olivia watched a sad-looking Mackenzie enter the class by herself.

Slut.

Bad friend.

Cheater.

Olivia couldn't help feeling bad for her.

Mackenzie sighed. *Even Olivia feels sorry for me now.*

Olivia blushed.

"Sorry," Mackenzie said. "I didn't mean it the way it sounded."

Renée looked back and forth between them. *Did she just say something to us?*

"Don't worry about it," Olivia said to Mackenzie.

Why's Olivia being nice? thought Renée. *She wasn't even invited to the Sweet! Neither of us were! Unless my invitation really was lost in the mail.*

Mackenzie flushed. *Oh, man. Olivia, did I not invite you?*

Well, we've never actually spoken before, Olivia thought.

Mackenzie nodded. *Right. There's that. Do you want to come?*

Too much pressure. Too much anxiety-producing activity. Small talk! Dancing! Walking in heels! Food between her teeth!

Oh come on, Mackenzie begged. *Please?*

Olivia hesitated. *Can I bring my boyfriend?*

Mackenzie's mouth opened in surprise. *You have a boyfriend?*

Olivia heard a tsk from a few seats over. *Mackenzie is so self-absorbed,* Courtney thought. *How does she not know who Olivia's boyfriend is? She's been thinking about that kiss all week!*

This time both Olivia and Mackenzie blushed.

I've had a lot going on, Mackenzie thought.

Jordana shook her head. *What, and the rest of us haven't?*

It's Darren Lazar, Olivia thought. She wasn't sure if Mackenzie would know who he was.

Oh! He's the short guy, right? Of course you can bring him. I like Lazar.

Courtney tsked again. *Not enough to have invited him in the first place.*

Mackenzie spun around. "Can you mind your own business?" *I'm kinda wishing I hadn't invited Courtney.*

Courtney gave her the finger. *If I hadn't just bought a dress, I wouldn't come.*

Levi banged his fist against his desk. *Catfight! Catfight! Catfight!*

Renée twisted her scarf around her wrist, obviously confused.

Mackenzie looked pained. *Am I going to have to drop out of school? Or at least cancel the party? It's going to be a disaster.*

"It won't be," Olivia said.

"What are you talking about?" Renée asked. "Did I miss something?"

"Do you guys want to come to my Sweet?" Mackenzie asked Olivia and Renée. "I'm sorry I didn't invite you earlier, but you can bring a date if you want, and it would be really fun if you came."

Renée smiled. *Hurray!* "Fantastic. We'd love to come!"

Olivia wasn't exactly sure she wanted to go, but the look on Mackenzie's face broke her heart. "Lazar and I will be there. Sounds fun."

"I'll bring you a printed invitation tomorrow. In fact, I should make sure everyone in 10B gets an invitation." *I don't need anyone hating me any more than they do already.*

Levi smirked. *Doing us all a favor, are you?*

Mackenzie rolled her eyes. *Give it up, Levi. You know you're coming.*

Cooper walked in, late as usual. He sat in an empty seat near the wall, diagonally from Olivia.

Olivia turned around and gave him a sad smile. *What you're going through sucks.*

You don't know the half of it, Cooper thought.

I do, Olivia thought, feeling her face go pale. *I think everyone knows.*

It's not just about Mackenzie.

I know, Olivia thought. *Your dad too, right?* She did not want to be the one to tell him, but someone had to.

"I think I'll wear my orange dress," Renée mused.

Cooper froze. *Everyone knows about my dad?*

Olivia nodded. *If you're thinking about it, so are we.*

Cooper put his head down on the desk. "Terrific," he said aloud.

Renée smiled at Cooper, completely oblivious. "Thanks, Cooper!"

"You're welcome," he said. *I have no idea what she's talking about.*

Don't worry about it, Olivia thought, but he had closed his eyes and she knew he couldn't hear.

CHAPTER TWENTY-NINE

NOWHERE TO HIDE

When Cooper walked into economics, he looked for a spot that was Espie-free. He tried to avoid us whenever he could. He couldn't stand our sympathy.

He saw an empty seat in the back corner and took it. The only one of us who was nearby was one of the twins, Dave—but he was a few seats away. Hopefully there would be enough interference between them that Dave wouldn't be able to hear him.

The sympathy was everywhere. In the halls. In the cafeteria. In class. All from us Espies. We knew everything.

By the time Cooper's dad had come home on Sunday night from Chicago, Cooper had convinced himself that the truth couldn't be as bad as he feared.

His mom was probably imagining the affair. She was tired and lonely and that was it.

But then they sat down for dinner. "How's everything going?" his dad had asked, his voice booming across the table.

The four of them were sitting at the kitchen table, eating takeout Haru.

"Everything's okay," Cooper lied. He certainly wasn't going to tell his parents about the ESP thing. He wasn't ready to talk about Mackenzie either. He wasn't sure what to say. He couldn't tell them that she'd cheated on him. His parents were good friends with her parents. His whole family was going to her Sweet.

Halfway through the meal, Cooper's dad took out his iPhone and scrolled through his messages.

Ooh, from Mandy, he thought.

Cooper's spine straightened.

I miss you already, his dad read. *When can I see you again?* His dad took a break for some tuna tartar and then typed back, *Wednesday at one. I'll book a room at the Westin. Wear what I bought you at La Perla.*

Cooper almost vomited his edamame.

"Can you put the phone away?" his mom asked. *He couldn't be reading his whore's emails right at the dinner table, could he?*

He could, Cooper wanted to say. *He is.* But Cooper kept quiet.

"It's family time, family time, family time," Ashley sang. "Then can I watch *Cinderella*?"

"I don't think so," his mom said. "It's late."

I'll ask Daddy. He never says no. "Daddy, can I watch *Cinderella* after dinner?"

"Sure, honey," he said absentmindedly.

"Yay! I love you so much!"

Way to undermine my authority, Cooper's mom thought. *This is exactly what I told Newton about.*

Newton? Who was Newton? Was his mom having an affair too?

"Can I have cookies after dinner?" Ashley asked.

His mom sighed. *I can't believe I thought having Ashley would save our marriage.* "One," she said.

"Two!" *Twoooooooo.*

Save their marriage? Before the ESP Cooper hadn't realized their marriage was in trouble.

We think Cooper must have been walking around with serious blinders on. Even Mackenzie suspected their marriage was in trouble. Cooper's mom and dad always looked vaguely pained to be in the same room.

That night after his parents went to bed, Cooper looked through his mom's Internet history and found out who Newton was.

One of Manhattan's top divorce lawyers.

His father was having an affair and his mother was suing for divorce.

He didn't tell his mom that he knew about the affair. He didn't tell his dad about the divorce attorney.

And he didn't tell either of them that he and Mackenzie had broken up.

Because he missed her. He knew it was stupid. He missed her voice. He missed her smell. He'd had a crush on her since his cubby was next to hers in nursery school. One day she'd taken his hand and taught him how to do a somersault. He'd begged his parents to make playdates with her after school.

Did he have to lose her? He didn't have a say in his family's falling apart, but he did have a say in what happened between him and Mackenzie.

Cooper, don't take her back, man, Cooper heard, the thought immediately pulling him back to the present. He jumped in his chair and looked around the classroom. Dave was looking at him and shaking his head. *Don't be pathetic.*

Not only did we all have sympathy, but we listened to everything. And we all had opinions.

Cooper moved to an empty seat in the front of the room.

CHAPTER THIRTY

THE FUTURE IS BRIGHT

Olivia took a long sip of water. The carnival hadn't even started yet and she was already exhausted.

"Is everyone ready?" Pi barked.

The doors to the gym opened in ten minutes. We all congregated at our Madame Tribeca fortune-teller booth. Adam McCall had an ear infection.

And Renée was sick.

"Sick?" Pi sounded incredulous. "She's sick? She can't be sick!"

Olivia nodded. "She texted me that she was barfing all night." Olivia had resisted the urge to tell her friend that maybe she should have gotten the flu shot after all. Instead, she texted back:

```
You didn't eat the chicken
   burgers, did you?
```

"We need someone to take over." Pi looked around our group. "Olivia, you're up."

Olivia's breath caught in her chest. No way. She did not want to play fortune-teller. *I can't talk to that many strangers!*

"That is a ridiculous reason," Pi said. "You'll be fine. Go get dressed."

"Why me?" Olivia wondered.

"You're the least likely to say something stupid."

"But I don't know what to do," Olivia said, her heart racing. "Or say."

"I'll help you."

"Okay, I guess. I'll do it."

"Good," Pi said. "Go inside the tent and put on your costume. The doors are about to open."

The booth looked amazing. The twins had brought an old tent they used for camping and we covered it with dark purple scarves. A desk outside the tent was covered with a dark purple tablecloth. It was lined with lava lamps. We were going to charge five tickets per reading.

At Pi's insistence, we divided the inside of the tent in two. In the main part, we taped up glow-in-the-dark stars, set up a small table, covered it with a midnight-blue scarf, and placed a crystal ball in the center. It wasn't really a crystal ball—it was actually one of Levi's old fishbowls. In the second part, we dragged over a chair for Pi to sit on while she helped Olivia.

After climbing inside the tent, Olivia put on the black robe that made up her costume and sat down, adjusting to make herself comfortable.

Pi came in a minute later and set herself up in the second compartment. Her goal was for no one to see her but for her to be able to help Olivia. First she unzipped the small mesh window above her head so she could continue to hear the words and thoughts of people outside. No reason for her to miss out on anything important that happened outside the tent. Then she set up the partition, which was an old brown sheet she duct-taped to the tent's ceiling. She'd cut the sheet down the middle and made sure it was a bit open so she and Olivia could hear each other and the people in the booth. *I know Mackenzie said she could hear her parents through a wall, but I'm not sure I believe her,* Pi thought.

She can't lie, Olivia said. *We'd know.*

So I guess you can hear me?

Yes.

Good. I'm here if you need me. "We're all set!" she hollered. "You can send in our first customer!"

The first person inside was a girl, probably around eleven years old. She was extremely pretty. She had shiny brown hair and bright eyes. Her mom, also gorgeous, bent to enter the tent behind her.

"Hello," the mom said, sitting down. "My daughter wants her fortune told. This isn't going to be scary, is it?"

"No," Olivia said quickly. Her hands were shaking.

Say hello, Pi told her.

"Hello," Olivia said.

Use a spookier voice.

They don't want me to be scary!

There's no way you're going to be scary. Just do it.

"Helllllllo," Olivia said again. Instead of deep and mysterious, she sounded like a monkey.

The girl laughed. "Hi."

The mom gave Olivia a fake smile. "So tell us what you see. I hope it's good." There was a warning to the mom's voice. *She'd better be nice! I don't want her freaking my kid out!*

Olivia pretended to look deep into the crystal ball. *Now what?*

Just make stuff up, Pi said.

Olivia contemplated the ethics of what she was doing. What would happen when the things she promised didn't come true? Wouldn't they feel ripped off?

Olivia, Pi thought. *They paid five tickets, each worth a dollar. They don't really think you're psychic.*

Oh. Right. "Is there anything specific you want to know?" Olivia asked.

The mom nodded. "Is my daughter going to be a famous pianist one day?"

Olivia didn't need to be a fortune-teller to know what the right answer for that question was. "Yes," she said. "Absolutely. It will take many years of toil and hardship, but she will one day become a concert pianist!"

Uch, the daughter moaned. *I hate the piano.*

Good, the mom thought. *Maybe she'll stop being lazy and start practicing again.*

Olivia heard a small snort from Pi.

Olivia's cheeks heated up and she looked back down at the crystal ball. "Hmm, maybe I misread it."

The girl leaned toward the table. "You did?"

"Yeah. It's, um, not piano."

"It's not?" she asked hopefully.

What are you doing? Pi wondered.

"What is it?" the girl asked.

"It's . . . um . . . it's . . ." Olivia rubbed her temples. She was about to close her eyes to look like she was channeling something, but realized that wouldn't help matters. She was listening hard and hoping that the girl would give something away.

The girl leaned even closer. *Is it the drums? Am I going to be a famous drummer?*

Aha!

"I definitely see music," Olivia said. "But it doesn't appear to be the piano. It's louder. It has more of a rhythm."

The girl's eyes widened.

"Yes!" Olivia cheered. "It's the drums. You're going to be a successful drummer . . . in a band! I think I see Grammys in your future!"

Olivia, didn't I tell you not to use the telepathy to tell their fortunes? Pi asked. *Were you not listening?*

This is ridiculous, the mom thought. "How did you know she wants to take drum lessons?" She turned to her daughter. "Did you tell her?"

You see! Pi yelled. *She's getting suspicious!*

"I didn't say anything, Mom! You were with me the whole time!"

Olivia gave a slight shake of her head. *Suspicious that I'm really psychic! Not that our homeroom has telepathy!*

We agree with Olivia. Pi was being majorly paranoid.

The mom glared at Olivia. "Did she put you up to this? Do you two know each other?"

Olivia tried to look as innocent as possible. She shook her head. "We don't. I swear."

"Mom, the fortune-teller is amazing!" the girl exclaimed. "She really knows her stuff! Mom, ask a question about you!"

Ella was probably drumming her fingers against the table or something. That's how the girl knew.

"So what about you?" Olivia asked the mother. "What would you like to know about your future?"

The woman just stared at her, her mind blank. Not helpful.

Olivia glanced at the woman's ring finger to see if she was still married.

She was.

Hmm. "Any questions about the future at all?"

Blank.

"About your career?"

"I don't work," the mom said.

She doesn't do anything, Ella thought. *Except bug me.*

Olivia pretended to look into the crystal ball.

Olivia looked up. "Even if you don't have a paying job, I can see you're going to be very busy this fall."

No kidding, the mom thought. *The Seaport committee is going to be the death of me. I don't know why I agreed to help with the Winter Wonderland. Geena totally roped me in. What a time suck. And I'm not even her co-chair.*

Aha! "It's something to do with seasons," Olivia began. "Summer . . . no, spring . . . no! Winter."

I know I'm supposed to be mad at you, Pi said, *but this is funny.*

The mom wasn't even listening. Instead she was thinking, *I really need to fix my highlights. And get more Botox. Maybe I should just get a face-lift. Why not? Geena did it. She can afford it, though. Her husband is about to make a fortune with all his Tableau stock. I don't know why Dave wouldn't buy any. Insider trading-shmading.*

Interesting, Pi thought. *What stock did she say?*

Tableau or something? thought Olivia. *Why?*

I want to write it down! I guess now that I'm sitting here I might as well be taking notes. Where's my notebook?

"Anything else?" the girl prompted Olivia.

It had been a full minute since Olivia had spoken.

She had to find something, stat. She peered into the crystal ball. She squinted to make it look more authentic. "I also see some major work being done in your future. Renovations, maybe?"

The mom's jaw dropped.

Pi snorted.

"You're doing something to your apartment? No. I don't think it's the apartment. I see your face featured very clearly."

The mom touched the side of her face. *Holy moly. How did she know?* "Would you mind telling me, then, if, well, if the renovations look good? Are they worth doing?" *I do not want to end up with one of those stretched-out faces like Romy Brohman.*

Olivia gazed back into the ball. "Honestly, you regret them. You wish you had left everything the way it was."

The mom's head bobbed up and down. "Thank you."

Olivia smiled. "Any time."

"You have really unusual eyes," she continued. "Are they purple?"

"They're colored contacts," Olivia said quickly. She'd noticed they started turning that morning.

I should buy some, the mom thought. *Cheaper than a face-lift.*

Maybe, Olivia thought. *But they're certainly not without baggage.*

She wondered who was next.

CHAPTER THIRTY-ONE

WORKING THE BOOTH

Tess was collecting tickets at the fortune-telling booth with BJ when Teddy popped up in line.

His homeroom was hosting a bake sale and he smelled like chocolate. *There she is. She can't get away now.*

Tess pretended to be very busy counting change.

"Have you been avoiding me?" he demanded.

"What? Me? No."

BJ coughed. *Bullshit.*

Tess glared at him. *None of your business.*

You can't be mad at him for liking someone else, BJ thought. He made change for a freshman and then looked pointedly at Tess.

Um, Tess was pretty sure she could. She couldn't stand listening to his lovesick thoughts. Sadie was so gorgeous. Sadie was so hot. Look at Sadie's awesome perky breasts. Yes, that was what he'd been thinking about during chemistry the day before. Tess had almost puked into her beaker.

You have better tits than Sadie, BJ thought.

She flushed.

Teddy leaned toward her over the table. "I've left you a million messages."

"I know, I'm sorry. I've been really busy." She shot a look at BJ. *Please don't use the word* tits.

I didn't say it. I thought it. Anyway, it's true. What would you rather me call them?

How about breasts?

Point taken. You have better breasts than Sadie.

Tess looked down at her chest. *I do?*

Yup. I've felt hers—and yours—so I know.

Oh, shut up.

Don't tell me you've forgotten about our time together in the closet? Do you still have that sexy white bra?

Tess's cheeks heated up. *Eighth grade. Seven minutes in heaven. Unsexy white bra. I haven't forgotten. So when did you feel up Sadie?*

He smiled smugly. *Eighth grade. And it was sexy. On you, any bra would be sexy.*

You had a very busy eighth grade, she fired back.

Teddy placed a chocolate cupcake in front of Tess. "For you."

"Aw, thanks," she said. *Too bad cupcakes aren't on my diet.*

Oh, please, BJ thought. *You do not need to be on a diet. Don't listen to Mackenzie.*

Maybe if I was as skinny as Sadie, Teddy would like me.

If you were as skinny as Sadie, you would have no boobs. And I like your booty too.

"I'll get out of your way," Teddy said, "but do you want to get coffee after the carnival?"

"Oh, um, I don't think I can today. I have plans."

His face fell. "Oh, that's too bad. Tomorrow?"

"Maybe. I'll call you if I can, okay?" she said.

He nodded. "Okay. Have fun. See you soon." He waved and walked away.

"What plans?" BJ asked.

"I'm going to try a SoulCycle class," she said.

"Is that the spin class?"

"Yup."

"Ouch," he said. "Sounds painful."

She nodded. *Maybe if I lose five pounds, Teddy will like me.* She eyed the cupcake. The moist-looking cupcake. It was calling to her. *Eat me. Eat me! I am delicious!*

BJ laughed. "Just eat it. A guy doesn't fall for a girl because of five pounds."

Tess shrugged. "Ten pounds, then. Can you eat it? It's taunting me."

"Let's share it," he said, picking it up and offering her half.

She couldn't resist. "But tell me this. If it's not the

five—maybe ten—pounds, then what is it? I know he thinks I'm cute, I know he likes spending time with me. According to you I have better—" *Breasts.* "So what is it?"

"Have you ever heard him thinking about your weight?" BJ asked.

"No," Tess admitted.

"Then it's not that."

"But maybe he just doesn't see me as sexy because of the extra weight. It's subconscious."

BJ shrugged. "Maybe he's just never thought of you that way. Maybe he'd change his mind if he knew how you felt."

"That's what Mackenzie said. When we were talking to each other."

"You won't know unless you try. Throw down the gauntlet. What do you have to lose?"

My dignity?

BJ laughed.

Tess flushed. *Like you know anything about dignity.*

"Ouch!" He held his hand to his heart. "I'm not the enemy here."

He was right. He wasn't the enemy. Teddy was the enemy. Sadie was the enemy.

"Just cover yourself in chocolate frosting and show up naked at his apartment."

Tess smacked him on the arm as a group of junior guys approached their booth.

All you think about is sex, Tess thought.

All anyone thinks about is sex. All the guy in front of us thinks about is sex, and he's *thinking about sex with his stepmom. Now, that's wrong.*

Tess laughed. *Not everyone thinks about sex all the time. I don't.*

Oh, please. Don't tell me you don't think about Teddy when you're alone at night.

Tess's jaw dropped. She did not! *Only sometimes! Omigod.*

BJ smirked.

She turned her back to him. *Agh! Stop listening to me! You're a good kisser. You should just kiss Teddy. See what happens.*

I am?

He nodded. *One of the best kissers I've been with.*

Her heart swelled. She couldn't help it. *Swear?*

Swear. His eyes brightened. *Do you know what you should do?*

What?

Kiss me right now.

Are you crazy?

Think about it. How jealous would Teddy be if you kissed me?

Not jealous at all. He doesn't like me.

He just doesn't think of you in that way. But if he sees you making out with me, he'll start.

You just want to make out with me. Or any other girl with a beating heart.

He shook his head. *Not any other. But you, yes. It's true.*

This whole conversation was ridiculous. Tess saw BJ's point, but she was not just going to make out with him.

You've probably made out with a hundred girls since eighth grade.

Forty-two.

She rolled her eyes. *Yeah, right.*

It's the truth.

Liar.

You can't lie in your thoughts.

You can if you want to.

He smiled. *Point is, we kiss. Teddy realizes he loves you. I win, you win.*

Tess stood on her tiptoes and looked around the room. She spotted Teddy near the balloon booth. "I'll think about it," she said. Incidentally, BJ wasn't altogether repulsive.

Why, thank you. BJ made a small bow. "I'm at your service should you need me."

"Hey, guys," Mackenzie said. "I'm up. Who am I replacing?"

Here she is, BJ thought. *The scarlet* M.

"I heard that," Mackenzie said.

"I know you did. I'm sure you've heard worse. And scarlet is my favorite color. I still think you're hot."

Case in point, Tess thought at BJ. *You'd hook up with anyone.*

Mackenzie looked hurt. *Hello? I thought we were friends.*

We are friends. But I'm still mad at you about the weight thing.

I'm sorry! I'm a moron! That isn't news!

You're not a moron. But I'm not ready to forgive you yet. She didn't look at Mackenzie while she thought it. "You can stay with BJ."

Mackenzie peered into the tent. "Who's inside?"

"Olivia and Pi."

"I think Levi is switching with me at some point," BJ said.

"Oh, joy."

"Is Cooper here?" BJ asked.

"I don't think he showed," Mackenzie said.

"Can't really blame the guy," Tess said.

We couldn't blame him one bit.

* * *

Spotting Mackenzie across the gym made Cooper even more miserable. She was talking to BJ as though everything were fine with the world.

Everything was not fine. Everything was a mess.

"Can I get my face painted now?" Ashley asked him, pulling his hand.

"Yup." He hadn't wanted to come, but he knew Ashley would enjoy it, and he wanted to make his sister as happy as possible before her world imploded.

He took her to get her face painted by two senior girls. She sat on a barstool trying to stay perfectly still as the girls painted cat whiskers on her cheeks. After this Cooper planned to take her to hair braiding.

Truth was, Cooper was enjoying spending the day with her. She was the only person he wanted to be around, since she was the only person who didn't lie. She said what she thought. She thought what she said.

Hey, Cooper, in defense of us and the rest of the world, Ashley was only three. She hadn't fully learned how to filter her thoughts yet.

Cooper just couldn't stand being around liars.

He knew he was sounding a little Holden Caulfield–esque calling everyone a phony, but he really did think everyone was a phony.

The senior taking his twenty bucks to get in the door? A phony. "Hey, man, how are you, good to see you. Glad you could come." *What's that kid's name again?*

The junior who sold him and Ashley cookies: "I hope you like them! I made them myself!" *I bought them at Crumbs, but no one will know.*

Cooper knew. We all knew.

Oops, thought the girl painting on a whisker. *Messed that up a little. Oh well.*

"You messed it up," Cooper blurted out. "Please fix it."

"What's wrong?" Ashley asked him. "Is it pretty?"

"Very pretty," Cooper said, "once she fixes her mistake." He glared at the girl and said, "Make it perfect, will you?"

The girl blinked. And then blinked again. *He wants me to make a perfect cat face?*

Yes. That was exactly what he wanted. A perfect cat face. Was that too much to ask? Did everything in life have to be messed up? He took a deep breath. He was overdoing it. It wasn't the face painter's fault that everyone was a liar. It wasn't her fault that Mackenzie had cheated and lied to him. It wasn't her fault that his parents' marriage was falling apart. He sighed. "Just make it as good as you can, okay?"

The girl nodded. She took a paper towel and wiped away a small line.

"That's better," Cooper said. Honestly, he couldn't tell the difference. But he appreciated the effort.

Cooper looked back across the room. Mackenzie was collecting money from a junior who was going into the Madame Tribeca tent.

She'd left a message on his phone that morning, asking if he was going. "I miss you," she'd said. "I heard what's happening with your parents. I'm here if you want to talk."

He missed her too. A lot.

He wondered if they should get back together. Sure, on the surface, breaking up seemed like the right thing to do. Girl cheated on guy, guy broke up with girl.

But now he saw that things weren't so black-and-white. Everyone lied. Everyone cheated. Everyone was full of it. At least Mackenzie knew she'd made a mistake. At least her lies were on the table. And he really could use someone to talk to.

Ashley jumped off her chair. "Meow!" *Meow meow meow meow!*

Someone who wasn't three.

"Can my brother go next?" Ashley asked the senior. "Can you paint Spider-Man on him? Or Superman? Or maybe Wonder Woman?"

"Sure," the senior said. "Is your brother a superhero?"

"He is," she said proudly.

"I can do Spider-Man," the girl said.

"Go for it," Cooper said, and sat down in his chair. Cooper did not feel like a superhero. But what the hell.

CHAPTER THIRTY-TWO

I HEAR YOU

Pi stretched her arms above her head.

Olivia had done a fantastic job at the fortune-teller booth. And thanks to Olivia, Pi had never felt more powerful. In her little hot hands, she now had everyone's secrets.

She'd gotten the goods on everything that was happening at our school. Crushes, college dreams, whatever. And it wasn't just the kids' secrets she knew. Grown-ups too. Bankers. Lawyers. Psychologists. Mostly parents who'd come with their kids, but still, the parents in Tribeca ran a lot of New York. She now knew about drug addictions, affairs, abortions, investment-banking deals, and more.

What could she do with all that information? How could she use it? Without, you know, resorting to bribery? Before she'd become an Espie, she'd barely bothered to learn people's names. Now she alone knew everything.

Olivia too.

But Olivia was hardly a threat.

Although Pi knew secrets would spread to the rest of us pretty fast. Not for the first time she wished she were the only one with telepathy.

"Hi!" she heard Olivia say now.

"Hey there, pretty," the guy said.

Pi opened her eyes. *Who is that?*

It's Lazar, Olivia thought.

Who?

My boyfriend.

"So what does my future hold?" he asked. "Does it see us going to another play tonight?"

"Should it?" Olivia asked.

"I think it should. Because I got tickets to *Night Walkers!*"

Another play? Olivia thought. *Can't we go out for dinner?*

What's wrong with plays? Pi wondered.

Nothing. But the ones he gets tickets to are so boring. Musicals I get, but these are the talking-talking-talking-about-nothing plays. And the seats are really uncomfortable.

Then tell him you don't want to go, Pi thought.

I can't do that!

"So?" Lazar asked. "Does it? *Time Out New York* gave it five stars!"

Maybe no one at Bloomberg was affected, a new voice thought from the other side of the tent window. A woman's voice.

Pi's back stiffened. *Who was that?*

I told you, Olivia responded. *My boyfriend.*

The voice continued: *Maybe that's why no one has come forward. Or maybe they're keeping the ability a secret.*

The hairs on the back of Pi's neck stood up. She didn't recognize the voice. It sounded older. It definitely wasn't one of us. *Is she talking about us?* Pi needed to see who it was. Immediately.

Pi tried to lift the side of the tent, but it was fastened down. She pressed her face against the small mesh window but couldn't see anyone. Pi had to find out whom those thoughts belonged to before the woman got away.

She dropped her notebook into her knapsack—no way was she misplacing that—slid the bag over her shoulder, broke through the sheet, pushed her way past Olivia and a surprised-looking Lazar, and stormed out of the tent. The light made her blink. It was busy out there. Really busy. But whose voice had she heard?

She circled the tent, listening for voices and thoughts of the people swarming around her.

Why does my son always smell like BO? I know he showers.

Can anyone tell how high I am? Cupcakes! Want cupcakes! More cupcakes!

I think I have lice.

Pi circled around and around the tent, trying to find the woman. Who was it? She'd definitely sounded like she knew about the vaccines. How did she know? Had someone spilled the beans? No. Pi would know if one of us had. We wouldn't be able to keep it from her.

This was not part of her plan. Not at all. She was in charge here. She would have to figure out who else knew what, and soon.

CHAPTER THIRTY-THREE

ONE MORE CHANCE

After an exhausting day at the carnival, Mackenzie wobbled home.

Just as she was unlocking her front door, she saw a text from Cooper.

> Meet me at that bench in Battery Park at 9 tonight if you want to talk.

Yes. Yes, yes, yes, she did want to talk. She wanted to do more than talk. She wanted to wrap her arms around his neck and kiss him until he forgave her.

Now here she was, sitting on their bench at Battery Park in front of the water, still waiting for him. He was going to show, wasn't he?

A few minutes passed before she heard his footsteps behind her. She also heard, *She's here.*

"Of course I'm here. I miss you," she said, and turned around. She couldn't help laughing. He had red paint all over his face.

I miss you. "I'm Spider-Man," he said instead.

"I figured. Listen, Cooper, I am so, so, so sorry about what—"

In the moonlight she saw that tears were dripping down his cheeks through the paint.

She hadn't seen him cry since . . . well, since second grade when he fell off the seesaw and had to get stitches. It broke her heart right in half. "Oh God, Cooper, I can't believe I did that to you." Her voice cracked. *I'm sorry, I'm sorry, I'm sorry.*

"It's not just you," he said slowly. He wiped the tears away with his sleeve, staining it red. *It's my parents. Everyone. The Yankees.*

"The Yankees?"

He hiccup-laughed. "Yeah." He stood beside her and stared at the water ahead. "It's everything. Do you want to walk?" he asked.

"Sure." As she stood up, she took his hand. He didn't stop her.

As they walked south, following the railing, he told her about his mother and father and about how everywhere he went he heard lies, and it was killing him.

"I'm sorry you had to learn such crap stuff about your parents," she said.

"Have you heard things about yours, too?"

"I heard them having sex," she said. "But that was it."

At least they're having sex with each other. "Lucky," he said.

"It didn't feel lucky at the time," she replied. From where they were standing, they had a perfect view of the Statue of Liberty.

"Let's run away," she said.

"To where?"

"Anywhere but here." She took a step closer to him. "Do you think you can ever forgive me?"

He looked deep into her eyes. *I don't know.*

You don't?

No. But I'm willing to try.

"You are?" she asked. Her throat choked up.

"Yeah."

She gulped, and the next thing she knew, tears were streaming down her cheeks too. She threw her arms around him. "I just love you so much." *I'll never take you for granted again.*

"I love you too," he said. "I just hate everyone else right now."

"Me too," she said. "Especially the other Espies."

"I know."

"And they listen to everything. With their beady

little purple eyes. Let's ignore them. What do we need them for?"

"They're hard to ignore."

"We can do it," she said, lacing her fingers through his. "We can make our own little bubble. It'll be us against them."

"Us against the world," he said.

She leaned toward him. *Can I kiss you?*

You're going to get red face paint all over you.

I would love to get red face paint all over me.

I hope I don't regret this, he thought, and then closed his eyes and kissed her.

CHAPTER THIRTY-FOUR

STILL GOING

We were so over it the next week.

We were used to our parents pretending to listen to us while they were really thinking about meetings, or what to make for dinner, or in Mackenzie's case, her dad's new Viagra prescription.

And we were getting increasingly annoyed with each other.

Homeroom was the worst. Renée and Adam—on the rare occasion he showed up—were suddenly the most popular people in the class. They were a wall of interference. Otherwise our thoughts spread through the room like germs after a sneeze.

Still taking those Addies, Courtney? . . . Levi, why don't you go to a dentist? . . . Are Cooper and Mackenzie back together? . . . Clearly—they're sitting in a corner

together. . . . What about Bennett? . . . I guess Cooper for-
gave her. . . . I wouldn't have forgiven her. . . . Good thing
I'm not you. . . . Cooper, ignore them. . . . I'm trying to,
but they're so loud. . . . Hey, Olivia, how's Lazar? . . . Did
you have to go see another boring-ass play? . . . They're
not that boring. . . . Don't lie. You were just thinking about
how boring they are. . . . Is something up with BJ and
Tess? . . . Why? . . . She's ignoring him. . . . Tess is in love
with Teddy. . . . But Teddy likes Sadie. . . . Is he using
mouthwash yet, Sadie? . . . It was only one time! He had
souvlaki for lunch. . . . Hey, Tess, are you fantasizing
about me yet?

Tess froze. Then she slammed her eyes shut. She
might have spent a few minutes reminiscing about
her seven minutes in heaven. But BJ could never,
ever know.

He knew. We all knew.

We all closed our eyes for as much time as we could,
but Ms. Velasquez was starting to get frustrated.

"Are you guys not getting enough sleep? Next person I find napping in class is getting detention!"

Just what we wanted—more time in school. At
least in our apartments no one could hear us.

Except for the twins. We all felt bad for the twins,
who shared a room.

The rest of our classes weren't as bad. Every hour of
every day was a barrage of other people's thoughts—
their secrets, their lies, their stupidities—but we
didn't have to worry about being heard ourselves.

We put multiple non-Espies between us as buffers. We needed space.

Except at test time. Then we all parked ourselves next to the smartest person in the room. Pi hated it. She hated it more when Jon was in our class and we all crowded around him. Jordana and Courtney even got into a telepathic fight about who sat next to him. Chair grabbing was involved. Jon thought it was because of his new cologne.

Lunchtime was awkward too. Cooper and Mackenzie left school for lunch. Olivia sat with Lazar. Tess avoided BJ. And Sadie. And Teddy, obviously, although he wasn't one of us. She started to skip lunch entirely and spend the time studying in the library. She only lost two pounds, but she aced all her work that week. She didn't even need to sit next to the smartest person in the class.

And Pi? Well, Pi was watching us. Pi was definitely watching everyone. Pi was always watching. She was watching the redheaded fake nurse who was wandering our hallways.

Olivia had been the first to see her. She'd gone to the nurse's room on Wednesday with a headache. She'd ignored it until eleven but then realized she needed some Advil or she'd have to go home. So she'd made her way down to Nurse Carmichael's office and knocked on her door.

Instead of Nurse Carmichael, a redheaded woman had answered.

"Hi there!" the woman said in a voice that was way too cheerful. "What can I help you with?" *Does she have it?*

Olivia wondered what this woman thought she had. Was something contagious going around school? The flu? Meningitis? "Where's Ms. Carmichael?"

"She's on vacation," the woman said. *Permanent vacation. Screwup.* "I'm Suzanna."

What screwup? What Olivia wanted to know was what Carmichael had screwed up, but of course she couldn't ask.

"Come on in," Suzanna coaxed.

Olivia did not want to get exposed to meningitis. "Oh, never mind. I thought I had a headache, but I feel fine now. It's gone."

She's panicking. Maybe she has it. The woman took hold of her arm. "Are you sure? Why don't you come in for a few minutes? And chat?"

Olivia was officially freaked out. "I should get to class."

"Wait. What's your name? What grade are you in? You have very unusual eyes," the woman said. *That's the color!*

Oh. She knew about the ESP. How did she know about the ESP? Olivia took a step back.

Olivia's mom had noticed her eyes the night before. "Are your eyes itchy? They look strange. Do you have pinkeye?" she'd asked.

"No," Olivia had answered, avoiding her gaze. "I'm just wearing purple eyeliner."

In theory, purple eyes were cool. But in reality, it was supremely creepy when one day our eyes were brown and the next they had a lilac tint. It was like we were turning into vampires or something.

"We're becoming undead!" Edward had cheered.

Olivia ran away from Suzanna without answering any questions. She recounted the story at our next Espies meeting.

"Who do you think she was?" Tess asked.

Do you think she knows about us?

Is she the person Pi heard by the tent?

Definitely seems like it.

She's spying on us.

Why would a substitute nurse spy on us?

Maybe she's not a substitute nurse!

I bet she's from the CDC!

She wants to round us up and have us quarantined!

She wants to take away our telepathy!

What should we do?

We should confront her.

"No," Pi said. "Even if the nurse suspects something, she doesn't know anything for sure. If she did, she would have said something to us. If we approach her, we're just going to look suspicious."

Jordana pointed a lime-green nail to her eyes. "We already look pretty suspicious."

"She's probably gathering evidence against us," Levi said.

"Maybe she is," Pi admitted. "So let's not give her any. Avoid her. And we all have to be on our best behavior. In school and outside of it."

We nodded.

Pi stood up. "That means in school no one visits the nurse's office. If you see her coming, walk the other way. Keep your distance. Don't blow it out of school either. Stay in control. No drinking."

No one spike the punch at Mackenzie's Sweet.

No pot either.

Or Addies.

Why would you take an Addie at a Sweet?

You guys are no fun.

"Just stay under the radar," Pi repeated. "Got it?"

We nodded. Once again we had a plan.

If only all of us had stuck to it.

CHAPTER THIRTY-FIVE

TWO DAYS UNTIL
THE SWEET

"Olivia, it's your turn," Mr. Roth said.

Here it was. The moment of truth.

Speech time.

Again.

Lyme disease, Lyme disease, Lyme disease.

She could do this. She was not the same person she had been two weeks earlier. She was different. She had a boyfriend. She could hear people's thoughts. She had confidence.

Or, at least, more than she'd had before.

She stood up. Slowly.

Is she going to pass out again?

She looks nervous.

Olivia tried to smile. *Lyme disease, Lyme disease,*

Lyme disease. Did she have Lyme disease? No, she did not.

She turned around to face the crowd.

She definitely looks nervous.

Lazar gave her a thumbs-up.

She's going to do it, Renée thought. *Go Olivia!*

Yes! She could do this! She knew how her speech started: *In Ridgefield, Connecticut!* She looked at Lazar and smiled.

He smiled back. *She's not going to fall again, is she? That would be so embarrassing.*

Olivia narrowed her eyes. Embarrassing for her? Or embarrassing for him?

The room started to sway.

"Olivia?" Mr. Roth asked. "Are you okay?"

She didn't feel okay. She felt sick. Her headache was back and it was a bad one. Oh God. She was going to pass out again. She was going to pass out and hit her head, and this time she really was going to die.

"You know what?" she said. "I think I need to sit down." Without looking at her teacher, she returned to her seat and slumped into her chair. Mission un-accomplished. Olivia felt like crying.

Lazar gave her a puppy-dog face. *At least she didn't pass out.*

Wow, Pi thought, *Olivia, your boyfriend is a real asshole.*

That's it, Renée thought. *She needs my help. I'm practicing with her after school.*

"Olivia, we'll need to discuss this after class," Mr. Roth said sternly.

When the bell rang, Olivia slumped her way over to Mr. Roth. "You're getting one more chance. That's the best I can do. Or you fail the assignment. Next week. Got it?"

She got it, all right.

* * *

Teddy cornered Tess after class. "You're coming with me to the ball fields to watch the baseball game. No excuses. Let's move."

"Fine," she said. It was a nice day. It wasn't a terrible idea to get some fresh air. Sit outside. Cheer on Nick. Support BHS against Millennium.

Most of us were going to the game. It was the semifinals. We wanted to support Nick. We might not all have been friends before this, but there was nothing like having ESP to bond you to a person.

Tess looks really good, Teddy thought.

Was he noticing her because of the two pounds she'd lost? Probably not. His attention was more likely because of her new V-neck that showed off her cleavage. BJ had been thinking about her breasts all through homeroom. And so had other boys, actually, as the day went on. Not one of them had said a word. Without ESP, Tess would never have thought a single one of these guys found her sexy. Maybe they always had, and she never knew?

They climbed up the stands. Nick was walking toward the mound. Teddy and Tess cheered loudly.

From where they sat, Tess could kind of see the catcher making those weird finger signals to the pitcher. When she focused on the catcher's thoughts, she heard: *Try a fastball.*

Then Nick's thoughts as he held the bat: *Fastball. Got it.*

The pitcher threw the ball; Nick swung and sent it over the fence.

"Home run!" the umpire yelled.

"Go, Nick!" Tess hollered along with everyone else.

"He's been playing so well this week," Teddy said. "I knew he could do it."

Yeah, he'd been playing well. With a little help.

Tess smiled. Nick was doing great. She was here with Teddy and he thought she looked good. In fact, lots of boys did. Life was good. Tess felt the sun on her face. She closed her eyes and enjoyed the moment.

Then she opened them and heard Teddy think, *There she is!* Her heart plummeted. Of course that was why Teddy had wanted to come. Keith was on the team, so Sadie would be there. Why hadn't it occurred to her?

A text dinged on her phone. BJ.

```
You look like you're about to kill
  him.
```

Tess looked up and spotted BJ sitting high in the bleachers. He waved. She typed:

```
He's thinking about her again.
```

BJ looked down at his phone and wrote back:

```
He only likes her because she's
  unavailable. You have to show
  him that you're unavailable.
Tess: And how do I do that?
BJ: Come kiss me.
```

Ha. She shook her head. Did he really think she was going to cross the field and kiss him in front of everyone?

```
Tess: Yeah right.
BJ: I'm coming over.
```

By the time she looked up, he was already walking toward them.

Oh God.

"Hi there," he said, and squeezed onto the bench beside her. "What's up, peeps?"

You are not going to kiss me, Tess thought.

You so want me to, he thought back. With a totally straight face, he put his hand on her knee.

She wanted to punch him. Kind of.

I'm growing on you, aren't I? He winked, then turned to Teddy. "Hey, Teddy, my man, what's happening?"

Teddy looked back and forth between Tess and BJ's hand on her knee. *What the hell is that?* "Not much," he answered. "Just watching the game."

He's freaking out, Tess told BJ.

Of course he is. Can I touch your breast now? That would really freak him out.

You are not to touch my breast.

Not even the left one?

No breast-touching at all. She laughed. She couldn't help it.

"Uh, what's new with you, BJ?" Teddy asked.

"Nothing much. Trying to convince your friend here to go out with me sometime, but she keeps turning me down."

BJ!

What? I'm helping you!

"She does?" *She never told me that.*

"She thinks she's too good for me, but she'll come around. It's only a matter of time."

Teddy clenched his jaw. *She's thinking about it? She cannot go out with that sleazeball.*

What's he thinking? BJ wondered. *You're right between us. You're blocking his thoughts.*

Tess smiled. *He's thinking you're a sleazeball.*

He turned to look at her. *Do you think I'm a sleazeball?*

Tess gave the question some thought. *I used to. But*

*I guess . . . well, everyone else is thinking the same things
as you. At least you're saying them.*

BJ raised an eyebrow. Then his hand began to
creep slowly up her leg.

I spoke too soon.

He gave a slight nod. *Let's play chicken.*

She put her hand on his. Then she leaned over
and very slowly gave him a long kiss on the cheek.
"Thanks for coming to visit."

BJ laughed. *Am I being dismissed?*

I don't like this one bit, Teddy thought.

Holy crap. He's jealous! It's working!

BJ stood up and saluted them. *Good luck. The offer
is still good if you want me to keep going.*

She shook her head. *Goodbye!*

"You're going to Mackenzie's Sweet, right?" BJ
asked.

"Yeah," Tess answered. Things with her and Mackenzie were definitely strange, but she wouldn't miss
the Sweet. That would be unforgivable. Plus there
would be dancing.

BJ jumped down the stairs. "Save me a slow dance!"

"I'll think about it!" she hollered back.

The girls in the row in front of her were buzzing.
Does BJ like Tess?

Tess could feel Teddy's eyes on her. "We can go to
the party together if you want," he said.

Huh? She turned to him.

I can't believe BJ was sleazing up my Tess.

Seriously? Since when was she his Tess?

He squirmed in his seat. "You're not really going to go out with him, are you?"

She tried to sound flippant. "I might. He's funny." *And honest.*

"Funny-looking," Teddy said. *She's so not his type. Although she is looking sexy.*

She was looking sexy? She preened in her seat.

"He's not funny-looking," she finally answered. BJ was a lot of things, but funny-looking wasn't one of them. He was hot. He had great shoulders. Really big hands. She felt herself flush. She was suddenly very, very, very glad that he wasn't sitting next to her right then.

* * *

Mackenzie and Cooper skipped the baseball game. They went to dinner instead. Like they had every night that week.

Cooper had been spending as little time as he could at his apartment. "I miss you!" Ashley cried, wrapping her arms around his leg. *Why does Cooper not take me with him all the time?*

He felt bad for Ashley. He missed her too, but he just couldn't take being at home. He couldn't face anything. Except Mackenzie. If he could just focus on Mackenzie, everything would be okay.

He was dreading Saturday.

"Gee, thanks a lot," Mackenzie said as they waited for a table at Kitchenette. "Aren't you excited to see me all dressed up?"

"You are going to look amazing," he said. "It's just everyone's going to be there, lying. My parents too."

"Sorry about that. My parents insisted on inviting some of their friends whose kids are coming. I didn't know, so . . ." She kissed Cooper hard on the lips. "I'm sorry they're coming. But I think it'll be okay," she told him. "As long as we're together. A team. It's us against them."

They thought they could hide. They thought they could separate themselves from us.

Impossible.

There was no escaping us.

CHAPTER THIRTY-SIX

PARTY PREP

The big day was finally here.

Sweet day.

We spent the afternoon getting ready.

Some of us got manicures. In Manhattan, there's a nail place on every corner, but most of us went to Beauty Charm on Chambers. It had the best massage chairs. Courtney and Jordana went to Drybar. Courtney got the straight-up blowout while Jordana got the just-got-out-of-bed look. Mackenzie, Mackenzie's mom, and Mackenzie's sister, Cailin, spent the day at Bliss SoHo getting everything done: hair, nails, pedicure, and makeup.

Mackenzie had been excited to spend the day with her sister.

But the excitement ended about five minutes into the appointment.

"So, how's school?" Mackenzie asked.

"Fine," Cailin said. *I can't believe Mom made me come in for this stupid party when I should be in the library.*

The appointment didn't improve.

"You have the most incredible eyes," the makeup artist told Mackenzie. "I'm going to use a teal green to really bring out the violet. They're so unusual."

Come tonight and you won't think they're so unusual, Mackenzie almost said.

"Did you get colored contacts?" her mom asked, peering at her face.

"No, they're just changing color. Puberty, I guess."

Under the circumstances, we thought that was a decent excuse. Tess's hair had been straight until her fourteenth birthday, when it had gone wavy, right? These things happened.

Cailin sighed. *I got zits and Mackenzie got exotic eyes. How is that fair? Ugh.*

Mackenzie wanted to tell her to shut the hell up, but she closed her eyes instead.

* * *

"Do we really have to go to this Sweet Sixteen party?" Lazar asked as they walked up West Broadway. "I could get us tickets to *The Eiffel Tower* at the Atlantic Theater."

If Olivia were being honest, she'd admit that she didn't really feel like going to the Sweet either. She was depressed. Her epic fail in public speaking class had been a punch to her stomach. "I promised Mackenzie I'd be there," Olivia said. She'd bought a gift. A set of cute mini metallic nail polishes. She'd "overheard" Mackenzie admiring Jordana's nail color one day in homeroom and had asked Jordana where it was from. Olivia had also borrowed a green dress of her mom's and a pair of sparkly flats. She even did her makeup just the way Lazar said he liked it on the day he'd finally asked her out. Well, not said. Thought. "It should be fun," she added. More fun than *The Eiffel Tower,* anyway.

"I don't dance," Lazar said.

"Oh, don't worry," Olivia said. "I'm not a great dancer either."

Such a waste of time. Why does Olivia care about Mackenzie? She's kind of a bitch. Olivia cares too much about what stupid people think.

Olivia stopped in her tracks. Maybe she should turn around and go home. She didn't want to drag him against his will. "Do you want to just go home?"

He turned to her, surprised. "I thought you wanted to go."

"I do want to go. But not if you're going to complain the whole time."

He blinked. "We can go," he said finally. "I'm just not really a party type of person." *I never know what to do with myself. I never know what to do with my feet. I should have taken dance lessons when I was younger or something.*

Aw, Olivia thought. Her heart melted. *He's shy. Just like me.*

Olivia laced her fingers through his. "We don't have to stay long."

They walked the last few blocks, hand in hand.

* * *

Mackenzie was in the bathroom at SoHo Tower re-applying her lipstick. It was seven-fifty-eight, which meant the party was starting in two minutes.

She wasn't sure how it was biologically possible, but her heart was pounding inside her head, her neck, her fingers. She was nervous. Very nervous. Not about one thing specifically. She was nervous about it all. Would someone think something they shouldn't? Would Cooper change his mind and decide he hated her after all?

Everything was set up. Her parents and siblings were there, the DJ was organizing his stuff, the bartenders were ready—no alcohol for anyone under twenty-one. She was sure some of the non-Espies would smuggle in booze, but she knew none of us would drink. Too risky. The waitresses had their hors d'oeuvres ready to go: mini pizzas, mini lobster rolls, spring rolls. The room looked fun, flirty, and modern but not cheesy, just the way the event planner had promised—white leather couches and chairs, glass bar tables, white candles in square silver candleholders, white roses in silver vases. No balloons. No streamers. A silver square dance floor in the middle of the room.

Everything was going to be fine, Mackenzie told herself.

Completely fine.

The Espies will behave themselves. I have Cooper. He's all I need.

Mackenzie pushed open the bathroom door and headed down the hallway to the hotel ballroom. People had already arrived. Olivia. Lazar. Jordana. Isaac. No sign of Tess, but most of the rest of us were there. Even Brinn, in a slightly ill-fitting black dress. Even Pi. She was wearing a navy blue dress, a navy blue jacket, and matching navy pumps. She looked like she was interviewing for a job on Wall Street.

Jordana clucked her tongue. *Way to make fun of your own guests.*

Oops. Maybe Mackenzie would tell the DJ to make the music loud. Really loud. *So loud the Espies won't be able to hear themselves think, never mind each other.* Would that work?

Mackenzie spotted her parents chatting with

Cooper's parents. Both dads were wearing black suits. The moms were wearing cocktail dresses. But where was Cooper?

He was alone at the bar, wearing non-wrinkled black pants, a black jacket, and a gray shirt. He looked swanky. He looked beautiful.

Mackenzie approached him from behind and put her arms around his waist. "Hey."

He turned and kissed her on the forehead. "Hi. Happy birthday."

She loved the fact that it was her actual birthday. How often did that happen? That a party celebrating your birthday really fell on the right day? For the first time in weeks she felt lucky. It was meant to be. Everything had been messed up until that day, but now everything would be fine. Magical.

"Sorry I couldn't be here earlier," Cooper said. "Ashley was throwing a fit."

"You should have brought her."

"She wanted to come. She put on a party dress and her party shoes."

"Aw, that's so sad. I wish she were here."

"I think my mom wanted a night out."

They both looked at his parents.

Cooper's father had his arm around his wife's waist. Was it possible Cooper had been wrong? Maybe he'd misunderstood?

Cooper shrugged. *Let's not talk about it tonight.*

You sure?

"Yeah. But . . ." *They seem happy, right?*

Absolutely. Mackenzie hugged him. Everything was going to be fine. Everything was going to be great. "Wanna dance?"

He took a sip of his Coke. "Boo-ya. Let's doooo this," he said, and Mackenzie could have sworn his words sounded like a song.

* * *

Tess and Teddy arrived together, her arm linked through his.

If we were surprised by the turn of events, Tess was even more surprised.

He'd called her earlier that afternoon and asked if they were still going together.

"Sure," Tess said. "Whatever." So he was going to walk with her? Big whoop. It wasn't a real date.

But then he offered to pick her up at her apartment. And he didn't ring from downstairs. He came up to get her.

"Let me get some pictures," her mom said when she saw them both in their fineries. It felt like a prom.

Did she lose a few pounds? her mom thought. *It's still not enough. She needs to lose at least another seven.*

That thought had almost ruined Tess's night, but she kept on her game face. Still, she sucked in her stomach.

Anyway, Teddy's reaction made up for her mom's.

She looks hot. And those eyes . . . Did she always have such gorgeous eyes? She has great boobs.

Is he staring at her boobs? her mom wondered. *He definitely is. I wish I had boobs.*

Ha! If she lost another seven pounds, she'd have no boobs. *Take that, Mom!*

They'd walked arm in arm to SoHo Tower. By the time they arrived, the room was packed.

"Let's go say hi to Mackenzie," Tess said. Their arms were still linked. Did it mean what she thought it meant? Was getting Teddy to notice her really that easy? Step one, show that other guys were interested? Step two, get dressed up and show cleavage? Was that all it took?

She found Mackenzie on the dance floor with Cooper. Cooper was a great dancer. He'd always been a great dancer. Maybe the two of them would be okay. She squeezed Teddy's arm. Maybe they'd all be okay.

She hugged Mackenzie tightly. "You look amazing," she said. "Happy birthday."

Does this mean you forgive me? Please forgive me? I'm sorry. I miss you. And you look amazing too. And happy. You came with Teddy! Is that on?

Tess blushed. *We'll see. All signs point to positive.*

I'm so happy for you. I want to hear everything. I know I haven't always been a great friend but I do—

Tess squeezed Mackenzie's shoulders. *We'll get through it.*

Good.

"What up, Coops?" Teddy said, and they gave each other one of those boy handshakes involving loud palm smacks.

"Come dance with us," Mackenzie insisted.

For a few minutes that's what they did. The four of them dancing, just the way Tess had always imagined. The music was pumping; she was moving, her hair flying all over the place.

For the next song, the music went old school and Marvin Gaye's "Sexual Healing" came on. Teddy and Tess moved closer together. His arms were around her waist and hers were around his neck, and they were dancing and kind of rocking back and forth.

Me and Tess? Teddy thought.

She could feel his hands on the small of her back. Was this really, finally, happening? Her heart was thumping so loud she could barely hear anything except the music. His eyes were closed, so she couldn't hear his thoughts, but she didn't need to. She could feel him pressed against her. She knew something had changed. Shifted. Even though they hadn't *done* anything, or said anything, they had crossed over from "just friends" to something more. This was going to happen. This was finally going to happen.

* * *

"It's so loud in here," Lazar whined.

It *was* loud. But still, Olivia was having fun. She

hadn't expected to have fun, but she was. All her friends were there. Look at that! She had friends! And after reading everyone's minds, she knew two things: one, she was looking cute, and two, she didn't have food in her teeth.

Olivia felt brave. "Come on. Let's dance."

He shook his head stubbornly. "I told you I don't dance."

"One song," she begged.

He sighed. "Fine."

They squeezed their way onto the dance floor.

It's so hot in here, he thought.

She couldn't help wondering if he ever stopped complaining. "Why don't you take off your jacket if you're hot?"

He scowled. *How did she know I was hot? Am I sweating? I must be sweating.* "Where would I put it?"

Close call. "On a chair?"

"What if someone takes it?"

Was he serious? Did he really think someone here was going to steal his jacket? He was the smallest guy here—it wasn't like his jacket would fit anyone.

She tried to ignore him and focus on the music. The last time she'd danced in public was . . . well, she couldn't remember. The truth was she liked to dance. A lot. She knew she wasn't the best dancer or anything, but it was fun. She danced in her room with the blinds closed, and while she was cooking dinner. In public she'd always worried people were staring at her—but now she *knew* no one was watching her. No one cared. Everyone was feeling the music and no one was looking. No one was judging her. She could do whatever she wanted to do. She lifted her arms above her head. Wahoo!

She's getting a little crazy, Lazar thought.

Olivia froze. Yeah, no one was judging her. No one except Lazar.

* * *

Pi was watching.

She sat on a barstool in the corner and monitored the room. She'd come to make sure no one did anything foolish.

She'd stopped at least three of us from trying to sneak alcohol. She didn't understand why we would take risks at a time like this.

She watched Olivia dance with that jerk boyfriend of hers. Tess was dancing with that guy she was obsessed with. Mackenzie was dancing with Cooper.

Everything was under control. Just the way Pi liked it.

She took a sip of her water and a bite of miso cod. At least the food was good. Nobu had catered.

Pi had surprised herself by going to Bloomingdale's and buying a new outfit for the party. She knew her suit was conservative, but she felt sophisticated and smart.

She'd bought some makeup for the event too. But when she opened the packages, she realized she had no idea how to use eye shadow or eyeliner. She wished she had someone to teach her.

Instead she watched an eye-makeup tutorial on YouTube and tried to follow along. When she was done, she studied herself in the mirror. She looked like a raccoon. She scrubbed the color off and hid the makeup in the back of a drawer.

Aw. Poor Pi.

She was about to take another bite of cod when she saw her.

The redhead. The fake nurse. Suzanna. What was she doing here?

She was wearing black pants and a black blouse, and she was sitting at a table across the room.

Pi had spent the past week ducking in the hallway whenever the woman was near. We all had.

Pi pushed her chair back and snaked her way to the other side of the room. She wanted to get close enough to the woman to find out who she was and what she wanted, yet stay far enough away that the woman didn't see her.

There were many people in her way. Pi struggled to get close enough to hear without being obvious and without being interrupted by random party-goers' dumb internal and external thoughts.

Suzanna: . . . *at least fifteen of them seem to have it.* . . .

"This party is the best!"

. . . I think Sadie forgot to wear a bra. . . .

Suzanna: *. . . eyes are definitely turning. . . .*

She was definitely referring to the Espies! She had to be!

. . . shouldn't hug people when he's so sweaty. It's disgusting! . . .

"I love this song!"

"Why aren't you dancing?"

. . . have some vodka in my purse . . .

. . . I think I just swallowed a toothpick. . . .

Pi's schoolmates were officially driving her crazy. She squeezed her way closer to the woman and heard:

At least we should have more of the antidote by Thursday.

Pi steadied herself on a table. Was the antidote for them? Would it get rid of the telepathy?

The woman turned around and saw Pi. *Why is she staring at me? Oh! Her eyes are purple! She's one of them! If she's one of them, she can hear me. Hello? You can hear me, can't you?*

Pi felt numb. Then, without thinking, she turned and ran out of the room.

* * *

Mackenzie was pretty sure it was the best party ever. Everyone was having a great time. The dance floor was packed. Even Olivia was dancing. Olivia! She'd never seen Olivia get down before, but there she was, partying it up.

"I am so sweaty," Cooper said. "Am I smelly?"

"You are not," Mackenzie murmured. "Trust me."

I wish I could. Cooper froze.

Mackenzie froze. She deserved that. She put her hand on his shoulder. "You will. Maybe not today. But you will."

He looked into her eyes. *I hope so.*

"Let's get something to drink?"

He took her hand and they walked back to the bar. *I'm going to get over it. I'm going to get over it. I need her.*

I need you, she thought. "I'll have a Diet Coke, please," she told the bartender. "Coop? What do you want?"

Romy Brohman, Jordana's mother, approached her. "Happy birthday, sweetie. I haven't seen you in ages! You look all grown-up and gorgeous!"

"Thank you! Thank you for coming," Mackenzie said. The woman's cotton candy perfume was overwhelming and almost choked her.

The woman motioned to Cooper. "Is that your boyfriend?"

"He is. Cooper, do you know Romy? Jordana's mom?" *We had our first kiss in her office.*

"Of course," he said. "How are you?"

"I haven't seen you in years! You're so handsome.

You look just like your dad." A smile danced on her lips. *I haven't seen him in ages either. Since that time I bumped into him and his wife at Odeon. He was so smooth too. Considering our history.*

Mackenzie bit her lip. She prayed Cooper hadn't heard that.

Cooper's eyes flashed. He had definitely heard.

"Cooper, let's go dance," Mackenzie snapped. She wanted him out of there before he heard anything worse.

His hand gripped his glass like he was trying to squeeze the life out of it. "Not yet. I have a few questions." He was definitely not singing now. His voice was cold. "What exactly is your relationship with my dad, Romy?"

Romy's eyes widened and she shrugged her thin shoulders. *Does he know about our affair?* "What do you mean?"

Cooper was about to blow. His face was turning red and it wasn't from the colored strobe lights.

"Cooper, let's get some air. Now." Mackenzie yanked his arm, causing his Coke to splash over the edge of his glass and onto her dress. It didn't matter. She needed to get him outside.

"I want to talk to her," Cooper protested as she pulled him through the room.

"No you don't. You want to talk to your dad."

"I want to punch my dad, not talk to him. Do you know what this means? The Chicago person isn't even the first time he cheated. He's such a bastard. I'm glad my mom's divorcing him."

He looked back at the bar, but the woman was now approaching Cooper's parents. *I can only imagine what she'll say. Or what she'll be thinking about. What my dad will be thinking about. What my mom won't know.*

"I'm sorry," Mackenzie said. She didn't know what else to say.

I hate them all. I hate his father for being a dick, I hate Jordana's mom for sleeping with him, and I hate his mom for divorcing him.

Mackenzie pulled open the door to the room and stepped into the hallway just as someone else was coming inside.

Bennett.

Mackenzie gasped. *Oh shit. Shit shit shit.*

Cooper turned to her. "What?"

She looks hot. Even hotter than she did in that black bikini, Bennett thought.

Cooper looked at Bennett and then back at Mackenzie. *Who is that?*

Mackenzie didn't want to say. She didn't want to think. Didn't want to move.

I guess that's the boyfriend, Bennett thought.

Shit, shit, shit.

"Is that him?" Cooper asked, his voice rising. "Bennett?"

"The one and only," Bennett said.

Cooper's fists tightened. *Are you freaking kidding me?*

And then, surprising us all, he punched Bennett in the face.

* * *

Tess and Teddy were holding hands and on their way to get a drink when they ran into Sadie. Sadie, who was looking gorgeous.

She was wearing a loose silver dress and silver heels. Her hair wasn't even done; it was just tied back. It screamed, *Look how pretty I am and I don't even have to do anything.*

Teddy stopped walking. *Sadie! And she's alone.*

Tess looked around for Keith but didn't see him.

"Keith's not coming," Sadie said. *We broke up.*

"You guys always break up," Tess said, tightening her grip on Teddy's arm.

"This time it's for real." *I just couldn't stand kissing him anymore. Or listening to him. You know what I mean.* She looked at Tess meaningfully.

Tess did know what she meant. Because right then she was listening to Teddy.

She's single? Does that mean there's a chance for me?

He let go of Tess's hand.

Tess couldn't stand hearing Teddy think about

Sadie right then. *She* was the one who was supposed to be with him. Tonight, Sadie was not getting in the way! Tess gave Sadie a look of desperation.

I'm not getting in the way, Sadie thought back. *I don't like Teddy!*

But he likes you!

But I don't like him! So it doesn't matter! I'll just walk away and you guys can be together!

I don't want to be someone's second choice!

Sadie shrugged. *I don't know what I'm supposed to say to that.*

Can you just go?

Sadie nodded. "I'll see you guys later." Before Teddy could react she disappeared into the crowd.

Now what? Tess looked at Teddy.

Teddy looked back at Sadie.

It's never going to happen with Sadie, he thought. *But maybe . . . well, maybe Tess and I can . . . I don't know. Tess is the best. We like so many of the same things. She gets me. Should I see where this is going?*

Yes! Tess almost screamed. *Yes, you should. Let's see what happens.*

Another slow song came on.

Her heart hammered in her chest and she tried not to think about what she was about to do. She was going to kiss someone she knew didn't feel the way she did.

She hated the stupid telepathy. If she didn't have it, then she would never have known Teddy had feelings for Sadie. They'd have had their dance and they'd be walking off into the sunset. She should just pretend that she hadn't heard his thoughts. That was what she should do. They would kiss and to hell with Sadie. Who cared if Tess wasn't his first choice?

"Let's go dance again," she said. She pulled him back onto the floor, and before she had a chance to think things through, she pulled him closer.

She smells good. Like vanilla, she heard him think. *I should kiss her. No. Yes. No.*

Yes. It's a good idea. It's a very good idea and it's going to happen right now. She pressed her body firmly against his. The music coursed through them both. It was going to happen. It was definitely going to happen.

The back of her head was against his neck, but she turned so she was facing him, facing his neck. If she opened her mouth, she could lick it. Not that she would lick his neck—that would be weird. But she opened her mouth a little so he could feel her breath.

His heart beat louder. *I should do it,* he thought. *Why not?*

Exactly, Tess thought. *Why not! Do it! Do it! You should do it!*

Ever so slowly, he lowered his head down to hers. A second more and their lips would be touching. *Don't think about it,* he thought. *Just do it.*

She agreed a hundred percent. She closed her eyes, waiting.

His lips touched hers. Soft at first. She pressed back. So soft. She hadn't expected his lips to be so soft. Sweet, even. It was weird to have known someone for so long, to know him so well, but not know what his lips felt like. To not know such an important part of him.

They were kissing, their lips opening and closing, so soft, so sweet, so gentle. It was all she had expected and nothing she had expected wrapped together in one feeling. It was everything.

When the song ended, he pulled back, blinking.

She was about to burst with happiness. "Hey," she said shyly.

And then he thought, *I hope Sadie didn't see.*

Tess's heart exploded.

* * *

Murmurs of a fight spread through the party, and we all went to see what was going on.

"Cooper!" Mackenzie yelled as she watched Bennett go flying back.

"What the fuck?" Bennett yelled from the floor.

"What do you expect?" Cooper yelled. "You hook up with my girlfriend and then show up here and don't expect me to punch you in the face? Are you an idiot?" Cooper was furious. He wanted to do more than hit the guy. He wanted to kick him. He wanted to kill him.

"I didn't know you knew, asshole." Bennett stood up and rubbed the side of his face.

Cooper lunged to hit him again.

Mackenzie grabbed his arm. "Stop it. What are you doing?"

"Why the fuck is he here? You invited him?"

"I invited him before!"

"Before what? Before you hooked up with him or before I found out?"

"Before . . . anyone found out." *I'm sorry. I shouldn't have invited him. I don't know why I did.*

Cooper couldn't take it anymore. "I picked out the invitations with you! I picked them out and then you sent one to him! What were you thinking?" He heard his voice crack.

"I'm sorry," she whimpered. *Please, Cooper, not here.*

"You're always sorry. Just not sorry enough."

To make things worse, that was when Cooper's mother and father walked over to them, looking stern.

"Cooper, what's going on?" his dad asked.

"Are you fucking serious?" he yelled. He knew he was losing it. He knew, but he couldn't stop. He felt like the Hulk just as he was about to turn green. "I'll tell you what's going on!"

Mackenzie grabbed his arm. "Cooper! Stop it!"

"Calm down," his father said. *What the hell is wrong with him?*

"Nothing is wrong with *me*. Something's wrong with all of *you*. I don't want to calm down. I want everyone else to stop being such fucking liars."

Is he drunk? his mother worried.

"No, Mom, I am not drunk. I am pissed off. At this jerkoff for showing up. At Dad for screwing Jordana's mother and some woman in Chicago. And at you for calling a divorce lawyer. Although Dad definitely deserves it."

His mom gasped.

We all gasped.

His dad shook his head. "I don't know what you're talking about."

"Yes you do. I know what's going on. Mackenzie knows what's going on. Everyone in this whole fucking room knows what's going on, because we can hear everything you're all thinking."

Shit.

Uh-oh.

Here we go.

He's definitely drunk.

Everyone at the party who wasn't us looked around in confusion.

"I think he's high," one of the party guests said. "Do you see his eyes? They look weird."

Nick and Isaac came up beside him. "Hey, man, let's go outside and get some air, okay?"

Cooper looked around at all of us. And then he deflated like a popped balloon.

Mackenzie reached out to try to touch him, but he stepped back. "No. Everyone leave me alone."

He pushed his way through everyone and into the stairwell. He ran down the one flight and ended up in the hotel lobby. He stood still for a minute, trying to calm down. No one even wanted to hear what he had to say. No one cared. His father had practically dismissed him.

"Cooper," said a woman behind him. He turned.

She had her red hair pulled back and was wearing black pants and a black blouse. She looked familiar, but he couldn't figure out from where.

Yup. His eyes are purplish. "I heard what you said up there," she said. "About hearing other people's thoughts. I want to talk to you."

Cooper took a step toward her. At least she wanted to listen.

* * *

"What a freak," Lazar said, shaking his head.

Olivia, who, like the rest of us, had witnessed the whole scene, felt her heart break for Cooper. "He's not a freak. He's just overwhelmed."

"He's a loser," Lazar said. "Can we go now?"

Suddenly, Olivia realized that Lazar *wasn't* like her. He wasn't shy. He was antisocial. She had always liked being around people—she just didn't know how to talk to them. He didn't like people. He liked judging them.

"Go without me," she said.

"What do you mean?" He took a step back. *I must have heard that wrong.*

"You didn't hear that wrong. I want to stay. If you want to go home so badly, go home."

He shook his head. *I don't need this attitude.* "We came together. We should leave together."

"But I'm not ready to leave yet. And you're clearly miserable, so go."

"You want me to leave by myself?" He looked incredulous.

"Yes. Goodbye! No one's keeping you here!" She wanted to forcibly shove him out the door.

Bitch, he thought. Then he stormed out.

For the first time all night, Olivia breathed a huge sigh of relief.

She spotted Tess, Sadie, Mackenzie, Jordana, and Levi in the corner and hurried over to find out what was going on.

Mackenzie was shaking.

"What happened to Cooper?" Olivia asked.

"He just blurted everything out," Mackenzie said. "And then he ran off."

"It's not like anyone believed him," Jordana added.

"Has anyone seen Pi?" Sadie asked. "She'll know what to do."

"I think she left," Levi said.

"I'll text her and see where she is," Tess said. *Stupid jerk.*

"Who's a stupid jerk?" Jordana asked her. "Cooper?"

"Not Cooper." Tess shot a look at Sadie. "I don't want to talk about it."

"I saw you and Teddy making out," Levi said to her. "What's up with that?"

"Nothing's up with that," Tess muttered. *Don't wanna talk about it.*

Mackenzie was still shaking. "I think I want to go home."

"You can't leave," Tess told her. "It's your party."

"I don't care," Mackenzie said. Her face was bright red. "I can't breathe. I need to get out of here."

Olivia put her arm around her. "Take deep breaths, okay? Let's just step outside and get some air. Someone tell her parents where we are. Someone get us some water."

Olivia led Mackenzie out the door and into the stairwell, leaving the rest of us behind.

"That was some Sweet," Jordana said.

Levi shook his head. *It was more of a sour.*

We couldn't help but groan.

CHAPTER THIRTY-SEVEN

WE'VE BEEN MEANING TO TELL YOU

They called us early the next morning.

7:02 a.m. *Ring!*

Mackenzie woke up immediately.

"Who the hell is calling so early?" barked her dad. *We did it three times last night! I am loving my Viagra prescription!*

Cooper's house line rang at 7:11 a.m. He was already awake and pouring his sister a bowl of cereal. He had barely slept all night.

"Nobody get that!" Cooper's mom yelled, storming into the kitchen and glaring at the phone. It went to voice mail. *No way I'm getting that. It's definitely Harry calling from his hotel.* She listened to the message two minutes later.

It was not Cooper's dad. It was Nathan Michaels, the school's principal.

The message requested Cooper's family to please call back immediately. They would be having an emergency meeting in the BHS auditorium at seven p.m. regarding their son's homeroom, and it was imperative that he and his parents go.

7:22 a.m. *Ring!*

Olivia heard her mom pick up and wondered who it could be. *What happened? Who died?* In Olivia's mind, all middle-of-the-night or early-morning calls were to report heart attacks, brain aneurysms, or plane crashes.

"But why?" she heard her mother ask. "What's this about? Is my daughter sick?"

Pause.

"Is she in any kind of danger?"

Pause.

"What about the flu shot?" Olivia's mom shrieked.

Pause.

"Unusual neurological symptoms? Are you kidding me?"

Of course, Olivia's mom ran right into Olivia's room.

"Wake up!" she yelled, throwing open the door. "What's going on? Are you okay?"

Olivia was already sitting up in her bed and waiting.

"What's going on?" her mom continued. "What happened with the flu shots? What aren't you telling me?" *Principal Michaels called! I thought someone died!*

You have complications from a tainted flu shot! They told us not to tell anyone! Her face was red and she was out of breath.

At first all Olivia could think was, *I can't deal with her now,* but when she saw the panic in her mom's eyes and heard her think, *If something bad happens to my daughter, I'll kill myself,* Olivia reached out her arms to hug her.

"I'm fine," Olivia began. "Sit down. I'll tell you everything. I'll show you what I can do."

And she did.

We all did.

* * *

We texted back and forth like crazy.

> Levi: What happened? How did
>   Michaels find out?
> Jordana: Does the whole school
>   know?
> Nick: School admin knows, teachers
>   don't. Except my mom.
> Isaac: That new nurse was at the
>   Sweet. Maybe she told Michaels?
>   Pi?
> Daniel: We saw Cooper talking to
>   her in the lobby.

```
Courtney: Cooper, did you talk
   to her?
Jordana: Cooper?
Levi: Cooper???
Tess: Pi, what do we do?
Pi: We go to the meeting and hear
   what they have to say.
```

What choice did we have?

* * *

We were all early.

Even Cooper. He showed up with both his parents, which was a bit awkward, considering his father had moved into the Conrad Hotel the night before. Cooper sat on the opposite side of the room from Mackenzie. He gave her a sad smile when he saw her, but quickly looked away.

"Thank you for coming," said the man on the stage. He'd introduced himself as Hank Soporic, executive director of the Centers for Disease Control and Prevention. He was tall and wore a blue suit and a traumatized expression. *I can't believe this is happening. This makes no sense. This is impossible.*

No kidding.

Suzanna sat by his side.

Hank coughed. "As I'm sure your children have

informed you, they seem to have developed some, um, complications from their flu shot."

Complications! Ha!

A sore arm is a complication. We've become mutants.

It's true. We're like the X-Men.

You know, the Espies would make an awesome comic book series.

We hear thoughts and fight crime!

I am so not wearing a leather catsuit.

Hank rubbed his forehead and continued. "It appears that the flu vaccine has caused your children to develop . . ." His voice trailed off and his face flushed with embarrassment. *I can't believe I'm saying these things out loud. They make no scientific sense.* "To develop headaches. Headaches and . . . a form of telepathy." He shook his head. *This is insanity.* "It appears that they can read other people's thoughts."

Our parents:

She wasn't kidding?

Impossible!

Oh dear, oh dear, oh dear.

"They've really been hearing everything we've been thinking?" Levi's mom asked.

"Yes," Hank said, still shaking his head. "That seems to be the case."

Everything?

Even the swearing?

Oh shit.

"How many people have been affected?" Isaac's dad asked.

"We can't share that information with you at the moment"—*because we have no idea*—"but we can tell you that we've traced at least three contaminated batches."

Contaminated?

Batches, plural?

There are others with telepathy?

Oh God. I hope it's not my French tutor. She's so hot.

"Were all the batches given to New York City students?" asked Courtney's mom.

"No. One of the contaminated batches was delivered to a nursing home in Jacksonville, Florida. One was delivered to a family clinic in Cleveland, Ohio, and one was delivered here, to Manhattan. To Bloomberg High School."

At least no one else at school is reading my thoughts secretly.

At least it's not my French tutor. She's so hot.

Olivia's mom thought she might hyperventilate. *What if this causes brain tumors?* "Are those the only complications? Telepathy and headaches?"

"No." Hank rubbed his forehead again. *It gets scarier.*

Scarier?

Now I'm nervous.

You're only nervous now?

"We've also noticed a slight pigment change in the subjects' irises. You might notice that your children have a purplish tint to their eyes."

Our parents all stared into our eyes.

I did notice that.

I thought she looked good.

I thought he was tired.

I thought he was on drugs.

"We're not sure what's causing the pigment change, but we believe it's related to the telepathy. We believe headaches may be another side effect. Symptoms tend to be severe immediately following the vaccine and tend to clear up. The risk of pigment change seems to increase as time goes on." *As does the risk of death.*

Huh?

"Death?" Olivia repeated.

"Are you kidding me?" Jordana called out. "We're going to die?"

A startled Hank nearly jumped off the stage. "Oh! I forgot you could . . . hear me."

Our parents started panicking.

"Death?"

"Who said anything about dying?"

We should have moved to Canada. This would never happen in Canada!

Hank cleared his throat again. "One patient who received the contaminated vaccination suffered a stroke and . . . er . . . expired."

Our parents:

Expired? As in died?

The vaccination killed someone?

My poor baby!

Us:

My mom's a lawyer!

We should sue!

We can't sue if we're dead!

I can't believe I'm going to die a virgin!

"But," Hank continued, his voice shaky, "he was also eighty-one. The stroke may have been unrelated. The autopsy was inconclusive."

"Why weren't we notified about this situation immediately?" Cooper's dad barked. "Did you know that contamination was a possibility when our kids were vaccinated?"

"Absolutely not," he said. *It's not like we believed the complaints. Telepathy? Gimme a break.*

"So there were reports of telepathy," Nick called out. "You just didn't listen to them."

Hank reddened. "Er, right. There were reports. Three weeks ago a clinic in Ohio contacted us. They'd had complaints from patients who'd received their flu shots and seemed to have developed . . . unusual neurological symptoms."

"You mean telepathy," Olivia's mom said.

"Right," he squeaked. "Telepathy. Patients claimed to have developed telepathy. We were, um, doubtful at first." *That's the understatement of the year. We joked about it over cappuccinos. Oops. They can hear that. Just kidding! We didn't joke about it! We don't drink cappuccinos! We work in a government building! We can't afford a cappuccino maker! I should just keep talking. Yes. Continue talking.* "In addition to the, um, unusual neurological symptoms, the patients in Ohio complained of headaches and changing eye color. We instructed them to monitor their symptoms. . . ." *How were we supposed to know that they weren't crazies? They sounded like crazies. This whole thing makes no sense. I miss SARS.* "Then we received some calls from a retirement home in Florida with reports of similar symptoms. By the time we followed up, the death had already occurred. The retirement home patients had in fact received their vaccinations before those in Ohio, but the nurses believed the patients were suffering from age-related dementia. It wasn't until there was a cluster of symptoms that the health practitioners took them seriously and informed us. Now we're tracing the batches we believe to have been contaminated. We thought one might have been sent to Bloomberg High School, but we didn't know which students had received the infected batch. Unfortunately, Nurse Carmichael improperly tracked them." *Idiot.*

"Why didn't you ask everyone who'd gotten flu shots if they had telepathy?" Jordana asked.

He flushed again. "It just . . . well, it seemed like a loony thing to ask. And we didn't want to cause a panic. We thought surveillance was a better idea. We removed Nurse Carmichael and installed one of our own agents—Dr. Dail—at Bloomberg, hoping that she would be able to find the affected parties."

Agents?

Suzanna!

Suzanna is CIA?

Who said anything about CIA?

This is so cool.

No it's not! We're going to die! Dying is not cool!

"Didn't the school have a responsibility to tell us?" Isaac's dad asked.

Hank shook his head. "The school didn't know. We didn't know. We suspected that an infected batch had been sent here, but we didn't have confirmation until last night."

Well, duh. If the school had known, we'd know they knew.

You're missing the point. Someone gave us up!

It was so Cooper!

We saw him with Suzanna!

It wasn't me.

Liar!

"But somebody died," Olivia's mom said. "You should have been cautious and called us immediately."

"There's no proof that the death was a direct result of the vaccination. It was likely just old age." *Although we can't say for sure.* "But! We have good news," he rushed to add. "We've been able to isolate

the compound in the vaccination that has been causing the, um, irregular neurological condition. It's a
reaction to a new preservative we've been using to
stabilize the vaccine, called NFG. And now that we
know what caused it, we've developed an antidote."

A what?

A reversal vaccine.

We can make it stop?

"It's one hundred percent effective. We've used it
on the group in Jacksonville and in Ohio, and both
groups' symptoms have disappeared. The telepathy,
the purple eyes, everything."

Our parents all heaved sighs of relief.

We weren't sure how we felt.

We didn't want strokes, obviously.

But were we ready to give up our telepathy for
good?

"Can our children get the antidote today?" Olivia's
mother asked.

"The next batch will be ready on Thursday," Hank
said. "One last thing to discuss is discretion. I'm sure
you can all understand the need to keep this quiet.
We want to avoid public panic. We don't know how
many other batches have been affected. We'd like to
steer clear of mass paranoia and conspiracy theories.
The vaccination manufacturer is requiring everyone
who receives the antidote to sign a confidentiality
agreement."

"Why would we sign anything?" Tess's dad asked.

"They have to give our kids the antidote, since they're responsible for this mess in the first place. We'll sue if we have to."

"You could," Hank said. *Please don't sue. What a pain in the ass that would be.* "The problem is that legal action takes years. And we don't know what the short- or long-term effects of the reaction to the NFG will be. Symptoms might progress. We're concerned about the potential for stroke. One of the Ohio patients also reported vision problems. We're apprehensive that eventual blindness might be a complication. We don't know what our time frame is here. We don't know what we're dealing with. We don't want you—a group of minors—to be our guinea pigs. Also, we can only imagine the media frenzy that would take place if this went public. We would not be able to shield your children from that. The pharmaceutical company has agreed to settle with you all now, with an immediate check for fifty thousand dollars to every affected person."

We all took a collective breath. That was a lot of money.

"But what if something goes wrong with the antidote?" Courtney asked. "What if we develop more 'unusual neurological symptoms' "—she made air quotes—"or our eyes turn orange?"

"There is a provision in the pharmaceutical company's agreement that if the antidote doesn't work, or if there are any additional unusual symptoms—

besides nausea and a low-grade fever for twenty-four hours after the vaccination—the agreement is null and void."

Our parents made their decisions.

Where do we sign?

She could use that money for college.

I'm not risking him having a stroke.

But we weren't as sure.

I don't want to die.

Only one person died.

But still—he died!

Fifty thousand is a lot of money.

It's not that much. My family spent more than that on our last trip to Cannes. We flew private.

Won't you miss it?

I'd miss being able to see more than I'd miss hearing your thoughts.

We turned to Pi. She'd know what to do. She always did.

Do we sign? we asked.

Pi nodded. *Yes, it's the only option. We can't risk our lives.*

If even Pi thought we should get the antidote, then we figured we really should.

So we agreed. We would take the antidote.

CHAPTER THIRTY-EIGHT

LAST CHANCE

It was a week of weirdness.

Levi's parents had him working overtime at Candy Heaven, listening for shoplifters. Over the course of the week, he was able to stop twenty jelly beans, three Blow Pops, and one bag of circus peanuts from disappearing from the store.

Courtney's mom and dad avoided her. They stayed out of her room. They even let her stretch out on the couch and watch all her CW and ABC Family shows by herself.

Isabelle's dad hosted his monthly poker game. With Isabelle by his side, he won six hundred and eighty bucks.

Mackenzie's parents attempted celibacy. Yes. Attempted.

Olivia's mom panicked and Googled stuff.

Tess's mom spent extra time at the gym.

Cooper's mom and Cooper had a long, long talk.

And the twins' parents . . . well, they pretty much just laughed and gave up.

In class, and in our spare time, we hung out together. We thought of it as our last hurrah.

We're going to have to start talking to each other again when this is done.

And studying.

At least we'll have some privacy.

So I can start imagining you all naked again?

As if you ever stopped, BJ!

* * *

Mackenzie was leaving school when Cooper caught up with her. "Can we talk?"

Mackenzie and Cooper hadn't spoken since he'd punched Bennett, except for across the room at the meeting the night before. He'd been avoiding her all day.

She wasn't sure she wanted to talk. *Talk* sounded ominous. Like he was going to break up with her again. Maybe it wasn't a breakup talk? Maybe the talk wasn't about her at all?

He sighed. *It's a breakup talk.*

Fuck.

"Can we walk?" he asked.

They waited for the light to change and then crossed the West Side Highway.

I don't want to have the breakup talk, Mackenzie thought at him.

I know.

So let's not.

We have to. He sighed. *We have to break up.*

She stopped in the middle of the street. *No.*

He put his arm on her elbow and led her to the sidewalk. *Yes.*

"No!" she yelled. "I'm sorry about what happened with Bennett! I'm really sorry!" Her chest hurt. Her feet hurt. She couldn't move off the sidewalk. Cars zipped by her. "I don't want to break up!"

He led her away from the street, closer to the water. "I think you do," he said. *At least, you did.*

She shook her head. *No, no, no.* "I didn't. I don't. I love you."

"Maybe you do. But we're not breaking up because of what you did with Bennett." He shook his head. "Well, not just because of that. I've been thinking a lot about this and . . . well, you do stuff like this all the time."

She didn't understand what he was talking about. "I cheat all the time?"

"No. You ruin things."

It felt like there was an elastic band tightening around her chest. "What does that even mean?"

"You self-sabotage."

"No I don't." *That's crazy.*

"Yeah, you do. You never study, so you get bad grades. You hand in homework late for no reason. Like that English essay. Mackenzie, why'd you quit gymnastics?"

"I don't like competing!" *I was afraid to lose!*

"No, you're afraid of winning. Of trying. And why'd you invite the guy you cheated on me with to your Sweet?"

I wanted you to know, she realized. Her eyes stung. She had invited Bennett so Cooper would find out what she'd done. So he'd break up with her. What was wrong with her? The tears spilled down her face.

"I can't . . . It's hard to hear what you're thinking when you cry," he said after a few minutes.

It's true. Crying garbles incoming and outgoing telepathy. Too bad we can't all cry on demand.

"I'm sorry," Mackenzie said, wiping her eyes with her jacket sleeve. "I'm fucked up."

"We're all fucked up," he said softly. "And what's happening to us is fucked up. And my life is really fucked up right now. And I just don't think we're the right people to help unfuck each other up. Am I making any sense?"

She shrugged, still crying. Now her nose was running too. She knew she was an ugly crier. She was glad she couldn't hear him noticing.

"I think I want to walk on my own." She hiccuped and dried her eyes again.

He shifted his weight. "You sure you're okay?"

"I'm fine." *And fucked up, apparently.*

I heard that.

She bit her lip. "So . . ." *We're really over?*

He nodded. *Do you want me to walk you home?*

Always a gentleman. No. Go. I'll be fine.

All right. Goodbye, Mackenzie. He turned and re-crossed the street. She watched him walk east. At first he moved slowly, but he moved faster as he got farther away.

She didn't want to go home yet, so she walked into Battery Park and kept going south. She walked until she could see the Statue of Liberty.

Maybe Cooper was right about the self-sabotage. Because now that she was truly free, she felt miserable.

* * *

Tess wasn't sure if she was avoiding Teddy or if he was avoiding her. Either way, it was Tuesday morning and they hadn't spoken since the Sweet.

After the kiss at the party, she'd run. She couldn't take it. They had finally had their perfect kiss and he was still thinking about Sadie. She couldn't deal.

Since he hadn't chased after her, she assumed he

thought the kiss was a mistake. And she . . . well, she thought it was a mistake too. How could she be with someone who liked someone else? She couldn't. She wanted more. She deserved more.

You totally do, BJ told her in homeroom. He'd started sitting next to her in the back row.

But we were best friends and now that's ruined.

It's only ruined if you want it to be ruined. He's confused. It's not that he doesn't like you, he just doesn't like you enough. He doesn't want to lose you. He doesn't want to hurt you. He doesn't know you know about Sadie. If you want to stay friends with him, let him off the hook.

She suspected BJ was right, so just before lunch, she texted Teddy to meet up and grab a bite.

When they met at the school door, he gave her a stilted hug. *She wants to talk about the party. I'm not sure what to say. We're best friends. She's cute. Why am I not into her? I should be into her.*

Tess died a little death with every unspoken word.

But still, she agreed with BJ. It was like the kids' song "We're Going on a Bear Hunt." The only way over this was through it. As they walked down the street, she said, "Teddy, I'm sorry about what happened. It was a mistake. See, the thing is, I like you. I've liked you since we became friends. Even when you had a girlfriend, I've had feelings for you—more than friendship feelings."

He nodded. "I guess I knew that."

"So I wanted what happened at the party to happen. But I know you don't like me like that."

His eyes widened. "But—"

"No. Don't say you do. I know you don't. I know how you feel about Sadie."

He blushed. "You do?"

She nodded. "I do. And I don't want to be the person you hook up with just because I'm there. I want to be someone's Sadie."

"I'm sorry I kissed you." *Not that sorry. It was a good kiss.*

It really was. She took a deep breath. "Good. Now that that's settled, where should we go for lunch? I'm starving."

"What are you in the mood for?"

"Shake Shack?" To hell with the five—no, seven—pounds. She wanted a cheeseburger, and a milk shake, and bring on the fries! She was absolutely sure she deserved it.

* * *

"Olivia?" Mr. Roth asked. "Are you sure you want to try your presentation again?"

"Yes," Olivia said, standing up.

She's totally going to bomb, thought Lazar. *She thinks she's too good for me. She's not even that pretty.*

Screw you, Olivia thought, and oddly, that gave her

the burst of confidence she needed. Olivia pushed Lazar's thoughts out of her mind and focused on her notes. "I have a new topic."

"What is it?" Mr. Roth asked.

"It's about Oprah."

He nodded. "All right, go ahead."

She could do this. She would not forget what she was talking about. She would not faint. She would not die. She would not care about what Lazar—or anyone else—thought. She cleared her throat. "Oprah was born . . ."

She focused on her own words and her own thoughts and didn't stop until she reached the end.

* * *

On Wednesday, BJ winked at Tess when he sat next to her in homeroom. *What's happening, gorgeous? How's Teddy?*

It's over.

Well, I'm not going to pretend I didn't know that already. You know he's not good enough for you, right?

I guess. I want to be someone's first choice.

Even though she was looking down at her notebook, she could feel him watching her.

You're my first choice.

She smiled. *I am not.*

You are too. Can I be your first choice?

That's it? You're throwing down the gauntlet?

He inched his seat closer to hers. *I'm throwing down the gauntlet. Putting it out there. You and me. What do you think?*

She wasn't sure. *What about Teddy?*

I thought it was over with Teddy.

It is over. But I, you know, can't pretend I don't still have feelings for him.

Do you know what would really help you forget about Teddy?

What?

Me.

Ms. Velasquez walked in and closed the door.

Tess smiled to herself. *I'll think about it.*

Does that mean you'll fantasize about me tonight?

Courtney turned around and glared at them. "You know we can still hear you, right?"

Oh, right.

* * *

One more day.

Pi could hardly wait.

She stood in the bathroom and checked under the stall doors to make sure she was the only one there.

She was.

Her shoulders relaxed. She was alone. Finally.

She exhaled a big sigh of relief. Controlling her thoughts all week had been exhausting. But she had no choice if she was going to do what she wanted to do.

After Suzanna had approached Cooper at the Sweet and he had shrugged her off, Pi had decided that she had to control the situation. The authorities already knew about the telepathy. The cat was out of the bag. Pi had to find out exactly what Suzanna knew.

Pi had approached her in the lobby. She had asked Suzanna to join her for a cup of coffee.

"Sure," Suzanna had said while thinking, *She must have received one of the vaccines. Her eyes are definitely purple. She must have ESP! She wants to talk.*

"I do have ESP, and I do want to talk," Pi announced.

Holy crap, she can really hear me! She's it! She's it! I found one! She's real! This is actually happening! Holy shit!

When they sat down across from each other, Pi began the meeting by saying, "How did you get into the party?"

"Mackenzie's parents invited me," Suzanna answered smoothly. *I slipped the doorman a hundred bucks.*

"You slipped the doorman a hundred bucks. Got it. But why were you there?"

She blinked repeatedly. *How am I supposed to keep things classified if she can hear everything? I guess I can't.* "I figured out that most of the students with probable ESP were from your homeroom. I was instructed to follow you all as much as possible."

"But how did you know that most of us were in the same homeroom?"

"I spotted four students with purple eyes. I tracked who they were and what grade level they were in and discovered that they—you—were all in homeroom 10B."

Pi kept on. "Why did you come to the party?"

"We suspected that a group of students had telepathy. But we didn't know for sure. We needed someone to admit it before we could move on."

"Move on? What does that mean?" Pi pressed.

Suzanna went on to tell Pi that once they knew who the affected students were, they planned to debrief our parents. Pi also learned about the other tainted batches, the other infected populations—including the old man who'd had a stroke—and the antidote. And she learned that they expected us all to take it. That everything would go back to normal. That there would be financial compensation.

"No," Pi said, sipping her coffee. "I'm not taking an antidote."

What? She has to! "But—but it's dangerous," she sputtered. "Someone's already died."

"Please. He was over eighty and in a nursing home." Pi dismissed Suzanna's concern with a wave of her hand. "What happened to me is exceptional. I am not getting rid of it. You can't force me."

"We can't take that risk with twenty-four students."

"We're only twenty-two students."

"The batch had twenty-four vaccinations in it. The additional two were given to other students. We're looking for them. We'll be offering them the antidote as well."

"So offer it to them. Don't risk their lives. Risk mine only." Her plan began to formulate. *I'll get everyone else to take the antidote. I'll remain the only one with telepathy. I'll be the last remaining Espie.*

I'll truly be exceptional.

She would need her father's permission, of course, but he would give it. He valued brilliance. Plus he could monitor her behavior and symptoms in case there was any real risk. Her mom would miss out on everything. She didn't deserve to be a part of it.

Is she crazy? I think she's crazy.

"I'm not crazy," Pi said. "Think of this as an incredible opportunity. I'll tell you everything you want to know. Plus I'll meet with you once a month so you can do whatever tests on me you want. I don't mind the risks. Imagine all you can learn. It would be brilliant research."

It would be fascinating . . . but there's no way they're going to go for it.

Pi slammed her coffee cup on the table. "Make them go for it."

She is hard-core. "I have to talk to my supervisor."

Pi nodded. "Do that."

Suzanna bit her lip. *Could we do this? Yes. No. Maybe. But what if the others find out that she's not taking the antidote? They could all decide not to take it. We'd have a major issue on our hands.*

"I won't tell anyone. You have my word."

"But they can hear what you're thinking!"

Pi smiled. "Not for long."

Keeping her plan a secret hadn't been easy. But if anyone could do it, Pi could. It took focus. And she had focus. She just could not let her mind wander. She hid. She discovered that humming helped block her thoughts. So she hummed at all times. She closed her eyes a lot. Plus she wore really, really uncomfortable shoes all week. Shoes that gave her blisters. That way she could focus on the pain.

Do you need a Band-Aid?

Why do you keep wearing them if they hurt so much?

Just get new shoes already. This is ridiculous!

She wished she could just stay home, but she feared it would be way too obvious, since she had a perfect attendance record.

She tried to teach herself to cry on demand, but unless she waved onions under her eyes, she couldn't quite master it.

Pi had made an interesting discovery one day when she'd bumped into Keren Korb in the bathroom.

Keren had taken off her dark glasses and was splashing water on her face.

Ahhh. My skin feels so oily today.

Pi almost laughed out loud.

We hadn't been able to hear Keren not because she was blind—but because she wore dark sunglasses. They stopped transmission. But Pi had worn sunglasses outside, hadn't she? Yes, she had. It hadn't stopped her from hearing other people's thoughts, had it? She didn't think so.

Maybe her sunglasses weren't dark enough.

After school, she went straight to the closest Sunglass Hut and tried on a few pairs. She bought the ones that blocked the most light.

It worked. She couldn't hear anyone in the store's thoughts. She assumed that meant we wouldn't be able to hear hers.

The problem was she wanted to hear our thoughts.

Plus, wearing dark sunglasses to class would make us too suspicious. Although Suzanna and her people might be able to use them. We were already suspicious of them.

Pi took the sunglasses off.

She'd figure it out.

It was a test. And Pi liked tests. She wanted to be number one.

CHAPTER THIRTY-NINE

WE MEET AGAIN

We were told to be at the nurse's office early, at seven a.m.

Our parents were asked to stay home so as not to raise suspicion among arriving students or faculty. We thought three men and one woman in dark sunglasses and navy suits surrounding us in the hallway might set off some alarm bells, but what did we know?

Hank Soporic greeted us in the hallway. "Good morning, everyone." He adjusted his dark glasses first and then his tie. "There are donuts for you in the cafeteria, so as soon as you're done, you can relax until your classes begin. Suzanna will be done setting up in just a minute."

What's up with the dark sunglasses?

They're trying to look like government agents.

They are government agents.

I can't hear what they're thinking.

Me neither!

Is it because of the glasses?

It must be!

How did we not know that earlier?

Too late.

It's disturbing.

Let's just get this over with.

"Who's going first?" Levi asked.

We all looked at Pi.

"I don't mind." *Hum, hum, hummmmmm.*

Olivia was behind Pi. Behind Olivia was Mackenzie, and behind her were Tess and BJ.

They couldn't stop flirting.

"We should just kiss now," BJ said.

"Why now?"

"Don't you want to see what it's like? To kiss with ESP? We'll keep our eyes open and everything. It'll be wild. It's our last chance. C'mon, you know you want to."

She laughed. "I'm not making out with you in front of the entire class!"

"Why not? No one cares." He turned around and addressed the rest of us. "Would anyone care if we made out?"

Go for it!

Please don't!

I haven't even had coffee yet.

Tess shook her head. "I'm sure we'll have time later. The vaccination took a day to kick in."

"The antidote might work right away," BJ warned. "We just don't know. Why take a chance?"

Tess put her arms on his shoulders. *I would do it if we were alone.*

He stood up straight. *Have you ever been in the guys' bathroom? Let's go.*

Gross, thought Mackenzie. *I'd go to the girls' bathroom if I were you.*

Tess put her hand on her hip. *I shouldn't. I know I shouldn't.*

Oh, just do it, Mackenzie thought. *Why the hell not?*

BJ nodded eagerly. *We have at least fifteen minutes.*

Tess laughed. *We're not kissing for fifteen minutes!*

There's other stuff we could do. Are you wearing the white bra? He waggled his eyebrows.

"Don't push your luck," she said. Then she added, *All right, let's go!*

His eyes lit up. He grabbed her hand and practically galloped down the hall, dragging her behind him.

Suzanna came out and smiled. "You're up, Pi!"

Pi went in.

We looked around at each other.

This is it. This is really it.

I can't believe how different everything is now.

"I'm going to miss the ESP," Olivia said.

Jordana nodded as she filed her nails. "Me too. To

be honest, I'm not exactly sure why we're getting rid of it."

Olivia turned back to Jordana, wondering the same thing. Why were they getting rid of it?

Levi snorted. "Because it's going to kill us?"

But would it? "We don't know that," Olivia said, her heart speeding up. "Maybe we should keep it," she said quietly.

Everyone looked at each other.

The two men in navy still outside shifted uncomfortably.

"Isn't it a little late?" Isaac asked. "We already signed the forms. I have plans for the cash."

Olivia felt her confidence—the confidence that had come from the ESP—build inside her. "So we won't take the checks. We'll rip up the forms. We don't have to do anything we don't want to do."

"But my eyes are purple," Courtney said. "And I don't want to have a stroke. Aren't you the one who usually worries about strokes?"

"Only one person had a stroke," Olivia said. "And he was eighty-one." Her heart was beating hard against her chest. Was she really suggesting keeping the telepathy? Staying an Espie? What would that mean for her future?

"We need that money," Dave said. "My family needs that money."

"So do I," said Michelle. *I don't have a fancy downtown apartment like the rest of you. We have mice.*

"We don't have to be unanimous," Olivia said. "We can each do what we want."

Courtney put her hands on her hips. "No way am I giving it up if I know some of you are keeping it. I don't want you reading my mind when I can't read yours."

"Me neither," added Levi.

"But what would we tell our parents?" Anojah asked, squinting.

Olivia stood up taller. Her mother was definitely going to have a heart attack. "It's not up to our parents. It's up to us."

"I'm with Olivia," Courtney said.

Levi nodded. "Me too."

Mackenzie wasn't sure. She thought about what Cooper had said about self-sabotage. Was keeping something in your brain that might kill you self-sabotage? Or was getting rid of a skill that could make you amazing self-sabotage? She decided it could probably go either way. "Me too," she said. "You all know how I feel about needles."

"But what if we get sick?" Anojah asked. "What if we do start to go blind? I can barely see as it is!"

Olivia definitely did not want to go blind. But losing her mind-reading abilities would also feel like a type of blindness. "I guess I just don't see what the rush is. We can still get the antidote. We just don't have to get it today. Can't we wait and see?"

We all started to nod. What was the rush? Why

were we in such a hurry to get rid of something that was so incredibly awesome?

Everyone in line was nodding, even Michelle. Everyone except Cooper.

Olivia looked up at him. "Not you?"

He shook his head. "I just want this to stop."

She nodded. She understood. He'd had a rough few weeks.

"I know it's been tough for you—"

He laughed. "My whole world fell apart."

Olivia took a step toward him. *Not because of the telepathy, though. Your whole world was already cracked. You just didn't realize it.*

No one said anything. Including Cooper.

"We all have to do what we have to do," Nick said.

Just then the door opened and Pi came out. "All done," she barked. "Who's next?"

Oops.

We forgot about Pi!

It's too late for her!

Pi's eyes narrowed. "What's going on?"

Olivia cleared her throat. "We decided—well, most of us decided—that we're not taking the antidote."

Her face paled. "What are you talking about?"

"We want to keep the telepathy," Jordana said.

Pi's eyes flashed.

She's pissed.

Her hands clenched. *Of course I'm pissed!*

How did she hear us?

"The antidote takes a day to kick in," Pi snapped. "I don't have time for this. Go get your shots. Now. Olivia, you're next."

Olivia stood her ground. "I'm not getting it."

"Yes you are."

"No I'm not. We're not."

Pi grimaced. *No! This isn't happening!* "We already came to a decision."

Olivia did feel bad about that. "Pi, we're so sorry we made a new decision after you already took the antidote, but—"

No! Pi stomped her foot. *I'm supposed to be the only one left!*

"Huh?" Jordana wondered out loud, putting down her nail file. "Left of what?"

"Left of . . . left of . . ." *Crap, what do I say?*

Left with telepathy?

Did she get the shot or not?

We circled closer to her.

Pi, take off your blazer.

She shrugged and removed it.

She's wearing a Band-Aid.

She could be faking it.

Why would she do that?

Why else? So she could be the only one.

"Care to explain?" Levi asked.

Pi took a step back. "There's nothing to explain. I got the shot. Now it's your turn." *Hum, hum, hum, hummmmmm.*

Without a word, Jordana reached over and ripped off Pi's Band-Aid.

Ouch!

Pi's arm was needle-mark-free.

"You are such a liar!" Anojah yelled.

"This is totally worse than giving us the wrong answers on a test," Daniel said.

Pi shook her head. "You don't understand. They don't want all of us to keep it. It's too risky. It makes the most sense for it to be only me."

The door opened. Suzanna smiled. We could see our reflection in her dark sunglasses. "Can the next person come in, please?"

She's in on this with Pi!

The sunglasses are blocking us from hearing her!

She's blocking us from hearing her!

They all are!

"We're not coming in," Olivia said.

"We know Pi didn't get it, and neither are we," Daniel announced.

Suzanna turned to Pi. "What are you talking about?"

Pi's arms shook. *I didn't tell them! They decided on their own!*

She can't hear you.

But we can.

Olivia stepped forward. "We're sorry, Suzanna, but we're breaking the deal."

Her smile faltered. "You can't," she said. "It's too

risky. We don't know what will happen to you. You could have a stroke. You could go blind. Hank! Come out here!"

"What we want," Olivia began, "is to not ignore this opportunity. What's the rush, anyway? We can always change our minds later, can't we?"

Hank stepped out of the office. "What's going on here?"

"They're refusing to take the antidote," Suzanna explained. She turned back and shook her head. "We don't know what the window is. What if you change your mind and it's too late?"

We exchanged glances.

"I don't think a few weeks will kill us," Mackenzie said.

"It might," snapped Pi.

Daniel laughed. "Says the person who wasn't getting the antidote anyway."

Hank shook his head. "You get the check when you get the shot. Don't you want the money?"

There goes my college tuition.

There goes my motorcycle.

There goes my pet pig named Pillow.

"Kids," Hank said in a cooing voice, "we're going to have to call your parents. They'll want you to take the antidote."

My parents are going to kill me.

They'll understand.

No they won't.

We'll make them.

It's our lives. Our choice.

I think mine were kind of disappointed I was giving it up.

"The school won't like it either," Hank continued.

They're not going to let us go to regular classes now if we can hear everyone.

And cheat.

They'll figure something out. They'll have to.

They're not going to tell the rest of the students, are they?

"This doesn't have to be a unanimous decision," Suzanna said. "If there is anyone who wants the antidote, I can still give it."

Cooper stepped up. "I do."

What?

Are you sure?

Don't do it, man!

He nodded.

"I'm calling your parents," Hank grumbled. He took off his sunglasses and rubbed his temples. *This is going to screw up everything.* "This isn't over." He stalked off in the other direction.

Suzanna took off her sunglasses too. "If any of you change your mind, I'll be here for the rest of the day. Cooper, come with me." *Lucky kids. If I were them, I wouldn't get rid of it either.*

The door closed behind them.

"You're all a bunch of morons," Pi snapped, and marched down the hallway.

"What do we do now?" Daniel asked.

Courtney licked her lips. "Get a donut?"

Brinn mumbled something.

"What did you say?" Jordana asked.

Brinn wrinkled her nose. *Maybe we should skip the donuts. In case they put the antidote in there.*

"Good call," said Dave. "But I'm starving."

Me too.

Me three.

We're all starving.

"Let's raid the vending machine," Courtney said.

We waved goodbye to the two remaining and useless bodyguards and followed her to the vending machine in the cafeteria.

* * *

That's our story.

How we became a *we*.

And that's what we are these days. A *we*.

When you're a group that can hear each other's thoughts, the line between *I* and *we* gets kind of blurry.

Along the way to the vending machine, Olivia stopped in the bathroom. She pushed the door open and interrupted a kissing BJ and Tess.

Can we do this forever?

We may have to eat at some point.

I think I can go without food.

Olivia jumped back. "Oops! Sorry!"

The couple pulled apart.

"Omigod, Olivia, you have no idea," Tess gushed. "Kissing another Espie is the most insane thing ever."

BJ motioned to Olivia. "You two should totally give it a try. I'll watch."

Tess punched him in the arm. "I guess it's our turn for the antidote, huh?"

"Actually," Olivia said, "there's been a bit of a change in plans. Some of us—most of us—changed our minds. We're not getting it. We're keeping the telepathy."

"Oh!" Tess said, her hand still on BJ's arm. "Cool."

"More Espie kissing!" BJ cheered.

"How long do we have until homeroom?" Tess asked.

"About twenty minutes," Olivia said. "I'm going to get a snack."

BJ waved. "We'll be here if you need us."

Olivia guessed she would have to find another bathroom.

She backed out and let the door swing behind her. When she turned around, she saw Cooper.

She couldn't help feeling sad for him. "You're done? Did it hurt?"

"No," he said.

"Well, that's good, at least."

"No, I mean I didn't do it." He smiled.

"You didn't? Why not?"

"I don't know. I just thought . . . well, Ashley already calls me her superhero. Imagine what she'd think if it were true."

Olivia laughed.

"I guess I just hated finding out that everyone was lying to me. But now no one will be able to lie to me, right?"

"Right," she said.

"And you were great out there," he said. "I was impressed."

Olivia blushed and smiled. "Thanks."

She's really cute, Cooper thought.

She blushed even more. *I think you're really cute too.* She didn't see Courtney, Jordana, and Levi approaching from behind, candy bars and gummy bears in hand.

Omigod, did you hear that? Olivia is hitting on Cooper! Does he like her?

Olivia spun around. "I . . . we . . ."

Ten bucks they're hooking up before the end of the month. . . . By the end of the month? By the end of the week! . . . They'll make such a cute couple. . . . Mackenzie is going to freak.

What can we say? We know everything.

ACKNOWLEDGMENTS

Thanks to my awesome agents, editors, publishers, colleagues, and friends: Laura Dail, Tamar Rydzinski, Wendy Loggia, Krista Vitola, Beverly Horowitz, Lauren Donovan, Colleen Fellingham, Trish Parcell, Tamar Schwartz, Rachel Feld, John Adamo, Dominique Cimina, Adrienne Waintraub, Deb Shapiro, Brian Lipson, Jess Rothenberg, Emily Bender, Anne Heltzel, Farrin Jacobs, Eloise Flood, Targia Clarke, Bonnie Altro, Brahm Morganstein, Judy Batalion, Lauren Kisilevsky, Alison Pace, Susan Finkelberg-Sohmer, Corinne and Michael Bilerman, Adele Griffin, Leslie Margolis, Kristin Harmel, Maryrose Wood, Tara Altebrando, Sara Zarr, Ally Carter, Jennifer Barnes, Julia De-Villers, Alan Gratz, Penny Fransblow, Maggie Marr, Susane Colasanti, Lauren Oliver, Aimee Friedman, Jen Calonita, Gayle Forman, Jennifer E. Smith, and everyone at *Justine* magazine.

Extra special thanks to Courtney Sheinmel, Elissa Ambrose, Lauren Myracle, Anna Kranwinkle, Avery Carmichael, E. Lockhart, Robin Wasserman, Jess Braun, and Elizabeth Eulberg, who read early drafts of this book and showed me how to make it so much better.

Love and thanks to my family: Aviva, Mom, Robert, Dad, Louisa, Gary, Lori, Sloan, Isaac, Vickie, John, Gary, Darren, Ryan, Jack, Jen, Teri, Briana, Michael, David, Patsy, Murray, Maggie, and Jenny.

Extra love and extra thanks and lots and lots of kisses to Anabelle, Chloe, and Todd.

A

Q&A

in Which We (Other Authors)

Ask Sarah a Bunch of Questions

and

She Answers Them

Q. From your first thoughts about writing *Don't Even Think About It* to your last revision, what concept or character changed the most? —SUSANE COLASANTI (Susane is the author of seven teen novels. She is thinking that visits to the nurse's office aren't what they used to be.)

A. The most radical change in my book was the point of view. When I outlined the novel, it was all from Olivia's perspective. But some early readers—hi, Jess Rothenberg!—suggested that the book might be better served by showing *multiple* points of view. So that's what I did.

Q. Hi, Sarah! Speaking of point of view, I love how the narrator in *Don't Even Think About It* isn't just one person—it's everyone! What were some of the biggest challenges you faced in writing from the perspectives of so many characters at once? —JESS ROTHENBERG (Jess is the author of *The Catastrophic History of You and Me.* She is thinking about how much more fun high school would have been if she could have read everybody's mind.)

A. The biggest challenge I faced was deciding when and how to jump into various characters' heads. I had to balance staying true to rules of first person plural with helping the reader care about the individual characters. I also had to choose whose thoughts I showed—and whose I left out.

Q. Should I write a book in first person plural? It seems hard. And I'm lazy. —ROBIN WASSERMAN (Robin is the author of *The Waking Dark* and *The Book of Blood and Shadow.* She is thinking about taking a nap.)

A. Since you've written over seventy books, I don't think the word *lazy* can be applied to you. But yes, it was hard.

And yes, you definitely should do it. A book in first person plural by you would be amazing. And likely scary. Oh! Oh! It should be from the perspective of a group of serial killers! Or murder victims! Or decades-old-secret-society members! C'mon, Robin. Everybody's doing it.

Q. Sarah, there is a character in this book named Courtney. She is not very likable. But you find me likable, don't you? —COURTNEY SHEINMEL (Courtney is the author of several books, including *Positively* and the Stella Batts series for young readers. She is thinking about naming a character in her next book after Sarah.)

A. Well, usually I like you. I mean, except when you bring brownies over to my apartment even though I have asked you not to. You know I can't control myself in the presence of brownies. But dear Courtney, of course I find you likeable. In fact, I find you absolutely delightful. Also super-smart and sweet and not at all addicted to Adderall. DEAR READER: UNLIKE THE COURTNEY IN *DON'T EVEN THINK ABOUT IT*, COURTNEY SHEINMEL DOES NOT POP ADDERALL. Hmm. Maybe I should check her purse before making such a statement. Okay, I've checked her purse. I have not located any amphetamines. I did find a box of brownies, though. Damn you, Courtney Sheinmel!

Q. In *Don't Even Think About It*, a group of high school students can suddenly read each other's minds and uncover the true feelings and deep secrets of their classmates. What is one thing your high school self would have been absolutely desperate to keep secret, if your high school classmates had developed powers of ESP? —LAUREN OLIVER (Lauren is the author of *Panic*, *Before I Fall*, and the Delirium trilogy. In light of Courtney's question, she is wondering why there is no character in Sarah's book named Lauren.)

A. One thing? One thing?! All right, here you go: I had a serious boyfriend for two years, but the whole time I was dating him I actually liked someone else—my guy best friend. That situation inspired the Tess storyline in the book. Can we keep that between us? Hmm, probably not.

Q. Sometimes I like to think I'm psychic. What is it about ESP that you think people find so fascinating? And did you do any research into psychics or mind reading while writing the book? —AIMEE FRIEDMAN (Aimee is the author of *The Year My Sister Got Lucky* and *Sea Change*. She is thinking, as she often is, about ice cream.)

A. I didn't do any explicit research, but . . . I once called a psychic hotline. I probably shouldn't admit that. But I did. I spoke to a guy named Stan. He told me I was going to do some traveling and I would not win the lottery. He's been right so far. I think people are fascinated by ESP because we all want to believe that there is something beyond the basic cognitive experience. Something extra. We can smell, we can taste, we can see . . . why can't we move things with our minds or tell the future? We're so close! Maybe with some extra focus . . . or a flu shot . . . maybe . . .

Q. A family of witches, kids who get sucked into fairy tales, flu shots that go haywire . . . your book ideas are always so much fun and so creative! How do you come up with them? —JEN CALONITA (Jen is the author of the Secrets of My Hollywood Life and Belles series. Jen likes to think about how she can con her way into an overnight stay in Cinderella Castle at Disney World.)

A. An overnight stay at Cinderella's castle?! Now, that is an amazing idea. Count me in. And I got the idea for this book when I walked by a supremely creepy building in Tribeca. It was tall. It was brown. It had *no windows*. I couldn't help but wonder: What was the building for? Why did it have no windows? Were aliens being hidden inside? Or perhaps . . . was it a top-secret school for students with ESP? Ding! Ding! Ding! I played around with that idea for a while, but then I thought it would be more fun if kids with ESP went to a regular school—but no one knew they had ESP. So that's what I wrote. The building is still there, and it's called the former AT&T Long Lines Building. I still have no idea what it is. But I'm 99 percent sure aliens have something to do with it. I've posted pics on Sarahm.com. Decide for yourself.

Q. You write for kids, teens, and adults. What do you find the most challenging? —LESLIE MARGOLIS (Leslie is the author of both the Annabelle Unleashed and the Maggie Brooklyn Mystery series. She is thinking that the building in Tribeca with no windows is seriously creepy. It'll probably give her nightmares and she hopes no one finds out she's such a wimp.)

A. Honestly, I don't find one age more challenging than another. For me, the only difference when writing middle grade, YA, and adult is the word count. But what I do find significantly more challenging to write are stand-alones or first books in a series. There are *so* many decisions to make. Setting! POV! Characters! Characters' likes/dislikes/siblings/heights/favorite chocolate bars! An entire world needs to be created. Sequels are a lot easier. The rules and a lot of the details have already been established. All I have to do is focus on the plot and story—my favorites.

Q. Sarah, I heard a rumor you are no longer in high school. But every time I read one of your young adult novels, I'm amazed by how perfectly right those years feel. So what's your secret to always delivering such a vividly realized high school experience? —ADELE GRIFFIN (Adele is the author of a number of YA novels, including *Tighter* and *Loud Awake and Lost*. She is thinking that nobody will notice if she finishes Courtney's brownies.)

A.: Thanks, Adele! I feel the same way about your books. I try to talk to a lot of teens, read a lot of teen books and magazines, and watch a lot of teen television shows and movies. That's to stay current about what fifteen-year-olds are thinking. And not, um, at all because I think Josh Hutcherson is adorable (Team Peeta! Woo!). But most of my research comes from my own high school diaries, pictures, and memories. Times may change, but emotions stay constant. Angst is angst. I'm guessing finding out your high school boyfriend cheated on you with an eighth grader named Kimmy would pretty much feel as miserable today as it did back then. Yes. Her name really was Kimmy.

Q. You are both a prolific and diverse writer and the mother of a preschooler and a toddler. How do you do it? No, seriously, how? Is there magic involved? A special "flu" shot? —GAYLE FORMAN (Gayle is the author of *If I Stay* and *Where She Went*, and *Just One Day* and *Just One Year*. She is also the mother of two young children and often doesn't quite know how she does it or if she does.)

A. Unlike the character Courtney, I don't take Adderall. But I do drink a lot of coffee. Regular coffee, mocha Frappuccinos, caramel Machiattos, espressos . . . also brownies, as I've already mentioned. Oh, have you tried chocolate-covered coffee beans? You will never sleep again.

Q. Hmm, I am also wondering why there is no character named Lauren, and I can only assume it is because for a writer to suspend her disbelief and create her world, she has to be able to separate herself from the real world. Perhaps I am so awesome that you couldn't possibly create a fake Lauren to replace the real me? But you asked for questions, not comments, so here is my question (and excuse me if I mumble; my mouth is full of one of Courtney's scrumptious brownies): Girls with magical powers show up in a lot of your novels, including this one. Also, you often write about strong, awesome friendships. If you, in real life, had to choose between having a magical power or an enduring friendship, which would you choose? –LAUREN MYRACLE (Lauren is the author of *TTYL* and *Shine*. She is thinking about how much she adores Sarah, and how she hopes Sarah adores her back. And her front. Well. You know.)

A. Mwah! And yes, you are *so awesome*. But I will still make sure that my next book has a Lauren! She will be the best character who ever was! She will be in kick-ass shape, plus have a zillion tattoos, plus have written multiple *New York Times* bestsellers. (Three traits conveniently shared by both you and Lauren Oliver.) But just so you feel extra loved, fictional Lauren will also adore pink glitter, rhino-dogs, and emoticons. Now as for your question, if I had to choose between magical powers and an enduring friendship I would choose . . . a magical power. I was totally supposed to say enduring friendship, eh? But c'mon! Flying! Mind reading! Spider-Man hands! Witchcraft! But don't be mad! I'll totally share my spellbook with you.

Q. The Magic in Manhattan series is set in New York City and so is *Don't Even Think About It*. What interests you most about New York, and do you see yourself saying anything about the city in these books? –E. LOCKHART (E. wrote *How to Be Bad* with Sarah and Lauren. She too is a fan of rhino-dogs. Also drittens. Alone she wrote *The Boyfriend List*, *The Disreputable History of Frankie Landau-Banks*, and *We Were Liars*. She is thinking about getting a flu shot now.)

A. The thing about living in New York City is that I would not be at all surprised to discover that magic does in fact exist here. The person in front of you at Starbucks is telepathic? All right. A practicing witch lives in the apartment below you? Of course. The streets in this city literally sparkle. Anything can happen here.

Q. You grew up in Canada and now live in and write about the US. What do you think are the biggest differences and similarities between US and Canadian teens? —ALLY CARTER (Ally is the author of the Gallagher Girls and Heist Society series. She wishes her hair were as pretty as Sarah's.)

A. *Oh, please.* I wish I were a blonde like you. As for the difference between Canadian and American teens—I'd say that Canadians watch less TV. This is not because they don't like TV, but because their channels aren't as good. Americans *definitely* watch more *Degrassi*. They're obsessed with it. Maybe Canadian teens don't watch as much TV because they are too busy on Facebook. Seriously, Canadian teens are on Facebook all the time. I think they get automatically signed up at birth. It's like Medicare. Canadians teens also say things like "eh?" and "keener." And they eat poutine (French fries, gravy, and cheese curds), Cherry Blossoms (yummy chocolate treats), and ketchup chips (self-explanatory). American and Canadian teens aren't that different, though. Both hang out at the mall. Both find their parents annoying. Both love books by Ally Carter.

Q. Do you have a playlist for *Don't Even Think About It*? —JULIA DEVILLERS (Julia is the author of many books, including the Trading Faces series coauthored with her twin sister, about identical twins who have "twin ESP." Julia is daydreaming about *Degrassi's* Joey Jeremiah and his fedora.)

A. If by playlist you mean what songs did I listen to while writing, I didn't. I prefer to write alongside other people, and I assume they'd find my desire to listen to "Call Me Maybe" on repeat a hundred times in a row annoying. (Did you know Carly Rae Jepsen is Canadian? Go Canucks!) Working with others makes me feel like part of a community. Also, when I spend too much time by myself I start to talk to the television.

Q. What's next for you? –JENNIFER E. SMITH (Jennifer is the author of several books, including *The Statistical Probability of Love at First Sight* and *This Is What Happy Looks Like*. She is thinking about where to travel next and hoping maybe Sarah will offer to show her around Canada. . . .)

A. There is nothing that would make me happier than showing you all my favorite Canadian haunts. Oooooh, can we do a book signing together in Montreal? Or maybe New York? Pretty please, with a Cherry Blossom on top? As for what's next for me: *Think Twice*, the sequel to *Don't Even Think About It*. More secrets! More scandals! More ESP! And now that I'm finished answering the fabulous questions from these amazingly talented and incredibly generous authors, I'm going to get back to it. Well, first I'm going to see if there are any brownies left, but then I'm going to write.